What Others Are Saying about Laura V. Hilton's *Healing Love*...

Laura Hilton brings to her readers not only "healing love" but also likable, realistic characters. She has created another story that kept me turning page after page with anticipation.

—*Robin Bayne*
Author of ten novels/novellas,
including *The Artist's Granddaughter*

Healing Love takes readers on a journey with two people from separate worlds whose lives collide in a heartwarming story.

—*Beth Shriver*
Author, the Touch of Grace series

Laura Hilton pulls this story together and leaves you ready and eager for more! I love the characters in this new series and have to hope I will meet Shane and Kristi again. Theirs is a beautiful story you won't be able to put down!

—*Cindy Loven*
Book reviewer, cindylovenreviews.blogspot.com

The Amish of Webster County is yet another endearing series from Laura Hilton. Hours of reading pleasure await you as Laura takes you to a place where time seems to have slowed but excitement and life overflow.

—*Susette Williams*
Author, *New Garden's Conversion*

Laura V. Hilton richly defines the line between the Amish lifestyle and the Englisch world in her new book, *Healing Love*. Amish fans will root for Kristi Lapp as she recovers from a buggy accident with help from her Englisch neighbor Shane Zimmerman.

—*Ruth Reid*
Author, the Heaven on Earth series: *The Promise of an Angel,*
Brush of Angel's W...

Healing Love

The Amish of
Webster County

LAURA V. HILTON

W
WHITAKER
HOUSE

Scripture quotation is taken from the *New King James Version*, © 1979, 1980, 1982, 1984 by Thomas Nelson, Inc. Used by permission. All rights reserved.

HEALING LOVE
The Amish of Webster County ~ Book One

ISBN: 978-1-60374-506-2
Printed in the United States of America
© 2012 by Laura V. Hilton

Whitaker House
1030 Hunt Valley Circle
New Kensington, PA 15068
www.whitakerhouse.com

Library of Congress Cataloging-in-Publication Data

Hilton, Laura V., 1963–
  Healing love / by Laura V. Hilton.
    p. cm. — (The Amish of Webster County ; bk. 1)
  ISBN 978-1-60374-506-2 (trade pbk.)
  1. Midwives—Fiction. 2. Veterinarians—Fiction. 3. Amish—Missouri—
Webster County—Fiction. I. Title.
  PS3608.I4665H43 2012
  813'.6—dc23
                                2012029237

1 2 3 4 5 6 7 8 9 10 11 ⨄ 19 18 17 16 15 14 13 12

Dedicated to:

Steve, *my best friend,*
Loundy, *my favorite song,*
Michael, *my adventurous one,*
Kristin, *my precious daughter,*
Jenna, *my sunshine,*
Kaeli, *my shower of blessing,*
And God, *who has blessed me with these.*

In loving memory of Allan and Janice Price, my parents; my grandmother, Mertie; and my uncle Loundy, each of whom has blessed me with some knowledge of our Pennsylvania Dutch ancestors.

Also, to Tamela, my agent, for not letting me give up and for giving sage advice.

Acknowledgments

I'd like to offer my heartfelt thanks to the following:

The residents of Seymour, for answering my questions and pointing me in the right directions.

Tonya and Steve, for providing medical expertise to help me describe Kristi's injuries.

Andrew and Mihir, for providing physical therapy advice. And Mom, whom I watched and learned from when she was undergoing her own physical therapy.

The Ozark Folk Center, for information on soup making, and the employees at Bakersville Pioneer Village, for letting me poke around and ask questions.

The amazing team at Whitaker House—Christine, Courtney, and Cathy. You are wonderful.

Tamela, my agent, for believing in me all these years.

My critique group—you know who you are. You are amazing and knew how to ask the right questions when more detail was needed. Also, thanks for the encouragement. Candee and Therese, thanks for reading large amounts in a short time and offering wise suggestions.

My husband, Steve, for being a tireless proofreader and cheering section, and my sons, Michael and Loundy, for taking over kitchen duties when I was deep in the story. And Kristin, for help with household chores.

Glossary of Amish Terms and Phrases

ach	oh
aent(i)	aunt(ie)
"Ain't so?"	a phrase commonly used at the end of a sentence to invite agreement
boppli	baby or babies
bu	boy
buwe	boys
daed	dad
danki	thank you
dawdi-haus	a home built for grandparents to live in once they retire
dochter	daughter
dummchen	a ninny; a silly person
Englisch	non-Amish
Englischer	a non-Amish person
frau	wife
großeltern	grandparents
grossdaedi	grandfather
grossmammi	grandmother
gut	good
"Gut morgen"	"Good morning"
"Gut nacht"	"Good night"
haus	house
"Ich liebe dich"	"I love you"
jah	yes
kapp	prayer covering or cap

kinner	children
kum	come
maidal	an unmarried woman
mamm	mom
maud	maid/housekeeper
nein	no
naerfich	nervous
onkel	uncle
Ordnung	the rules by which an Amish community lives
Pennsylvania Deitsch	Pennsylvania Dutch/Pennsylvania German, the language used most commonly by the Amish
rumschpringe	"running around time," a period of adolescence after which Amish teens choose either to be baptized in the Amish church or to leave the community
ser gut	very good
sohn	son
verboden	forbidden
"Was ist letz?"	"What is it?"
welkum	welcome
wunderbaar	wonderful

Chapter 1

October

*K*risti Lapp flicked the reins impatiently. "Kum on, Samson. 'Slow' isn't the only speed you're capable of, ain't so?" She needed him to pick up the pace. Silas Troyer had banged on her door earlier to alert her that his frau, Susie, was going into labor, and then he'd raced down the lane in his horse and buggy to notify their family members of the imminent birth.

Kristi was especially excited about this boppli. Susie had four girls, all of them a year apart, and she'd been expecting to have a boy this time, based on how different it had felt carrying him. Mamms usually sensed these things. And Kristi predicted she was right.

Several deer stepped onto the road right in front of her, none of them even glancing her way. Smiling, she pulled the reins slightly to the right to direct Samson away from them. A similarly sized herd had meandered its way through her family's backyard the other day, and she'd always admired the animals for sticking together as they did.

She tightened her grip on the reins and gave them another flick, hoping to encourage Samson to move more quickly.

As the deer were crossing the center line into the other lane, the powerful roar of an engine broke the serenity of the setting. A red sports car crested the hill up ahead, barreling in Kristi's direction at a speed she'd never witnessed on this road. She heaved a breath of exasperation. Any idiot would have noticed one of the several signs that read, "Watch for Buggies." They were impossible to miss, and Kristi had passed four of them in the last mile alone.

As the car whizzed toward her, the herd of deer scattered, darting in different directions. The driver swerved sharply into Kristi's lane to avoid them, and she gasped, frantically trying to steer the buggy over toward the shoulder. A chill ran up her spine at the sight of the steep embankment and deep ditch below.

One of the spooked deer pivoted. Made a mad dash straight toward her horse. Samson reared and immediately took off at a run, straight toward the ditch.

"Whoa, Samson!" Kristi planted her feet against the front of the buggy and pulled back on the reins with all her might. Leave it to Samson to shift into high gear at the worst time.

The car sped past, but Samson wouldn't slow down. He was heading straight for the drop-off. Panic surged through Kristi, constricting her breath. Should she try to jump out? She dropped the reins and scooted to the edge of the seat.

She was too late. The buggy lurched as Samson ran headlong over the embankment. As the vehicle tipped, she was propelled out the side. Hours seemed to pass before her body collided with the ground and pain engulfed her.

Teetering on the edge of consciousness, she thought briefly of Susie. How desperately she wanted to be there to assist with the birth of her boppli! Especially considering the problems she'd had with her first delivery.... And then she blacked out.

Shane Zimmerman flipped on his fog lights to illuminate the low-lying clouds, which created interesting shapes and shadows against the dark backdrop of woods lining the rural Missouri highway. He scanned the area for deer ousted from their natural habitats by hunters. Not that he hunted. He did treat many a pet that had been injured accidentally by a hunter, such as the Great Dane boarding at his clinic while she recovered from the surgical removal of an errant bullet. Of course, rutting season also brought deer out of hiding.

Shane reached inside the console for a CD—the latest release from LordSong—and slid it into the player. As the uplifting music filled the car, he flexed his shoulders in an effort to relieve the tension of the busy day behind him. He looked forward to getting home and kicking back to read his Bible and watch the evening news.

As his Jeep crowned the hill, he tapped the brakes at the sight of a wrecked Amish buggy. He scanned the area, but there was no sign of horse or driver. The animal must have been released and carted home. Or put down, if its injuries had been severe enough.

Returning his gaze to the highway, he slowed. A young buck lay on the road, still alive yet struggling.

Shane pulled his Jeep to the shoulder, put it in park, and clicked on the hazard lights. Leaving the keys in the ignition, he got out, his heart pounding in time with the obnoxious dinging sound of the car. Cautiously, he approached the deer. Its brown eyes fixed on him, wild with fear. The animal lurched to a standing position for a second but quickly collapsed again on the hard pavement, where it remained. Its labored breaths intensified. Whoever had hit it had driven off, leaving it to die. Was the same person to blame for the buggy accident? He'd probably never know.

"It's okay," Shane spoke softly.

The deer flicked its ears and struggled to get on its feet again.

"I'm here to help you." Shane stepped closer, keeping a wary eye on the rack of antlers. It was hardly the biggest he'd seen, but even small antlers could do hefty damage.

With another flick of its ears, the buck managed to achieve a semi-standing position and limped off to the edge of the road and into the forest. It would surely die, but Shane couldn't do anything about that. He wasn't about to chase an injured wild animal through the woods. He didn't carry much medical gear in his Jeep, anyway, aside from a few larger tools used for treating farm animals.

He started back toward his vehicle, but a glance at the buggy lying on its side gave him a strong urge to check it out. No point in hurrying. He rubbed his eyes, weary after his long day at the clinic, and surveyed the scene. The buggy appeared to be abandoned.

Then, he moved to the edge of the embankment and gazed down the leaf-covered slope. Something caught his eye. A woman? Shane squinted. Sure enough, there was an Amish woman, wearing a maroon dress and a black apron. Gold hair peeked out from underneath her white prayer kapp, and a black bonnet hung loosely around her shoulders. "Hello?"

No answer. His breath hitched. Had she hit the deer? Or had the deer hit her? He frowned. Accidents caused by deer affected more cars than buggies, by far. Where was the horse?

Heart pounding, he scrambled down through the brush into the ditch. As he crouched beside the woman, his nose caught the metallic odor of blood. The brilliant red on her dress wasn't part of the fabric. He lifted the hem just enough to spot the injury. Her left leg lay at a weird angle, with a bone protruding from the skin. Definitely broken.

His heart sank. His expertise was limited to animals.

But he was the only one there. And she needed help—urgently.

"Hey." He touched her left hand. It felt warm. He noted the shallow rise and fall of her chest. His fingers moved down to her wrist, feeling for her pulse. Alive but unresponsive. He reached into his pocket, pulled out his cell phone, and dialed 9-1-1. When the dispatcher answered, he said, "I'd like to report a buggy accident. We need an ambulance. The woman is unconscious and bleeding with a badly broken leg. Looks like a serious injury." He added their approximate location.

Glancing again at the bone sticking out of her skin, Shane shuddered. Animals, he could handle. Humans were too easy to identify with; their injuries hit too close to home. He leaned down and gently pushed her hair away from her neck. Her pulse was extremely rapid but weak. He breathed a prayer that help would arrive quickly.

As he studied her face for the first time, recognition nearly knocked him off balance. This woman lived right next door to him. What were the odds of that? Her backyard was overrun with weeds, a stark contrast to her meticulously maintained garden in the side yard. He'd seen her working there many a time. She had the most beautiful dog he'd ever seen, a Siberian husky. And the thought had dawned on him, more than once, that the dog's owner was more than commonly beautiful, as well.

She wasn't married, as far as he knew. The only other people he'd spotted next door were an older couple, presumably her parents. Their last name was Lapp, if the stenciling on their mailbox was current.

Shane would have to stop by the house to let her family know about the accident. They would probably be worried sick when she didn't return.

The young woman moaned, drawing Shane's attention. He saw her eyelids flutter slightly, and then her eyes opened.

"It's okay," he said, gazing as calmly as he could into her grayish-green eyes. "Help is coming."

"The pain...my head...my leg...." She winced as tears filled her eyes. "Who are you? I've seen you before."

"I'm Shane Zimmerman. Your next-door neighbor." He reached for her hand, hesitated, then folded his fingers gently around hers. As their skin connected, he was startled by the jolt that shot through his fingertips and gained intensity as it traveled through his hand and up his arm. He had no explanation, other than his being overly tired. "You'll be fine," he assured her.

She only moaned again and closed her eyes.

Shane stared down at her bloodstained skirt and saw that the fabric was saturated. He grimaced. She needed help fast, or she'd bleed out. Animal or human, he didn't want death on his hands tonight.

God, help me. Shane let go of her hand and yanked his sweatshirt up and over his head. He lifted her skirt again and pressed the garment against her wound, knowing he could be introducing harmful germs. But there wasn't a choice. He tried to make her as comfortable as he could without letting up the pressure. Even though she didn't rouse again, he explained every measure he took, from applying pressure to strapping his belt as a tourniquet around her leg. Then, he sang a couple of Amish songs, the ones he remembered learning from his grandparents. His father had left the Amish as a young man, choosing to marry Shane's mom, who wasn't Amish. But Shane had often spent entire summers with his grandparents.

Time hung in the air as he waited for help to arrive.

Finally, there was a screech of brakes and a rumble of gravel on the road above, followed by the sound of a vehicle door opening.

"Down here!" Shane called.

Seconds later, an EMT carrying a medical bag peeked over the embankment. "Ambulance is right behind me. You didn't move her, did you?"

"No. But she's bleeding profusely. I did what I could to slow it down."

The man half climbed, half slid, down the slope toward Shane. "I've got some emergency flares in the back of my truck. Mind setting them out while I take a look at her?"

"Not at all."

Shane did as he'd been asked, then walked over to the buggy to inspect it more closely. The leather harness straps dangled with frayed ends, indicating that the horse had broken free, possibly when the buggy tipped. He checked the immediate area and even wandered a ways into the woods for signs of a wounded animal, but no clues turned up. The roar of sirens in the distance beckoned him back to the site of the wreck.

In his Jeep, he found a rag and wiped off his bloody hands while he thought out the statement he'd make to the police.

An ambulance screeched to a stop beside the pickup, lights flashing, and a police cruiser pulled up alongside. It wasn't long before the ambulance wailed away again, spiriting its nameless passenger toward the hospital in Springfield.

After Shane had finished answering the police officer's questions, he started the two-mile trip home, keeping his eyes peeled for an injured horse. He passed his own small plot of land without any sign of the animal.

Shane pulled into the driveway next door, hurried up to the house, and pounded on the front door. No response. After several moments, he knocked again. He knew that the Amish generally kept their doors unlocked, but he didn't feel comfortable opening the door and hollering into the hallway of a stranger's house. He rapped one more time, just to be sure.

"Hey!"

He turned around and saw a man on the front porch of the house across the street.

The man started down the steps. "Can I help you?"

"I'm looking for Ms. Lapp's family. She was in a buggy accident."

The man came closer. "She hurt bad?"

Shane nodded. "Bad." Would she survive the trip to the hospital? His heart clenched.

"Donald Jackson. Me an' the wife live here."

Shane stretched his mouth into a tight smile. "Shane Zimmerman. Neighbor on the other side."

"Oh, the new guy. Vet, right? Welcome to Seymour."

"Thanks." It hardly seemed appropriate to exchange pleasantries when someone's life was hanging in the balance. Shane shifted his weight. "Does she have any family?"

Donald shrugged. "Everyone has some. See her parents and other people around from time to time. Sometimes lots of buggies over there. Besides, ain't the Amish all related? Heard that somewhere."

"Seems that way sometimes." Okay, this man was no help. A howl from the backyard reminded Shane about the Siberian husky. "I'm going to check on the dog." He strode down the porch steps and made his way around the side of the house.

Donald trailed him. "Barn's always unlocked, I'm pretty sure, so you could get the dog's food. I never see her lock it, anyway. But then, I don't watch her twenty-four-seven or anything."

Shane raised an eyebrow. This Donald apparently watched her often enough to know about the barn door and the dog food. "Nice meeting you, Donald. I'll just make sure the dog has fresh water, and then I'll go." He needed to find someone Amish to notify.

Seeing the red and white Siberian husky in a large kennel in the backyard, Shane opened the gate and went in, shutting it behind him. The dog whined and jumped up, wrapping him in a sort of canine embrace. He hugged her back. This breed was so affectionate. He rubbed her neck, then stepped back, picked up her metal water dish, and headed for the outside spigot, which he'd spotted on his way to the backyard. The dog followed closely at his feet, growling in a friendly way, as if she carried on a one-sided conversation. At the spigot, he filled the dish with cold water, then checked the barn door. It was unlocked, as Donald had said it'd be.

Shane stopped and scratched the dog behind her ears. "I'll be back later to get you some food." He hesitated. "No, I'll do it now." He turned back to the barn and slid both wobbly doors open, going into the darkness. He paused, wishing for his flashlight, then remembered that his Amish grandfather had always kept a lantern near the door. He turned back and groped along a shelf, finally feeling the familiar metal base of a lantern. Next to it was a book of matches, one of which he used to light the wick. It didn't seem right, being in a stranger's barn, but the dog would be hungry.

He found the dog food and bent down to scoop some into the dish. Then, he straightened and looked around. This was an Amish farm. There'd be other animals to bed down. Cows. Chickens. Horses. He sighed.

A nicker sounded, and Shane turned to the door. Ah, the prodigal buggy horse, dragging the frayed strands of a harness. He spoke softly to the animal as he grabbed hold of one of the harness straps, and then he led it back to an empty stall. The dog followed, whining all the way. Shane gave the sweaty horse a rubdown, checking it for injuries. Nothing seemed amiss, other than the wild look in its eyes and the way it kept tossing its head, evidently responses to the trauma of the accident.

When Shane had calmed the horse as best he could, he glanced around again. He knew the basics of managing an Amish farm, thanks to the years he'd spent helping his grandparents, but it was more than one person could handle alone. Another Amish family would probably take on the rest of the chores.

Still, he wanted to go to the hospital to check on Ms. Lapp. Why did she still weigh so heavily on his mind? He'd done his duty to her, a stranger.

His decision made, he returned the dog to her kennel. Before closing the door, he gave her another rub behind the ears. "I'll be back."

The dog flopped down on the ground with a reproachful whimper, as if he were abandoning her in her time of greatest need.

"Your master was in an accident, but she'll be okay," Shane explained. "I hope." He crouched down to the dog's level. "I'm going to the hospital right now to check on her."

With another whine, the dog lowered her head to rest on her front paws. Apparently, she had resigned herself to his departing.

Shane drove home for a quick shower, then got back in his Jeep to head to the hospital. First, though, he stopped by the farm on the other side of his property, which he hadn't really taken notice of previously. The mailbox there also said "Lapp," and he figured the residents had to be relatives of the injured woman.

Seconds after he pulled into the driveway, a man came out into the yard. Shane introduced himself and asked for confirmation that this family was related to the other Lapps, specifically the young woman with the Siberian husky.

The man frowned. "Jah, we're family. I'm Kristi's onkel. Name's Timothy. I'm caring for their livestock while her parents are visiting family in Sarasota. I was getting ready to head over there."

Shane proceeded to tell Timothy about the accident. For a relative of Kristi's, he processed the information rather stoically, Shane thought.

"Can I give you a lift to the hospital?"

Timothy took a step back. "Nein, I'll contact the bishop, and he'll get the word out. And I'll make a call down to Florida to tell her parents."

Timothy headed to the barn, and Shane drove away, wondering why he was taking the time to go to the hospital and check on a woman he didn't even know. He probably wouldn't find out anything, thanks to the strict privacy policy. But still, something drew him.

At the hospital, Shane went directly to the emergency wing and approached the front desk. "Kristi Lapp, please."

The receptionist nodded and checked something on her computer. Then, she looked up with a sympathetic smile. "If you'll take a seat in the waiting room, a doctor will be out to talk with you in just a few minutes."

Her condition must be as serious as he'd feared. Shane went down the hall to the waiting area, where he was grateful to find a coffeemaker. He poured himself a coffee and watched several minutes of the sitcom playing on the TV mounted on the wall overhead.

As the only person in the room, he had his choice of seats. He selected a chair in a corner and picked up a magazine from the end table next to it. However, the contents didn't appear to be any more interesting than the drama he'd been watching, so he put it back. Instead of reading, he prayed for Kristi and for the doctors working on her. It felt strange praying for a woman he didn't know and waiting for an update from the doctor, as if she meant something special to him. But it seemed she did, even though he'd just met her. Did their brief interaction even count as a meeting? He wasn't sure. All he knew was that he hadn't felt this strong a connection with a woman since Becca. He immediately dismissed the thought.

He was glad he'd found out her name. Calling her "Ms. Lapp" seemed so wrong. Plus, he probably wouldn't have been permitted to see her if the hospital staff thought he was a stranger.

Several people came into the waiting room and exited again during a period of time that felt like hours.

At last, a doctor entered the room. "Family for Kristi Lapp."

Shane blew out a breath. Family he wasn't, but he was the only person there for her. Hopefully, the doctor wouldn't ask how he was related. He got up, feeling a twinge of guilt at his act of impersonation.

The doctor led him into a private conference room and gestured for him to sit down. "She's in recovery. We've given her a blood transfusion, and we'll be monitoring her hemoglobin and hematocrit—that is, blood values. As soon as we're sure they are in the normal range, she'll be referred to an orthopedic surgeon for a procedure we abbreviate as ORIF: open reduction internal fixation."

Shane nodded. He was familiar with the procedure, but the doctor was probably accustomed to having to explain it, so he continued.

"Open reduction—that's how we put the bone back in the position it's supposed to be. And internal fixation is how we stabilize it—with a rod down the center of the bone and plates on either side, to keep it in position until nature takes her course and it heals completely. The plates may be removed later, as long as the bone heals well. Also, her femoral artery was nicked, but she'll be fine. Lost a lot of blood. We had to give her three units. She's going to have substantial bruising and probably be in considerable pain."

"Has she regained consciousness?"

"Not yet. But brain activity is normal, and we expect no complications."

"Thank you." Shane stood up and started for the door.

"If you want to wait, I'll have a nurse come and show you to her room."

Shane stopped in the doorway. "I'll come in tomorrow."

The doctor frowned. "I'm sure your wife will want to see you when she wakes up."

❧

Kristi woke up in an unfamiliar room filled with odd beeping noises. Straight ahead, a television was mounted on the celery-green wall. To her right was a beige-colored curtain; to her left, a big, dark window. The hospital. How did she get here? Someone must have found her. What about Samson? What had happened to him?

Had Susie birthed her boppli? Kristi groaned and shifted on the bed, noticing the bedside table with a plastic pitcher of water and an empty tumbler. And…flowers? She smiled at the vase holding six pink rosebuds, a cluster of baby's breath, and some other greenery. Who would have sent a bouquet? Maybe the person who'd found her.

With great effort, she reached with her right arm toward the table, pain washing over her anew. It seemed every part of her body ached. Despite the discomfort, she extended her arm just far enough to snatch the white envelope from the plastic forklike thing tucked into the bouquet.

Her left hand had an IV needle stuck in it, taped down. She grimaced at the sight. She'd have a bruise there, probably, but that would be the least of her injuries. Even with her now pain-blurred vision, which made it seem as if the room was spinning, she could tell from the shape of the blanket that covered her legs how swollen they were. Her left leg, in particular—that's where most of the pain radiated from. Wincing with effort, she tore open the envelope, pulled out a plain white card, and squinted at it. The message written inside was simple:

You're in my prayers.

    Shane Zimmerman

Sweet, but it must have been intended for another patient. She didn't know anybody by the name of Shane Zimmerman. Or did she? Her head pounded as she tried to figure it out. No one came to mind.

Maybe this mystery man would come to the hospital to see her.

She pressed the card to her chest and closed her eyes, imagining a tall, handsome Amish man. Hopefully, when she fell asleep, he would visit her in her dreams.

Chapter 2

Shane hesitated in the hallway outside Kristi Lapp's hospital room. It made no sense, his continuing to visit a complete stranger like this. For whatever reason, ever since he'd discovered her in the ditch last week, this Amish woman had haunted his thoughts. At least his prayer life had improved as a result.

He took a sip of the coffee he'd picked up at McDonald's on his way to the hospital. Then, with a deep breath, he entered the room.

She was asleep, just as she'd been when he'd dropped by yesterday. And the day before. And the two days before that. He glanced at the vase of flowers he'd sent. No sign of wilting yet, but he figured he should probably stop by the florist and order a replacement in the next couple of days.

Or not.

Coming here was plain foolishness.

But that didn't stop him from stepping further into the room. He paused beside her bed and gazed down at her beautiful face. Even the bruises on her cheeks and jaw couldn't disguise her fine bone structure.

She shifted slightly, opened her eyes, and blinked, studying him with a look of surprise. After a moment, she narrowed her eyes, evidently searching her memory bank to place him. But the light of recognition didn't dawn in her expression.

Shane felt foolish for coming. Disappointed that she didn't recognize him.

"Are you a doctor? Or a...therapist?" She grimaced at that word.

He shook his head. "Your neighbor. Shane Zimmerman." He gestured toward the bouquet. "I live on the farm next to yours."

She followed his gaze to the roses, then looked back at him. "You aren't Amish."

"Um, no, I'm not." Did it matter? Would it help if he told her that his grandparents were?

She readjusted her position as pain clouded her eyes. "You aren't Creepy Guy."

"Creepy Guy?" She must mean Donald. He fought a grin. "No one has ever called me that to my face, but I'm sure some animals have felt that way about me."

"Animals?" She leaned forward and pressed a button on the edge of her bed, which began making whirring sounds as it lifted her into an upright position. "You're the one who rescued me?"

He hardly felt like a rescuer. "I found you, yes, and called nine-one-one. I'm a veterinarian, not an EMT."

"Danki—I mean, thank you for the flowers. And for rescuing me."

He smiled and took another sip of his coffee, then set the cup down on the bedside tray and gestured to a chair. "May I?"

She smiled. "Of course."

He pulled the chair closer to her bed and sat. "So, how are you feeling?"

She shrugged. "As well as can be expected."

"How's the pain?"

She frowned. "They're...managing it."

"Good. Did you have the surgery on your leg yet?"

She nodded. "I don't know when, exactly. A couple of days ago, maybe. They said they put a rod in my leg to hold the bone together." Her forehead wrinkled. "I've started physical therapy."

He remembered what the doctor had told him about the procedure they had planned. "Good. You should start to heal, then." His mind scrambled to find something else to talk about. "Your horse made it back home safe. A bit scared and nervous, but safe."

"Gut." She grinned. "I'd wondered."

"And your dog is a real sweetheart. I refilled her water dish and food bowl. Hope you don't mind."

"Thank you, again." She smiled. "Daed thinks it's silly to have a Siberian husky as a pet. But she is such a beauty. Her name's Chinook."

Shane tilted his head. "An Indian name. How'd you come up with that?"

"I thought it sounded Alaskan. Someone told me it was a type of wind." Her eyes started to blur with tears. "I may have to let her go to another family. She needs a lot of exercise, and I'm not sure I…." She glanced down at her leg.

Shane saw an opportunity and decided to seize it. "I go jogging just about every day. Usually twice a day, actually. I'd be happy to take her along on my runs."

Her head shot up, eyes wide. "You'd do that?"

"No problem. I can do it until you're able again. It'd be a pleasure." It would be a pleasure, especially if it would mean seeing Kristi on a regular basis.

He sucked in a breath, one that burned in his chest, and felt like a teenage boy with his first crush. He glanced away briefly before returning his gaze to Kristi. "Your parents are away?"

She nodded. "They went to Pinecraft, Florida, to take my großeltern down for the winter. Grossmammi—my grandma—can't handle the cold so well. It makes her arthritis flare up. My onkel Timothy—his farm's on the other side of yours—called them about my accident. They'll kum home sometime next week."

Shane couldn't imagine that. His parents had always been there when he needed them. He found what he hoped was a teasing smile. "And has your sweetheart been here to see you?"

Would she see his question for what it really was—an attempt to fish for her romance status? He shouldn't even be here. What was he doing?

Natural appreciation of female beauty. That had to be all it was. Nothing more.

She blushed slightly, then frowned as an expression close to sadness crossed her face. "I have nein beau." With an impish grin, she added, "And if I did, it'd be none of your business, Mr. Neighbor. Courting couples are supposed to keep their relationships secret."

"Secret? Why is that?" He twisted his body to face her more fully.

"It's always been done that way."

He picked up his coffee and took another swig, waiting for her to expound on her statement. Or maybe on her sad expression of a moment ago.

Instead, she fell silent and reached for her water cup. She stared down at the plastic lid for a few seconds, then leaned forward and took a sip through the bent straw.

"It's not kept secret in my world," Shane supplied. "We date openly."

She looked up. "It's supposed to be done under the cover of darkness."

He had nothing more to say on the subject. Pursuing it might take him down a path he didn't want to travel.

He searched for another topic. "It was beautiful out today. Temperature was about seventy degrees, and there was a nice breeze. Leaves are really starting to fall. It's supposed to drop to about fifty tonight."

She nodded and looked out the window. Not that she could see much from there. From his vantage point, he saw only the darkening sky and the rooftops of some buildings.

A nurse bustled into the room. Shane's cue to go. He stood up. "Well, I should be heading home. I'll stop to check on Chinook, if you'd like. And your horse."

Kristi glanced at the nurse, then looked back at Shane. "Onkel Timothy is supposed to take care of the livestock."

"Including the horse?"

"Jah. Samson."

The nurse stepped around Shane. "I need to change the IV bag."

"Of course. Excuse me." Shane picked up his chair and moved it out of her way. He met Kristi's eyes. "I'll try to come by sometime tomorrow."

No promises, no commitment.

But, Lord have mercy, he couldn't stay away.

At eight o'clock on Saturday morgen, Kristi became acutely aware of masculine footsteps clomping down the hall. It didn't sound like the familiar gait of Onkel Timothy, or even Bishop Dave. And it definitely wouldn't be Eli. Not after his brief visit Thursday afternoon, when he'd called off their courtship. In all fairness, even though she felt hurt and rejected, this was probably for the best. She'd been flattered by his attentions, for sure, but he didn't seem to have much zest for life. In fact, she'd found him pretty boring. She couldn't imagine being married to him. So, if the footsteps in the hallway weren't from any of the Amish men she knew, and if it wasn't her doctor.... She held her breath and watched the doorway with anticipation.

When Shane appeared, he stopped and raised a hand to knock. Their gazes met before he did, and she nodded quickly, as if to sanction his entry.

She tried not to stare, but it was next to impossible. The straw hat on his head, similar to the one Daed wore in the summer; a royal blue button-down shirt that made his sky-blue eyes seem even more vivid; form-fitting blue jeans; rugged-looking cowboy boots; and probably a day's growth of hair on his pronounced jaw all added up to one drool-worthy man—"Man with a capital *M*," as her Englisch friend Starr would say.

And here she was in a frumpy, pale green-checkered hospital gown, her hair gathered messily beneath her smashed kapp, her eyes probably bloodshot with dark circles beneath, considering how many times she'd been awakened in the nacht for another blood pressure reading or IV change. She tucked several loose strands of hair behind her ear.

Yet Shane's eyes lit up when he saw her, even before he smiled, and the concern in his expression shifted into something resembling tenderness.

Her steady heartbeat jumped into a gallop, and her mouth went dry. She reached for the glass of orange juice on her breakfast tray and gulped it down, almost choking on the bitter liquid. This was nothing like the fresh-squeezed orange juice Daed made with the fruit he brought back from Florida. She should have asked for grape juice.

"Good morning." Shane removed his hat and came to stand at the foot of the bed. Then, he focused on the tray of uneaten breakfast still balanced on her lap. "Did I come at a bad time?"

With her spoon, she poked at the lumpy substance she supposed was oatmeal. "No. Now's a gut time." Maybe it'd give her an excuse not to eat. Until now, she hadn't thought it possible to ruin oatmeal. She longed to go home and make herself a proper bowl.

He studied her tray again. "The toast wouldn't be too bad with jam. And the scrambled eggs might be good. Don't they give you coffee or tea with breakfast?"

"They asked if I wanted some. I didn't think I did. Now I'm not so sure."

"Want me to run down to the coffee kiosk and order you something?"

She furrowed her brow. "Do they serve tea?"

"I don't know. I'll find out." He glanced at the wall where her wheelchair and walker waited. "Maybe you'd like to come with me."

She considered his suggestion. It'd be nice to escape the confines of her room for a reason other than to hobble down the hall with a therapist holding a belt attached to her, as if she were an elderly woman likely to fall. Then, she remembered the stares she usually got from the other patients and visitors. "Ach, nein."

He stepped back and turned toward the door.

"Nein, no tea, please. Really, it's okay." She poked at the oatmeal again, then dug out a large lump and took a bite. Maybe it would stick to her ribs. Not that her recent activities were enough to work up an appetite.

"Good girl. Eat up." Shane slid a chair toward her bed and sat down. "Chinook ran five miles with me this morning. She's a good jogging partner. Only got sidetracked twice: once when a rabbit dashed across the road in front of her, and again when someone's cat dared to show its face. She treed it." He leaned forward. "And I ran faster than I've ever run before."

Kristi gave up on the oatmeal and reached for the packet of grape jelly on her tray. Maybe it would make the toast taste better. "I usually let go of the leash when she runs too fast for me, but I worry she won't kum home. It's hard to leave her in the Lord's hands."

He nodded. "Siberians are bred to run."

Kristi couldn't believe how quickly the rest of the morgen seemed to pass. Several nurses came in during the course of Shane's visit, claiming they needed to check her IV. Kristi suspected their true motive was to check out the good-looking man sitting there with one foot propped on the opposite knee. She could hear the whispers and giggles out in the hall, and she doubted Shane was oblivious to them. But he focused on her, like she was the only woman in the world. It'd be fun to have a friend next door. It'd be even nicer to have an Amish man pay attention to her in this way.

But that would never be. Not with her injured leg. Not when an Amish man had already left her because of it.

All too soon, an aide brought in her lunch tray. Instead of simply dropping it off, she took the time to tear open the wrapping of both the straw and the plastic silverware, all the while casting sidelong glances at Shane.

Hadn't these women ever seen a man before?

As the aide started to peel back the lid on a Styrofoam cup of soup, Shane rose to his feet. "Well, I need to be going. Nice visiting with you, Kristi. I'll be by later. Tomorrow, after church."

She nodded and opened her mouth to reply, but the aide beat her to it.

"Oh, don't let me run you off, honey. I'll be glad to bring a tray in here for you so you can stay with your…"—she openly glanced at his left hand—"friend."

Shane's smile was polite. Nothing more. "Thanks, but I'll pass this time. Kristi needs to rest, and I have some things I need to do."

He turned to Kristi and winked, then put on his hat and strode out the door, leaving her heart racing like a runaway horse. She didn't fail to notice that the aide's smile of two seconds ago had been replaced by a sour expression.

The rest of the day dragged by. Kristi was thankful for the book the bishop's frau had brought. The identification of poisonous mushrooms probably wasn't a topic too many people found fascinating, but Kristi's attention was rapt for at least a few hours.

On Sunday morgen, after a slow and painful trip down the hall with her walker, Kristi begged the nurse to help her take a shower. She initially objected, saying something about needing a doctor's permission, but she finally acquiesced to a sponge bath and sent someone to help wash her hair.

Afterward, Kristi picked up the thin hospital comb she'd been issued. It didn't seem strong enough to do the job. She flexed it back and forth a few times, then shrugged. Strong enough or not, it was all she had. She attempted to run it through her thick, damp tresses, yanking on the tangles she encountered. There were many. She'd need a stronger comb—or some assistance. Would the nurses be "too busy" to help style her hair so she'd look nice for Shane?

Shane paused in the doorway at the sight of Kristi sitting up in bed, struggling to pull a comb through her curly mane. Her hair hung down in a cascade of waves that reached her waist. He couldn't tell if the waves were natural or if they were the result of her hair being twisted up in a bun all the time. Either way, he longed to tangle his fingers in their silky length.

He must have made a noise, because her attention snapped to the door. Just as quickly, she released the comb and hastily gathered her hair with both hands into a ponytail.

"No, wait. I can help you get the tangles out." Shane hurried across the room and picked up the comb.

Color flooded Kristi's face. "Nein, you—. No one is supposed to see my hair down. Except my husband, someday."

He raised his eyebrows. "Really? Why?"

Eyes downcast, she shook her head. Her only answer.

"I already saw it down. And I offered to help. You didn't ask for it. It'd be easier for me to get the tangles out. I can see, and your arms must still be sore from the accident. Scoot forward a little."

She sat still for another second. Two. Three. He was about to hand her back the comb when she slid forward a bit. Shane lowered himself onto the bed behind her and, with the comb, started from the bottom of her hair and worked his way up, carefully removing the snarls as he went.

"You've done this before?" Her voice was barely louder than a whisper.

"Uh, no. But I watched my mom do my sister's hair when she was little." His wife had kept her hair short—"wash-and-wear," she'd called it. She'd always added some foamy stuff to give it a spiky texture.

"You're early. I thought you said you were coming after church. It isn't even noon."

"I had an emergency call early this morning. A cow went into labor and was having trouble delivering. I went home afterward, took Chinook for a run, and then showered before coming here." He ran his fingers through the soft, silky lock of hair he'd just untangled. "You have beautiful hair."

She dipped her head.

Shane sighed. He probably shouldn't have said that. He picked up the section he'd finished, draped it over her shoulder, and selected another part to work on. "Our run was pretty uneventful. We didn't even see a squirrel. I think Chinook was disappointed."

Kristi made a strangled noise, then reached back and yanked her hair into a ponytail, frantically twisting it.

"Hey, I wasn't done yet." Shane grasped her hand to still it, and that's when he noticed the Amish couple standing in the doorway.

The woman covered her mouth with her hand. The bearded man merely stared at him with narrowed eyes.

Shane released Kristi's hand and jumped off the bed. It was clear he'd made a huge mistake, and he seriously hoped these weren't Kristi's parents. He gripped the comb tighter.

"Mamm! Daed! I—I wasn't expecting you until tomorrow."

Go figure. That explained the almost murderous look in the man's eyes.

"Jah, dochter. I can see."

Kristi's chest rose and fell. "This is Shane Zimmerman. He's the one who saved my life."

Her father stepped into the room. "We're grateful." His stern gaze could have pinned Shane to the wall.

Shane fumbled with the comb and glanced toward the door.

"Shane, this is my daed, Ira, and my mamm, Barbie."

Shane turned back, nodding sheepishly. "Nice to meet you."

Neither parent returned his greeting.

Shane sucked in a breath and took a step forward. What should he do? Go, and leave Kristi to shoulder the fallout alone? Or stay and ignore the tension?

"Daed, Shane lives next door to us. And he's a veterinarian. He took over the practice of our last vet."

Ira grunted.

Shane swallowed hard. If word got out that he'd touched an Amish girl inappropriately, he'd be banned from every Amish farm in the state. An outcast. Unaccepted. Unused. And ultimately out of business, with the way the Amish stuck together. He should have thought of that earlier. But the sight of her hair, loosened from the constraints of a bun and the covering of a kapp, had made him lose all ability to reason. Or maybe he'd simply decided it was worth the risk.

How could he fix the mess he'd made?

His mind scrambled for something to say but came up empty. He wished he hadn't left his coffee in the car. At least that would have given him something to hold in an effort to still his quivering hands. Something other than the incriminating comb.

"We are grateful to you for saving our Kristi's life," Ira repeated, but he didn't sound quite like he meant it. Or maybe his words simply sounded stiff since they were directed at an outsider.

Shane nodded. After a moment's hesitation, he held out his hand to Ira. "I'm sorry. I didn't mean anything inappropriate there. I was just trying to help…." He looked down at the comb, then handed it to Kristi.

"I asked the nurse who helped wash my hair for some apple cider vinegar to smooth out the tangles," Kristi explained, filling the awkward silence, "but she said they didn't have any."

"Ach, jah," Barbie said. "They use something called conditioner. Not sure how well that works."

Kristi shook her head. "They didn't even use that. Just shampoo."

"You had many tangles, ain't so?" Barbie stepped closer and fingered her daughter's hair.

"Jah, and not all out yet, I'm afraid."

Ira cleared his throat. "Well then, I'll let your mamm help you while I see this young man out." He moved toward the door, clearly expecting Shane to follow.

Shane's emotions had already been as tangled as Kristi's hair, and now there was a new snag in their relationship. He glanced back at Kristi, who sat on the bed, her head bowed, her face flushed. Not knowing what else to do, Shane walked out. He dreaded the conversation that was sure to transpire between Ira and himself as soon as they were a fair distance from the room.

Chapter 3

$\mathcal{K}$risti fought back tears as Mamm yanked the comb through her hair. Perhaps more painful than the tugs at her scalp was her gnawing guilt. She shouldn't have granted such liberties to a man—especially an Englischer. What would Mamm have to say about this act of impropriety? Or would she leave the lecturing to Daed?

Kristi shivered, remembering the heat of Shane sitting close behind her. She almost couldn't believe he'd been on the bed. With her. Not just seeing her hair, but touching it, even running his fingers through it, as his breath brushed her neck. Her skin tingled at the memory.

Jah, she'd been very sinful to act so immodestly. Whatever punishment her parents decided upon would be deserved. Would they make her go to the bishop and confess?

"There you go." Mamm stepped back and separated a cluster of Kristi's hair from the teeth of the comb, then dropped both into the trash bin in the corner. "That comb is worthless. I'll bring a gut brush the next time I kum."

An aide shuffled into the room, carrying a lunch tray and clicking her tongue. "That hottie of yours is some piece of eye candy. Did he stop in here already? He's outside in the hall right now, talking to some man."

"My daed." *And that "hottie" isn't mine.* Kristi reached for the packet of plastic silverware and unwrapped it, refusing to

38

look at Mamm. Whatever would she think about this woman using such terms for Shane? And what were he and Daed talking about? *Me.* Her stomach churned.

After the aide had left, Mamm smiled at Kristi. "Eye candy...that's a new one to me. He is certainly gut-looking. The new vet, you say? Guess we'll be seeing a lot of him." She chuckled. "You go ahead and eat. When your daed returns, he and I will go down to the cafeteria and order something."

Mamm didn't sound concerned. Maybe it wouldn't be as big a problem as Kristi feared. She bowed her head for a moment of silent prayer, then glanced up at Mamm. "I'm sorry you had to cut short your time at Pinecraft."

"We're just glad you're okay. It certainly was a gut thing that young man came by when he did. The doctor told us you wouldn't have survived the accident otherwise." Mamm smiled again, then stepped behind Kristi, tied her hair into a bun, and pinned it up. Next, she picked up her white kapp from the bedside table and secured it on her head. "Your daed brought back some oranges and grapefruit. He'll get more when we go back in the spring to pick up your großeltern." Mamm came around and sat in the chair at the foot of Kristi's bed. "I sure enjoyed seeing all of our snowbird friends. You can go down with us next time."

Kristi shook her head. "I don't know. My schedule will be pretty unpredictable."

Mamm frowned. "You aren't thinking about going back to midwifery, are you? Can't you just leave it for the other midwife, Matthew Yoder's Shanna?"

"She can't handle it all alone, Mamm. Shanna trained me because it was too much for one person. It seems everyone wants an Amish midwife. Even some Englisch folks do."

"Well, she'll have to handle it while you heal and until therapy helps you regain the use of your leg. Who ever heard of putting a metal rod inside a body? I wonder if it's permanent." Mamm looked pensive for a moment. "Anyway, the doctor said it'll be three to six months before your leg heals completely. I'm sure Shanna can manage for the time you're in Florida." She nodded, as if the matter had been settled.

Kristi pursed her lips. No point arguing about it now. Hopefully, Mamm would be more lenient about letting her stay home when springtime came. Protesting further might result in Mamm's making her move to Florida to live with Grossdaedi and Grossmammi. As much as she loved her großeltern, she didn't want to be separated from her friends and the rest of her family.

Or from Shane Zimmerman.

With her fork, she drew a pattern in the mashed potatoes on her lunch tray. Who was she kidding? Shane had no place in her future. He was only a friend. She had no reason to factor him into her long-term plans.

Why, then, did she get the feeling, deep down, that he was meant to be something more?

When Shane had followed Ira out into the hallway, the older man had hesitated outside the door, glancing at the hospital staff that swarmed around the nurses' station and bustled in and out of other rooms. Apparently, he'd decided the spot wasn't private enough for what he needed to say. Motioning for Shane to follow him, he'd started down the hall toward the elevators. "Nice and warm in Florida still. Feels downright chilly here. But the leaves sure are pretty, ain't so? I love the fall colors."

The small talk didn't fool Shane. Nor did it settle his churning stomach. Sure enough, once they reached the recessed area by the elevators, the chatty façade and friendly demeanor faded altogether. Ira stopped and faced Shane squarely. "You had no right to be in a room alone with my dochter, much less on a bed, touching her hair. You shamed her."

Shane flinched at his bluntness, then nodded. He'd been in the wrong. He'd known as much from the moment he'd met her father's fierce stare. "Yes, sir."

There was so much he wanted to say in his defense. But he'd already explained that he was only trying to help, and Ira seemed unlikely to overlook his offense just because of his good intentions.

"I appreciate your saving her life, but this is as far as the relationship goes, understand?" Ira gave Shane a hard stare. "I saw how you looked at her. How she looked at you. You are not someone I want my dochter to marry."

Ouch. "I'm not looking for a wife."

Eyes flashing angrily, Ira stiffened, as if that was the worst thing Shane could have said. "So, you're seducing an innocent Amish girl for sport? Looking for a casual lover?" His voice remained low, controlled.

"What? No!" Shane sucked in a breath. "No. I was just trying to help her. The differences in culture…I guess I didn't realize…." Untrue. He felt a stab of guilt.

"The thing is, we're different from you Englisch. We have different beliefs, different values. A woman's hair…that's personal. Private. And reserved for her husband alone. Do you understand?"

"Yes, sir." Shane pulled in another breath. "I'm sorry. I didn't know."

Ira nodded. "I forgive you. Again, I do appreciate you for saving Kristi's life. And for taking time to visit her when we couldn't be here. The doctor told us you've been faithful to kum every day. You really have gone above and beyond the call of duty. I respect that. However, I think it's in Kristi's best interests if your visits end here and now." He jabbed the elevator button. "You stay away."

Pain knifed through Shane's heart. He gulped. "Yes, sir."

"Glad we understand each other. Have a nice day, now." Ira spun on his heel and strode down the hall. He didn't look back.

"Have a nice day"? Shane watched the man until he disappeared around the corner. With a dinging sound, the elevator doors whooshed open. Shane stood there another moment, then forced himself to step into the elevator and push the button for the lobby. The doors slid shut.

Would it be wrong to deliberately disobey Kristi's father?

It might be too late to return to the hospital later today, but he'd be back on Monday. Kristi was a grown woman. Plenty old enough to tell him to get lost, if she wanted to.

"I saw how you looked at her. How she looked at you."

Shane hung his head. He'd have to be very careful what he said and did from now on. He couldn't allow her to get the idea he was interested in a relationship with her.

For that matter, he couldn't allow himself to get that idea.

But he was afraid the damage had already been done.

Kristi's therapist, whom she'd dubbed "Tom the Torturer," had yet to give her permission to practice walking on her own. To make sure she didn't try, he typically parked her walker on the far side of the room, out of the way. But on Monday, after the afternoon session, he left the walker beside her bed. Within reach.

The temptation was too much to resist. That evening, Kristi leaned on her walker and struggled to her feet. She bit her lip to hold back a cry. The pain had diminished only slightly, even though the doctor had assured her it would eventually vanish. She put weight on her left leg a little at a time, hoping none of the nurses would walk in on her. But they'd been talking about discharging her, so she needed to be able to walk, right? She eyed the wheelchair in the corner. She would *not* be dependent on it forever.

If only she had taken a different route to Susie's to deliver the boppli. If only this were a bad dream, and she would wake up and find her leg fully functional again. Maybe that was all it was—a horrible nightmare.

But then, would a nightmare feature someone like Shane?

Nein. But he was a dream. He had to be. In real life, would an unusually handsome vet voluntarily spend time visiting a lame Amish girl in a hospital? No way. Of course, even if Shane were real, the lecture Daed had surely given him had put an end to whatever relationship they might have had. Kristi's oldest brother, Justus, had left the church and was shunned, and Daed wasn't about to let that happen to another of his kinner. He would make sure she had no further opportunities to be around Shane.

On second thought, she didn't know that for certain. Daed had returned to her hospital room alone, with no further mention of Shane.

Out of the corner of her eye, she saw a figure appear in the doorway. She turned her head in that direction. Her heart leaped.

Shane looked around the room, as if checking to see if she was alone, then came in. "Wow, look who's up." He grinned. "I was in town to pick up some supplies and thought I'd stop by for a few minutes. Is this a bad time?"

"Physical torture time." Kristi took a couple of steps forward, pushing the walker as she went.

"There you go!" Shane's grin widened for a second, but then he glanced at the walker and sobered. "Are you supposed to be doing this on your own?"

"Tom, King of Torment, didn't say I couldn't."

"Hmm. Did he say you could?"

She looked down. "Ach, you know, I didn't ask. But the doctor said I'd be discharged soon, and I'll be walking at home."

Shane watched her for a few seconds.

"You're not going to make me stop?"

He shook his head. "If the therapist has been doing these exercises with you, then it shouldn't do any damage. Besides, you seem so determined, I doubt I could dissuade you. But, here—let me stand beside you, just in case you need help."

She really hoped she wouldn't stumble in front of him. "I'm glad you came today. I was afraid you wouldn't."

Was that a look of discomfort that flitted across his face? It disappeared so fast, she couldn't tell. It might have been confusion. He shook his head. "Why wouldn't I?"

Hadn't Daed warned him to stay away from her? Maybe all they'd had was a casual, get-acquainted conversation. Unlikely, but she wasn't about to pry by asking Daed about it. He would say it was none of her business.

Shane glanced at his watch. "I don't have long. I'm due at a ranch in forty minutes or so. If you're going to walk, let's do a lap down the hall and back again. We'll get you settled in a chair before I go."

Settled in a chair, as opposed to in bed. She supposed that was wise.

Gritting her teeth to deal with the pain, Kristi pushed the walker toward the door. Shane must have noticed her limp, but he never mentioned it. "You're doing great, Kristi. Keep going."

He stayed slightly behind her, murmuring encouragement, as she struggled all the way to the end of the hall.

A nurse came out of a room and smiled at them. "Who needs a therapist when you've got a man like him?"

Shane gave a nervous chuckle.

Kristi rolled her eyes and started retracing her steps. When she reached her room, Shane helped her to ease into a chair. "A nurse will probably be in soon to help get you in bed. I'd better get going." He hesitated, as if he wanted to say something else, but then he started backing toward the door. "I might not see you tomorrow. I don't think my schedule brings me this way."

Kristi shrugged, hoping her face didn't betray her disappointment. "It's okay. The doctor said he might send me home this week, maybe even as early as tomorrow. You could kum over sometime. I'll cook you dinner. After all you've done for me, it's the least I can do."

"That sounds great, but I'm not sure...." He shook his head. "Well, we'll see. Right now, I really need to go." He turned around abruptly—and froze.

Mamm stood in the doorway, gazing at Shane with her head tilted and one eyebrow raised. "Well, if it isn't Dr. Eye Candy." She grinned.

Kristi released the breath she'd been holding and looked at Shane. A brilliant shade of red crept up his neck.

"Uh, hello, Mrs. Barbie," Shane stammered. "I was, uh, just leaving."

Mamm smiled again. "You're safe—for now. Ira decided to stay in the van to see where the driver would park so that we could find it later."

He nodded, a quick down-and-up motion to signal acknowledgment. "Bye, Kristi. Mrs. Barbie." Then, he strode out the door and disappeared, without another word or a backward glance.

It felt strangely like a final good-bye. But they were neighbors. Friends. It couldn't have been.

The next day, to her delight, Kristi was released from the hospital. Tony, the driver, brought Daed back in the van to pick her up. She wished Shane could have taken her home, instead. The way he'd left last nacht still bothered her.

He couldn't have meant "good-bye" the way she'd interpreted it. He'd been rushed, of course, with obligations to tend to. Yet he'd taken the time to walk with her the length of the hall, offering constant encouragement.

She would see him again. She knew it. Plus, he had a standing date with her dog, didn't he?

When they reached the haus, Tony helped her out of the van and immediately unloaded her walker. The hospital had also sent home the hated wheelchair, which she intended to keep collapsed in a corner.

She glanced at the porch swing swaying in the breeze and imagined sitting there with Shane while they sipped hot cocoa and talked about their days. She tried to hide a shiver of anticipation. She couldn't wait to get to know him in a context outside of the hospital.

When she'd been discharged, some of the hospital staff had been under the assumption that Shane was her boyfriend—and, presumably, that he'd continue helping her with her therapy. She'd been wrong to allow them the misconception, but part of her secretly relished it. After all, Shane was far more attentive than Eli had been, even on his best days. She'd promised to keep exercising on her own and to call her doctor if she wanted to see a professional therapist. They said she could even schedule home therapy, which had sounded good until she'd found out she'd be haus-bound, not permitted to go anywhere.

That was way too restrictive. She was anxious to get back to work helping expectant mamms. Back to real life. Frolics and singings. Visiting family and friends. And Shane.

Maybe he would work with her on her therapy when he had time. She wanted to wean herself off of the walker and move as she used to. *One step at a time*, she reminded herself. She'd use a cane after graduating from the walker.

Daed stayed close beside her as she labored her way up the path to the farmhaus. When they reached the steps, he carried the walker while she pulled herself up by the railing. She'd need to practice vertical motion so that she could get in and out of the buggy. As soon as she could, she'd go back to work. She couldn't wait.

Mamm flung open the front door. Behind her, Kristi could see her brothers and their wives gathered in the kitchen. All except for Justus, of course. She missed him. "Welkum home, Kristi!" they shouted in unison.

Her pregnant sister-in-law, Marie, came up and wrapped her in a hug. "Hurry and get well so you can deliver my boppli when it's time."

Kristi returned the embrace. "You know I'll do my best."

Marie released her into her brother Peter's arms. "Why didn't you kum see me in the hospital?" Kristi asked him. "I've missed you."

He shrugged, and his face flushed. "Needed to get the hay harvested, ain't so?"

"And it's deer season." Marie gave her husband a look. "I think he bagged a whole buck for every man in the family. We'll have plenty of venison to put up." She turned to face Kristi's other sister-in-law, Roxy, who held a twin dochter in each arm. "We're having a canning frolic for Saturday, ain't so?"

Kristi's own arms ached to hold a boppli. "I need to sit down." She headed for the chair Peter pulled out for her.

Then, seated comfortably, she reached out her hands toward Roxy. "Let me hold one of those sweet blessings. Ach, they've grown so much." She tickled the tiny, sock-covered foot of her niece Mandy, giggling when the six-month-old jerked her fragile leg in response.

Mamm poured koffee for everyone and set a platter of her prize-winning cinnamon rolls on the kitchen table.

Kristi's brother Luke came up and squeezed her shoulder. "Gut to have you home again, Kristi. Now, you'll have to work hard to walk again. Can't let your little nieces beat you, ain't so?"

Kristi grinned at him. "I'll be back to normal in nein time. You'll see. The doctor said six months before I'm completely healed. I say three months, tops."

Roxy sat down beside her. "Will the therapists kum here, then?"

Kristi shook her head. Her grin widened as she glanced around at her family members. "They discharged me from therapy since they knew Shane would be so faithful to work with me. I didn't argue."

"Shane?" Daed stared at her, his Adam's apple bobbing. Then, his gaze darted to Mamm, sending her some nonverbal message by way of his furrowed brow.

Embarrassment washed over Kristi like a heat wave. She never should have mentioned Shane. But Daed hadn't forbidden her to see him. Her insides roiled. If only she could take back her statement.

Peter's arm remained suspended over the platter of cinnamon rolls.

Luke frowned. "Is there something we don't know?"

Kristi shook her head. "Just a misunderstanding." She swallowed a lump. "I'll practice walking. With so much to do around here, and my bedroom on the second floor, I'll have nein choice but to get better, ain't so?"

"The doctor said to keep you on the first floor until you're ready to climb stairs regularly," Daed said, turning his attention back to her. "Your mamm and I will sleep upstairs until then."

"It won't be long." Kristi shifted the baby to her left arm and reached for a cinnamon roll with her right. Then, she glanced out the window and across the sunlit yard toward Shane's haus, barely visible through the trees. If only he'd been invited to her homecoming party.

At least she'd see him tomorrow, when it was time for his run with Chinook. Surely, he wouldn't come by without checking on her.

Her heart thumped into overdrive as she envisioned their reunion. She would save him a cinnamon roll. Maybe he'd spend a few minutes at the kitchen table with her and her family in the morgen. Daed would like him as much as Mamm did, as soon as he got to know him. And especially once he realized that Shane was just a friend.

Even if Kristi wanted him to be more.

She shook her head with a sigh. Friendship was the only option when it came to Englisch men.

It would be wunderbaar living right next door to her new best friend.

Chapter 4

February

*I*t had been four months since Shane had spoken to Kristi. It hadn't seemed right to just end their relationship the way he had. For the thousandth time, he regretted failing to tell her that he wouldn't be coming around. But then, he would have had to explain why, and he didn't want to give her a reason to resent her father. He wasn't about to drive a wedge between them.

Still, it saddened him to think he might have hurt Kristi. And it hurt *him* to know Ira had singled him out as unworthy of his daughter—the first woman to have turned Shane's head since the death of his wife. It was obvious Kristi was permitted to have English friends. He'd seen various cars pull into the driveway, pick her up, and drive off. Evidently this firm boundary excluded him alone.

He missed their visits, casual though they'd been. Did she miss him?

He didn't have to wonder too long. As usual, Shane saw Ira that morning when he went over to the Lapps' to take Chinook on a run. Ira seemed to have become accepting of him as a neighbor and a vet, but he apparently hadn't changed his mind about wanting Shane to keep his distance from Kristi. When Shane asked about her progress, Ira pulled at his beard before answering. "She's doing well. Not quite where I think she should be, but at least she's walking."

Shane opened the kennel and snapped a leash on Chinook's collar.

Ira straightened his shoulders. "I hope she'll get married this wedding season."

Shane felt a stab of pain, even though he knew that was as it should be. However, he hadn't seen any Amish men coming courting. But that wasn't to say they hadn't been. After all, Kristi had said courting was done under cover of darkness.

Wanting to change the subject, Shane inquired about the white van he'd noticed parked in the driveway. Ira murmured something about leaving in a few minutes for a trip to Florida, then turned and headed for the barn.

Would it be wrong to approach Kristi while her parents were away? Try to pick up where they'd left off with their budding friendship? He hesitated a moment. And then shook his head. Like it or not, he needed to honor Ira's wishes and leave his daughter alone. He should have left her alone in the hospital, especially after being expressly forbidden to see her.

He glanced toward the house again and noticed a bit of movement in one of the downstairs windows. Then, he forced his attention back to the kennel and Chinook. Time for a run to clear his mind.

Kristi cupped the steaming mug in her hands and peeked out of the open window to watch Shane's daily routine of releasing Chinook for an early run. She could not figure out this devastatingly handsome man. He lived on a farm but didn't use the land, instead renting the acreage to someone for crops and boarding animals in the barn and pastures. From what she could tell, he had no pets of his own—odd for a vet. Odder still was that he'd picked a farm in the middle of Amish country.

His affections for her dog were evident on his face. If only those feelings were directed toward her, too.

Her breath caught. After all this time, why did she still want him to pay attention to her in that way? They were complete opposites. Besides, he'd made his feelings more than clear when he'd dumped her that day in the hospital. He'd ended their fledging friendship just when she was about to be released—just when a relationship could have become a lot easier.

She stepped away from the window, ashamed of her fascination with an Englisch man, and took a sip of her tea. She wouldn't spy on him anymore. She needed to practice self-control.

Chinook made a whining sound. Despite her fresh resolve, Kristi leaned toward the open window again and watched as dog and man interacted like old friends. Kind of the way she and her cousin Martha had greeted each other on Martha's wedding day last year.

Kristi was glad that her dog had the friendship of Shane Zimmerman. But she wanted his friendship, too. She smiled at the sound of Chinook "talking" to Shane in her own language of happy yelps and whimpers as he unhooked the gate and clipped a leash on her. The dog danced and wagged her tail with excitement as he led her out of the enclosure.

Ache ripped through Kristi's heart anew to think of how their friendship had died. Why had Shane abruptly stopped visiting her once she'd come home from the hospital? She'd seen him chatting with Daed out by the road from time to time. He'd even come over to check on a cow that was having trouble delivering her calf. Daed had gone for him, insisting Kristi stay inside, out of the way, while Dr. Zimmerman was there. She didn't know why. Surely, Daed recognized what a gut man Shane was. It couldn't be that he wanted her to stay away from him. At least, he'd never said as much. Plus, it wasn't as if Daed would have been trying to protect her from the sight of a cow giving birth. She'd witnessed plenty of animal births before, and she helped deliver human boppli all the time.

That left her with one conclusion: Shane had requested that she stay away whenever he was around.

If that was true, then it must have been out of a sense of pity alone that he'd come to the hospital and visited her. And the attraction she'd sensed between them had been strictly one-sided. Not mutual.

She'd seen Shane laughing with Mamm once or twice, but whenever he'd noticed her coming, he'd given a quick nod, made some brief excuse about a visit he needed to make, and left.

He was a vet. Maybe he really was that busy.

Kristi sighed. There was no convincing herself that his excuses had been legitimate.

Shane had never asked her what she did for a living. Maybe, since she was Amish, he assumed she spent every day at home, cooking, gardening, and sewing. He probably thought her support system was such that she no longer needed his friendship.

Carrying her tea, Kristi limped from the kitchen to the front room so she could watch Shane and Chinook jog down the dirt road. It'd be her birthday gift to herself. No need to sneak around or be quiet. Mamm and Daed had just left for Pinecraft. She was glad Mamm had relinquished her earlier determination to take her along.

Kristi reached the front window and lifted the partially pulled shades. It was a chilly February day, with temperatures in the mid-thirties, yet Shane still wore his bright-red jogging shorts and a white T-shirt. She hated that she couldn't tear her eyes away from him. That made her almost as bad as the man across the street who ogled her all the time. She shuddered, remembering the time she'd caught him surveying her window with a pair of binoculars, right after she'd washed her hair and left it down to dry. It was a sin for a man to see the uncovered head and hair of any woman but his frau.

Yet Shane had not only seen hers, he'd also touched it.

She pushed the memory away, trying to ignore the sensation of warmth rising in her face, and took another sip of tea.

She'd die of shame if Shane caught her staring at him. It was bad enough Mamm had caught her once. She'd gotten a stern talking-to about how she needed to find a "gut Amish man" and get married, settle down, and start a family.

Evidently Johnny Miller fit her parents' definition of a "gut Amish man." She'd seen Daed talking with Johnny's daed last church Sunday, both of them casting occasional glances in her direction. Probably trying to make a match.

That would never happen, though. She knew Johnny was courting another girl. She wondered what Mamm and Daed would think if they knew that Eli had been courting her and had unceremoniously dumped her after her accident. As for Kristi, she was interested in…. Her stomach clenched. Someone she shouldn't be interested in.

After Shane and Chinook had disappeared from view, Kristi moved away from the window. She needed to shower and get ready for an appointment with an expectant mamm. The time they'd arranged to meet was an hour earlier than she usually started her workday. She sighed, wishing she could go back to bed. Take a nap, at the very least. She'd been up all night delivering Peter and Marie's beautiful baby bu, her nephew. They'd named him Aaron.

When a mamm-to-be insisted that seven o'clock in the morgen was the only time she was available, what else could Kristi do? Her schedule was at the mercy of her clients. She wouldn't gripe. She rubbed her eyes and glanced at the battery-operated clock. It was after six o'clock. She needed to hurry.

Once she had showered and dressed, Kristi filled her travel mug with steaming water and added a tea bag. On days like this, she needed a double dose of caffeine. Then, after donning her black coat and bonnet, she grabbed her cane and hobbled out the door. She hitched Samson to the buggy and came around to the driver's side to climb in.

That's when she heard sneakers pounding the pavement. The runners had returned.

Shane's blue eyes met hers for a second, and then his gaze darted away. "Hope you don't mind I took the dog out."

Why would she mind? He'd been taking the dog for a run every day, often twice a day, for the past four months.

"Uh-uh." *Pathetic response.* "I hope you had a gut run."

A dimple appeared at the corner of his mouth, and a smile danced on his lips, which were neither too full nor too thin. Just…perfect. Kissable.

She shouldn't think such things. She forced her attention up to his eyes, instead.

"We did. Isn't that right, girl?" Shane ruffled the fur on Chinook's head, and the dog whined, as if she understood every word and was dutifully holding up her side of the conversation.

Kristi had once felt close to her dog, but they'd grown apart since her accident.

She tossed her medical bag into the buggy.

"Well, it was nice seeing you." Shane started to move away, Chinook at his heels.

"Wait." Kristi took several steps toward him.

He paused beside Samson and turned around.

She drew in an unnecessarily deep breath. "I don't know much about you. And, well, it seems I should, if I'm going to let my dog keep dating you. Don't you think so?"

He grinned, flashing his dimple again. "You know my name, where I live…what else is there to know?" Then, he shrugged, the same way he had when he'd blown off every one of her personal questions during his hospital visits. He'd always managed to change the subject.

Kristi could think of a trillion things she'd like to know, starting with why he'd ended their budding friendship so abruptly. Did he have a girlfriend? It was none of her business, of course, especially considering their cultural and religious differences. She'd be in serious trouble if anyone ever discovered her infatuation with the Englisch vet. That'd probably warrant a visit from the bishop.

With a sigh, she glanced at Shane's haus and noticed the bare flower beds lining the front walk. Her fingers itched to plant something. Bulbs, like tulips and jonquils, would be nice, but they needed to be planted in the fall. Maybe some marigolds or moss roses could go in once spring arrived. A red geranium would look lovely in a hanging planter on his front porch. The place needed a woman's touch, plain and simple.

When her gaze returned to him, she was startled by his steady, silent regard. Apparently he wasn't going to volunteer any information. She desperately wished he would. She'd like to give their friendship another chance. She wanted to get to know the man she was attracted to. The man who'd saved her life.

She opened her mouth to voice these thoughts but promptly shut it again. Maybe he didn't want to be known by a woman who hobbled around with a cane. She was well aware that the accessory didn't enhance her appeal to the opposite sex.

She edged closer to him and rubbed Chinook's ears. The dog grinned up at her.

"She's very sweet." Shane ruffled the dog's head once more, then glanced at his watch. "Well, I'd better get going. See you later." He turned away again. "Come on, Chinook."

Kristi let him go, having nothing else to say to hold his interest. Plus, she needed to get going herself. A glance at the rising sun told her she would be late for her first appointment of the day. She headed back to the buggy. Instead of climbing in immediately, she paused and looked back at the kennel.

Shane waved Chinook inside and shut the gate. Then, he turned and started back toward the buggy. She straightened her posture and surveyed the sky, hoping he hadn't noticed her gawking. "Looks like it's going to be a beautiful day."

He nodded. "When springtime comes, let me know if you want any help getting rid of those weeds in your yard. I mowed them once in the fall, but it looks like they're making a comeback. Maybe I could spray the area with some weed killer."

He had mowed her herb garden? And he wanted to poison it? She'd known someone had cut it down while she'd been in the hospital, but she'd figured it'd been Creepy Guy. Not Shane.

She spun around to face him so quickly, her bad leg buckled.

Her cane was too wobbly to hang on to for support, so she dropped it and grabbed for the side of the buggy. But missed. She closed her eyes and clenched her teeth, getting ready to crash-land on the gravel.

Instead of painful stones, strong arms broke her fall. She opened her eyes and saw Shane leaning over her, like some hero on the cover of a tawdry romance novel. Not that she'd read any. She'd seen them on a shelf at the library.

Even though she was cradled in his arms—the perfect posture for kissing—the truth was that he wasn't kissing her. Wasn't about to. So, she really had no excuse to faint.

But she couldn't help slipping into the dark of unconsciousness.

❧

Shane's heart stopped when Kristi went limp in his arms. Why had she fainted? Low blood pressure, maybe? Or hypoglycemia? He shifted his arms and lifted her toward his chest. Glancing from her farmhouse to his, he determined that hers was closer. But there was that issue of walking uninvited—and unwelcome—into a house that didn't belong to him. Even if no one was home.

Besides, his cell phone was at his house. If it became necessary to call for an ambulance, he'd need it.

His decision made, he picked her up, turned, and started across the lawn.

"Hey!"

Shane's steps stuttered, and he turned in the direction of the voice. *Donald.* He stifled a groan.

"I saw her go down. What happened?" The neighbor man hurried across the street, shrugging into a jacket.

"She fainted. I think she might have skipped breakfast."

"She usually takes her breakfast with her when she leaves so early. Pancakes and such."

"I don't think she has anything with her today."

"Hey, you're probably in a hurry to get off to work. You usually leave about now, don't you? And it looks like you still need to shower and change. I can take her off your hands. Just carry her on over to my house. The wife won't mind."

Shane glanced across the street at Donald's house and saw that the carport was empty. Donald's wife was probably at work—first shift at a factory in Springfield, if Shane remembered correctly. For some reason, he didn't feel right handing Kristi over to Donald. He seemed harmless enough, but his apparent obsession with spying on neighbors was pretty disturbing. "Thanks, but you're...uh, she's...I'm a doctor."

"I thought you were a vet."

Caught in a lie. Shane sucked in a breath. "That's true, but some of the treatments are the same for humans and animals. This, I can handle. So, if you don't mind, I'll get her settled."

Shane turned his back on Donald and strode away. It was a little alarming that Kristi hadn't come to. And here he'd been, talking and wasting time. He climbed his porch steps, opened the front door, and stepped inside, where he deposited her on the couch.

Hopefully, Donald wouldn't tell Ira he'd been with Kristi—alone—in his house.

Chapter 5

Kristi became aware of someone patting her cheeks, and her eyelids fluttered open. It took a few moments for the blurring to subside. When her vision had stabilized, she saw Shane crouched on the floor next to her, so close that she could smell peppermint on his breath.

She must have fainted. How long had she been unconscious? Definitely long enough for him to carry her here—his haus, she presumed. Her eyes scanned the room. It was sparsely decorated, furnished with only the couch she lay on; a blue recliner across the way; presumably a small table at the other end of the couch, holding up the lamp she could see; and a large flat-screen TV mounted one of the grayish-blue walls. On another wall was a framed photograph of a ship docked in a harbor. Two books were stacked next to the recliner on the beige carpet. One of them appeared to be a Bible.

A Bible? No matter. If anyone found out she'd been alone with him, in his haus...well, it wouldn't be pretty, for sure and for certain.

He met her gaze and rocked back on his heels. "Feel better?"

Kristi pushed herself into an upright position, ignoring how her vision swam as a result. "Jah. Danki. I've never done that before."

"Did you eat breakfast?"

"Nein." *Because you were busy playing Peeping Polly.* "Just a cup of tea." That reminded her—she'd been holding her travel mug of hot tea when she'd fallen. It was probably on the ground near the buggy, along with her cane.

"You need to eat something. Let me get you some toast. Would you like a couple of eggs, too?" He stood.

"I really need to go. I have an appointment at seven, and—"

"Didn't your mother ever tell you breakfast is the most important meal of the day?" He smiled, flashing his dimple. "Besides, you need to keep up your strength. How about an egg sandwich to go?"

Kristi shrugged. It seemed she had no choice. He'd decided she needed to eat. She was already late for her appointment; waiting on an egg sandwich wouldn't make much of a difference. Besides, it was sweet of him to make her breakfast. She could call her patient and let her know. However, the client's file, including her phone number, was in Kristi's bag in the buggy. And she hadn't programmed the number in her cell phone. She patted her pocket to see if the phone was still there. It wasn't. It must be in her bag, too. Either that or it'd slid out when she'd fallen.

Holding the armrest of the couch for balance, Kristi stood to her feet, waited for her vision to settle, and took a tentative step toward the kitchen. An ache throbbed through her bad leg. Should she ask Shane to run and get her cane? Nein. He'd probably tell her to sit still. At least her leg hadn't buckled again. Maybe the dizzy spell had more to do with her having been out all night than not having bothered to eat breakfast. While she usually preferred to eat oatmeal or another hot cereal, an egg sandwich sounded surprisingly tempting. She envisioned farm-fresh brown eggs cracking open and their yellow insides sizzling in a buttered cast-iron skillet.

She took a few slow, lurching steps. It was more difficult without the cane than she would have imagined. She hesitated beside the end table, which displayed an array of framed photos. Kristi picked up a snapshot of a couple—Shane and a woman with short, spiky red hair. His arm was draped around her shoulders.

Her vision blurred again, though, this time, dizziness wasn't to blame. She blinked away some of the moisture and studied the photo another moment before putting it back. The woman had no resemblance whatsoever to Shane; she was definitely not his sister, unless one of them had been adopted. Figured. The first man she'd ever really been attracted to was already taken.

She'd have to get over it later.

Besides, she'd never had him. And, with their cultural differences, she never would.

A couple of steps more, and Kristi entered the kitchen. Shane stood at the stove, whistling to himself as he poured a milky-looking substance from a carton into a small skillet.

Egg Beaters—ick. She knew about them only because her Englisch friend Starr loved them. But Shane couldn't honestly expect her to eat them, right?

She slid her gaze to the table. There was a plate with two pieces of lightly buttered white toast—taken, no doubt, from the store-bought loaf in a colorful bag on the counter. Squishy, cheap stuff that probably tasted like cardboard. How could the man eat like this and look as great as he did?

Other than the bread bag, a cookie jar and a toaster were all that adorned the countertops. A small table with two chairs occupied one corner of the kitchen. A microwave oven was suspended from a cabinet above the stove.

Kristi wondered whether her haus was visible from here. She stepped nearer to the window above the sink to find out.

Shane turned and smiled. "Almost done. You should have stayed seated. I would have brought it to you."

"Is this what you had for breakfast?" She waved her hand toward the food. If one could call it that.

He looked puzzled for a second. Then, he shook his head and crossed the room to the refrigerator. He opened the freezer door, letting out a rush of cold air, and studied the array of boxes inside before pulling out a yellow carton. "I had frozen waffles. Should have offered you one."

Kristi shuddered. Processed food—it wasn't natural. Maybe the redheaded woman in the picture would teach him some healthy eating habits.

Kristi glanced back at the stovetop, where the pan of egg product still bubbled away, and tried to prepare herself to choke it down, just to be polite. How long until she could make her excuses and leave? If she could get the breakfast to go, as he'd suggested, then she could dispose of the sandwich discreetly without hurting his feelings.

Shane stuffed the box of waffles back inside the freezer and shut the door. His gaze dropped to Kristi's legs. She knew he couldn't see anything he wasn't supposed to, as they were covered almost to the ankles by her functional, if not fashionable, dark green dress. After a moment, his eyes flickered back to her face. "Does your leg still hurt?"

"Sometimes, jah." She didn't want to sound like a complainer, but he'd asked, right?

"Have a seat. Breakfast is just about ready." Shane returned to the stove, shut off the burner, and used a spatula to slide the heap of scrambled "eggs" atop one piece of toast. Then, he placed the other slice on top, grabbed a knife, and sliced the sandwich into four triangles—not four squares, as

Mamm always did. They were cute. And definitely easier to handle than a whole sandwich. The other men Kristi knew would have handed her the whole thing—that is, in the unlikely event that they fixed something in the kitchen.

"Danki. Would you mind if I took it to go? I am running late...."

Shane shook his head. "I'd rather you didn't. I want to make sure you're feeling okay." He moved closer. "I know you said you have an appointment, but—"

"I'm fine." Kristi considered twirling around to show him how fine she was, but she didn't think her leg could handle the movement. Definitely not without the aid of her cane. It would work against her if she fell to the floor mid-twirl. Although, if it landed her in his arms again, it might be worth it.

The photo in the living room flashed through her mind. Why did she insist on fantasizing about someone who was already in a relationship?

"I'm fine," she repeated, wanting to reassure him. Or maybe it was to convince herself.

"I need to get to work, too, but a few more minutes won't hurt either of us." He glanced at his watch. "Let's make a deal. You eat half the sandwich here, and I'll feel better about letting you go." He grabbed the plate from the counter with one hand and touched her elbow with the other.

Sparks shot up her arm. Kristi glanced down at the point of contact, half expecting to see flames.

"Please, sit down."

"But...."

It was no use. With a heart-stopping grin, he steered her over to the table and pulled out a chair.

Kristi sat.

Shane turned the other chair around and straddled it, clearly prepared to make sure she ate. *It's just half a sandwich*, Kristi told herself. She picked up one triangular quarter and took a tentative bite. Maybe it would help to imagine these were farm-fresh eggs on homemade bread. She closed her eyes and chewed, trying to keep her expression neutral. She could do this. She could do this. She could—

"Let me get you some juice, too."

Kristi swallowed and opened her eyes. One bite down. To her surprise, these eggs tasted pretty normal, though they lacked the strong odor of farm eggs.

A moment later, Shane placed a small tumbler of artificially colored orange liquid in front of her.

"Danki."

"No problem." He smiled. "Eat up."

Encouraged by the ease with which she'd kept the first bite down, Kristi proceeded to finish the rest of that quarter, and a second one, thereby fulfilling her requirement. If only all her patients could be so easily persuaded to comply. Suppressing a grin, she rose to her feet. "Danki for everything."

Shane nodded. "If you're sure you're fine, let me see you out to your buggy." He grabbed the remainder of her sandwich and wrapped it in a paper napkin. Then, he touched her elbow again, and the sparks flared to life with such intensity that Kristi was sure he must have felt them.

He jerked away as if he'd been singed and took off at a trot toward the front door.

Her face burning, Kristi tried to match his stride, but her leg throbbed, and she was afraid to keep up that pace without any support. She slowed down and rubbed her left thigh, where the pain was the worst.

When Shane stopped at the front door and turned around, she moved her hand away. He didn't need to see her babying herself.

"You're moving a bit stiffly," he observed.

Kristi bit her tongue. As she moved into the front foyer, she spied her black bonnet and her coat draped over the back of a chair. She put on her coat, then snatched up the bonnet and secured it over her head as she hobbled out the door.

"Walking is gut for me," she finally said as he shut the door behind them.

"Yes, it is. Use it or lose it." Apparently, he thought she needed to walk more. He came to her side and tucked her arm in the crook of his elbow, supporting her. Her heart rate tripled.

She didn't want to talk about her leg. She wanted to ask why he never came by. Why he'd let their friendship die. But that picture in his living room had made the answer more than clear. He was involved. With someone else.

She swallowed. "I was looking at some of the photos on the table in your living room. Who's the redhead pictured with you?" Part of her didn't want to know. But part of her also thought that hearing him say "My fiancée" would put a stop to her crazy infatuation.

What if he interpreted her question as an attempt to fish for his relationship status? Ugh. The half sandwich in her stomach threatened to come up.

Shane remained silent as they crossed his front yard and approached her buggy. He probably wasn't planning on rewarding her nosiness with an answer.

Kristi straightened her spine. Just as well. It wasn't any of her business, anyway. And he was probably about to say so, judging by the way he'd stiffened.

"My wife," he finally muttered.

Kristi's heart sputtered to a stop. He had a frau? That didn't seem possible. He lived in a haus that screamed "bachelor," and ate meals that came from cardboard boxes. Plus, he'd lived in Seymour for more than a year, and she'd never seen anyone else over there—certainly not an attractive redhead. There was something he wasn't telling her.

As they rounded the front of the buggy, her curiosity got the best of her. "So, where is she now? Trying to sell the haus where you used to live? Planning on joining you later?" Her tongue had a mind of its own.

"No. She's…no longer with us."

She put her hand on her stomach, hoping to encourage the sandwich to stay down. "I'm so sorry." He didn't show anger at her nosiness, but neither did he sound heartbroken. Just resigned, and maybe a little bit sad. It must have happened long enough ago that he'd adjusted. Mostly.

There was a measure of relief in knowing she wasn't attracted to a married man. That would have made it so much worse. But, still. He'd lost his frau. Tears welled in her eyes.

"Where do you need to go for your appointment?" He changed the subject before she had a chance to apologize for prying. "I could give you a ride, but you'd have to find your own way home." He bent over and picked up her cane and the travel mug.

Kristi climbed into the buggy. She deserved his inquiries, considering the major blunder she'd just made. And, since he'd reacted with candor and kindness, he'd earned the same from her. She drew a deep breath. "I need to go to a farm to meet with a frau who's expecting. I'm her midwife."

Silently, mouth set, Shane handed Kristi her travel mug and the napkin containing the other half of the egg sandwich. He slid her cane in next to her.

Kristi bristled, bracing herself for another round of the argument she'd had with several non-Amish in the past—people who scoffed at her lack of a medical license and didn't consider her qualified to deliver babies.

But Shane didn't say a word. Maybe Kristi had been wrong to expect wariness on his part. With a deep breath, she picked up the reins. "Well, danki—"

"So, you…deliver babies. At home. And you prescribe… herbal remedies?" He turned and nodded at her yard. "Explains all the weeds."

She couldn't fully read his tone. But she knew that there was far greater nutritional value in one of those "weeds" than in the "egg" sandwich sitting next to her. She merely nodded, and he made no reply.

∽◡◠◡∾

A midwife? Shane's heart took a sharp dive toward his heels. He couldn't believe that the captivating woman seated in the buggy before him specialized in the very profession he'd come to despise.

Painful memories flooded him: his wife jubilantly announcing that they were expecting their first baby. Her excitement at the prospect of having a home delivery with the help of a midwife.

Shane had expressed his concern, but Becca had assured him that everything would be fine. They'd had a major argument, but, as usual, he'd given in to her wishes.

And maybe everything would have been fine. Except that Becca had reacted fatally to the herbs the midwife had insisted she take. It had been hours later when Shane had come home and found her.…

Admittedly, the autopsy had revealed that a brain aneurysm was to blame; nothing the midwife had done could be linked conclusively to his wife's death. Still, Shane suspected that the herbs the midwife had supplied had raised Becca's blood pressure and ultimately resulted in the artery bursting.

He tried not to glare. To keep the disappointment that coursed through him from showing on his face. Kristi had the right to choose her own career. He had the right not to like it. But he had nothing to say. Not when he wanted to lash out at her for something she'd had no part in. He didn't want to hurt her feelings.

It was all he could do to step back, flash what he hoped might be the facsimile of a grin in her direction, and mutter, "I need to get to work."

Chapter 6

$\mathcal{K}$risti smoothed the dark green fabric of her dress over her knees and watched him walk away. His casual indifference toward her "weeds" had offended her a little, but at least he hadn't openly questioned her profession. It wasn't as if she misled women. Her clients knew she wasn't a licensed physician. They elected to hire a midwife because they were seeking a more comfortable, more natural birthing experience than most hospitals had to offer. Granted, there were women who needed more medical help than she could provide, but she always directed them to seek professional assistance.

Her shoulders tightened as she picked up the reins again and clicked her tongue, signaling Samson. The horse plodded down the drive toward the road. She checked for traffic and, seeing none, urged Samson forward. Did she have the energy to pull herself out of her slouch? What would be the point? The walls of her heart seemed stuck to each other like a deflated balloon. Why did Shane's opinion matter so much? It shouldn't.

But it did. Because she was infatuated with the man.

Kristi shrugged. In a way, this morgen had been like the death of a dream. Not that she'd been earnestly planning on a relationship with Shane. It was just that her heart didn't always listen to her head. And something inside her wanted a chance with him.

But what good was a chance? It wouldn't lead to anything. There was no way it could. She sighed. It would be best for them to remain mere acquaintances. Nothing more.

If only the memory of his gentle touch didn't cause her stomach to clench and her skin to tingle.

She was too smart for this.

She jerked on the reins, directing Samson over to the side of the road and then pulling back so he would stop. Then, she turned to the bag resting on the seat beside her and shuffled through her file folders, selecting the one for Karen, her first appointment of the day. She wasn't Plain. In fact, she was far more modern than Kristi would have thought possible. She probably just wanted to brag about using an Amish midwife.

At least Kristi had a cell phone. She smiled as she opened the file and located Karen's home phone number. Then, she reached inside the small interior pocket of her bag, pulled out her cell phone, and dialed the number.

Karen's husband answered on the second ring. Kristi swallowed, hoping for a sympathetic response. "Mr. Baysinger? This is Kristi Lapp, the midwife. I'm so sorry, but I'm running late. If Karen still wants me to kum, I'll be there as soon as I can."

"That's fine. I'll tell Karen." He disconnected without calling to his frau. Probably just as well. Karen was the kind of woman who always had someplace to go. She served on many volunteer committees. It was more than likely she had another appointment somewhere. But the delay hardly could have been helped.

When Kristi arrived at Karen's, her client waited on the front porch, a steaming mug in her hands.

Kristi climbed out of the buggy and greeted her as she tethered Samson's reins to a fence post. "If that's koffee, I hope that's the only cup you plan on having today."

Karen smiled as Kristi approached the porch. "Sometimes a booster shot of caffeine is the only thing keeping me going."

Kristi caught a scent of the strong brew and wrinkled her nose. "Your body needs to use a lot of energy to develop the new life inside of you. A nap would do both of you a lot more good than koffee, and you wouldn't have the side effects."

Karen shook her head. "No time for naps."

"Caffeine is a drug." Kristi tried to soften the words with a wink.

Karen merely grinned. "Come on in. I have a meeting at nine."

Smiling, Kristi complied.

Forty-five minutes later, having finished up with Karen, Kristi stood on the porch and waved as her client backed out of the driveway in her car, then sped off to her next appointment.

When the coast was clear, Kristi retraced her steps to the buggy. The other half of her artificial egg sandwich still lay on the buggy seat. Hunger pangs gnawed at her, but she wasn't about to finish it at this point. Food poisoning wasn't on the agenda for today. Or any day.

Still, it had been sweet of Shane to fix a meal for her. He could have sent her home to eat, or simply let her go off to work without insisting she eat. He hadn't. That meant something. Just what, Kristi wasn't sure.

She untied Samson, climbed into the buggy, and drove the short distance to the local grocery store to find something she could eat. A small carton of strawberry yogurt, a banana, and a bottle of apple juice would tide her over until lunch.

As she carried her purchases back to the buggy, Kristi noticed a veterinary clinic across the street. Not Shane's, apparently. According to the sign out front, the veterinarian's name was Mike Stevenson. She needed to figure out the name of Shane's clinic and where it was located. Despite their heated encounter that morgen, he certainly deserved her patronage. It was the least she could do to repay him for taking such good care of Chinook.

Dogs were supposed to be excellent judges of character. And Chinook certainly loved Shane.

Kristi emptied the contents of her grocery bag onto the seat, slid the napkin containing the toxic "egg" sandwich into the empty bag, and then settled in to eat her snack. She had an hour before her next appointment, which was only a twenty-minute ride away. She was thankful to have time for a late breakfast and a little Bible reading.

Around noon, when Kristi arrived at home, she noticed Chinook lying next to the fence of her kennel, her blue eyes fixed on Shane's haus. His Jeep wasn't in the driveway.

At the sound of the wagon wheels, the dog perked up. She starting wagging her tail and whining.

Kristi stopped the buggy in front of the barn, set the brake, and eased herself out. She made her way over to the dog's enclosure, where she opened the gate, bent down, and petted Chinook.

"Are you lonely, girl? I know the feeling. I wish I could take you on a walk. Or on a run, like Shane does." But she couldn't run, even if she were physically able. She'd been taught not to. Besides, the dresses she wore were hardly conducive to jogging.

Kristi gave the dog another pat and then refilled her water bowl.

As Kristi walked to the haus, her shoulders drooped once more with disappointment. She missed the walks she'd taken every evening with Chinook before her accident. Now, she couldn't even go on a short walk without the help of her cane. The dog would be too much for her to handle.

In the kitchen, she made herself a cup of hot tea and then went back outside to sit with Chinook just outside her kennel. The dog sat at attention, her focus fixed on Shane's haus. In spite of Kristi's presence, the dog didn't budge. Nor did she show any interest when Kristi fixed a sandwich—all-natural peanut butter and honey on twelve-grain bread—and offered her half. Granted, it wasn't the most exciting meal in the world, but Chinook used to gobble it down with just as much gusto as she might a filet of fish.

Funny thing was, Kristi struggled to find her own appetite.

She was still studying her half of the sandwich when her cell phone rang. She glanced at the caller ID. It was Starr, the Englisch girl who'd been one of her best friends since they'd met as teenagers. Glad for a distraction, Kristi picked up the phone. "Hi, Starr. What's happening?"

"Nothing, really. I'm in the mood for a chocolate milkshake. Want to come to McDonald's with me? I can pick you up."

Kristi thought for a moment. "I'll meet you there. I need to make some prenatal visits after lunch."

She set her half of the sandwich next to the one she'd left for Chinook, in case the dog changed her mind. "I'll be back a little later, girl, okay?" She rubbed Chinook behind the ears, but the dog didn't bother to wag her tail. In fact, she hardly acknowledged Kristi, other than to give her a heartbreaking glance before returning her gaze to Shane's haus. Pathetic. "He'll kum see you when he gets home," Kristi assured her. "Unless I scared him away for gut."

For Shane, the morning stretched on in an endless procession of cats and dogs. It certainly didn't help that he couldn't get Kristi out of his mind. Of all the careers available to an Amish woman, hers had to be the one he loathed. Why couldn't she run a bed-and-breakfast or a bakery? Work in a greenhouse? Stitch quilts for sale? Anything besides practice midwifery.

It just wasn't right.

Although, he had to admit that before medicine had evolved to make birthing safer in a hospital setting, midwifery had been a valuable profession. He thought of the midwives who'd saved all the babies in Moses' time and been rewarded by God. And of all those women on the prairie who'd needed midwives. But nowadays?

God must be looking down from heaven and laughing at this one. Kristi was the first woman he'd been attracted to since his wife had died, and she was unacceptable, in more ways than one. Amish. Her parents disapproved of him. And her career choice was the sole profession he resented.

Even so, his fingertips tingled at the memory of touching her skin. Had she felt the sparks, too?

Maybe Ira had been right to draw the line so early in the relationship.

And maybe Shane had been right to honor Ira's wishes.

This whole situation with Kristi made it obvious why Amish couples courted under the cover of darkness. It kept the relationship confidential. Top secret.

Safe from a father's disapproval until it was too late for him to do anything about it.

But, if that were the case, how was Ira to presume that Kristi would get married later this year?

Shane should have stepped in when he'd had the opportunity. It was so confusing. The immediate connection, the almost tangible sparks between them…but everything else was wrong. She was just a distraction. Nothing more.

Right?

"Should haves" didn't change a thing. Kristi was still Amish. Still a midwife. And still subject to her father's wishes, which didn't permit a relationship with him.

Besides, Shane wasn't looking for a wife.

A companion? Maybe. A friend? Most definitely. But if he wanted a committed relationship, then his single-and-on-the-hunt receptionist at the clinic would fit the bill.

He shuddered at the thought. He'd gone out of his way not to give Patsy the wrong idea.

Shane shook his head, hoping to clear it, and reached for his office phone to call a farmer who'd asked him to come vaccinate some cattle. He glanced up when a shadow crossed in front of his door.

His too-available receptionist leaned against the doorframe. "I turned the sign to 'Closed for Lunch,'" she said in a sultry voice. "I know you're busy all afternoon, but what are you doing this evening?"

Chapter 7

$\mathcal{K}$risti couldn't remember the last time she'd gone to a fast-food restaurant, and now she realized why. She could smell the grease from a mile away.

As she stood in line with Starr, she perused the menu posted behind the counter, keeping her eyes out for healthier options. Salad seemed to be her only choice.

Realizing she'd been holding her breath, she inhaled. And felt her arteries clogging by the second.

Ten minutes later, she carried her side garden salad and small ice water to the booth where Starr was seated with her tray of food: a fried chicken sandwich, a medium order of fries, and a chocolate milkshake with whipped cream and a cherry on top. The shake looked tempting, actually—at least compared to the sandwich and fries.

When Kristi slipped into the booth across from Starr, her friend scowled at her selection. "Rabbit food, Kristi? You should have at least gotten a milkshake. It's your birthday, for goodness' sake!"

Kristi laughed but refrained from commenting on Starr's eating habits. Her friend had heard her lecture plenty of times before.

Starr glanced around the restaurant. "This place is so crowded."

Kristi surveyed the space, seeing that every table was filled. And then her gaze connected with a familiar pair of brilliant blue eyes. She froze, and her face heated.

Shane started his approach, clutching a carryout bag in one hand and a brown McCafé cup in the other. A few strides brought him to their booth.

"We should stop meeting like this." He placed his bag on the table but kept his grip on the fold at the top.

Kristi smiled and tried to remain calm. "Hi, Shane. This is my friend Starr Belmont. Starr, this is…Chinook's new vet, Shane Zimmerman."

Shane quirked his eyebrows at her, then turned his smile on Starr. "Nice to meet you, Starr."

"Likewise." Starr shook his hand, then looked back at Kristi, her eyebrows arched in a way that Kristi had learned meant, "He's so cute!"

"Want to join us?" Kristi asked, certain he'd say no. It looked as if he was ready to go.

Shane hesitated for a moment, his grip tightening around the enclosure of the bag, which made a crinkling sound. Then, he nodded. "Sure."

As he sat down next to her, Kristi scooted closer to the wall to make room, but not quickly enough to avoid a brush against his blue-jeaned knee. She tried to ignore how her whole body tingled. Why was she so keenly aware of this man?

He opened his bag and pulled out a box printed with the words "Big Mac," followed by a large container of fries and not one but two apple pies. He slid one in Kristi's direction. "It's almost cheaper to buy two than just one. Want it?"

Kristi shook her head. "Nein, danki."

Starr snorted. "English, Kristi. He might not speak Pennsylvania Dutch."

"I do, actually." Shane nodded at Starr. "My grandparents are Amish."

Kristi had known he was practically perfect. Total perfection would mean he was Amish—not just his großeltern. She longed to hear the story but couldn't find the courage to ask.

Shane offered the apple pie to Starr, but she declined, also, pointing to her half-finished chocolate milkshake. "So, you have Amish grandparents, yet you're not Amish. That's a story. Do tell."

Shane turned his heart-stopping smile on Kristi and placed the apple pie next to her salad. "A woman can't live on lettuce alone. You have to get at least a few grams of fat here and there."

"Good luck making her." Starr took a bite of her sandwich. "We're waiting. The story is…?"

Shane chuckled. "You're tenacious. But, if you insist, my dad left the Amish to marry my mom. End of story."

That couldn't possibly be the end of the story. Not even the beginning. It was just a summary. But Kristi couldn't keep from noticing the parallels. His dad had left for an Englisch girl. Would she end up leaving for an Englisch man?

Ach, nein. She couldn't think that way. Maybe he'd embrace the Amish faith for her.

Not likely.

Shane opened the carton containing his Big Mac, and his arm brushed Kristi's. She sucked in a ragged breath and focused on her salad of lettuce, cucumbers, tomatoes, shredded carrots, and other healthy ingredients—not one drop of oily processed dressing, even though the cashier had given her a strange look when she'd said "No dressing, please" and had placed a packet on the tray, anyway. She was glad she'd sprinkled her lettuce with sugar, as she always did, before Shane had shown up. She didn't need to give him further proof that she was weird.

His arm brushed hers again.

This wasn't going to work at all. Except that she had no place else to go. She was already as close to the wall as she could get. Shane had more space he could use, toward the end of the bench, but he didn't seem to consider that.

Maybe he would if she scooted closer to him. For a second, she was tempted. She tried to summon the courage.

But she couldn't. Besides, it might backfire. Instead of getting the hint that she needed more space, he might wrap his arm around her shoulders, and....

Too tempting.

Feeling the heat rise in her cheeks, she tried once more to force her attention back to her salad. Away from the man sitting next to her, close enough to touch yet far beyond reach. Completely off-limits.

For a few moments, Starr's eyes flicked back and forth between Kristi and Shane. Finally, she put down her sandwich and shook her head. "Okay, I give up. How do you two really know each other? And don't expect me to believe you met when Kristi took Chinook for her shots. You two are chummier than the average vet and client."

Kristi slumped in the seat, not wanting to tell the truth. Besides, what could she say? That he was her hero? That she had a major crush on him? Starr probably could tell as much. She always said Kristi's face was an open book.

Shane took another bite of his burger, as though no one had said anything. That left the answering to Kristi.

She grimaced and shifted on the hard bench. "Um…he's my next-door neighbor. And he's the one who found me at the scene of the buggy accident."

"Ooh." Starr's attention shifted to Shane. "So, you're the one who saved her life!"

He glanced at Kristi, then looked away. "I guess."

"And you're neighbors, too. That's so romantic!" Starr's eyes sparkled with speculation.

Romantic? Kristi supposed that was one way of looking at it. Too bad the romance didn't go any deeper than appearances. Well, except for the tingling she felt when she was near him. And her obsession with watching him out the window. But their friendship had petered out when she'd been released from the hospital. And this morgen's good-bye seemed to have sealed the deal. So, why the tingles?

She didn't have any idea.

Shane pulled out his cell phone and read a message on the screen. "I'm sorry. I have to run." He swallowed the last of his sandwich, then bagged one of the apple pies and what was left of his fries. As he stood, he reached into his shirt pocket and then dropped a business card on the table. "Make sure you eat the pie."

He walked out the door before Kristi had the sense to pick up the card and read it.

Talk to the Paw Veterinary Clinic
Shane Zimmerman, DVM

It was followed by a phone number and his address.

When Kristi looked up, she saw his Jeep passing the window. He waved.

Starr gave her a huge grin. "Was it just me, or were sparks really flying between you two?"

Shane drove out to the ranch. He was ten minutes ahead of schedule, but he figured the rancher wouldn't mind. He'd needed to get away from Kristi before he did something stupid, like reach for her hand. Enfold her in a hug. Or, at the opposite end of the spectrum, tell her about his problem with midwives. That a midwife had been somehow responsible for the deaths of his wife and unborn baby. The death of his dreams.

A new woman haunted his dreams now.

He frowned. Best to get to work and get her out of his mind.

He shouldn't have joined Kristi and her friend for lunch. He'd been so desperate to escape Patsy's clutches, he'd left his bagged lunch sitting in the refrigerator at the clinic and headed to McDonald's. He needed to have an honest talk with his receptionist and let her know he wasn't interested.

Not something he looked forward to.

Shane opened the door of his Jeep. His cowboy boots had barely touched the ground when a cloud of dust announced the presence of the rancher, Marc Ellis, mounted atop his favorite steed.

"I'm glad you're here, Doc. Just had a call from one of the hands. A cow is having difficulties with a birth."

Shane grabbed his bag and shut the door. "I'm right behind you."

◈◈◈

Despite her disgust at fried foods, Kristi decided to sample the apple pie Shane had left for her. The flavor wasn't remotely close to fresh-baked, homemade pie; even so, she nibbled away at it while she continued visiting with Starr.

When only crumbs remained, Kristi looked at the clock on the wall. Time to go. "This has been great, but I need to get on to my prenatal visits." She stood and threw away her trash. "Thanks for making my birthday special. I'll see you again soon, jah?"

She had traveled a couple of miles when she noticed that Samson seemed to be favoring his right hind leg. Moreover, his speed was even slower than his typical snail's pace. Alarmed, Kristi pulled over to the side of the road and into the parking lot of a building that appeared to be abandoned. She didn't remember ever seeing cars or trucks parked here. But the sign on the building indicated it was some sort of plumbing shop.

No matter. She didn't need any help. Samson probably had a stone stuck in his hoof, and she knew how to check. She'd done it before. Once. Of course, Daed had stood over her the whole time, directing her.

Her biggest concern was Samson. He was a stubborn horse who typically did not let anyone near his back end. And, when he was in pain, he became even more cantankerous and tended to kick and nip.

Getting knocked out by an angry horse was not on her to-do list today. Where was Shane when she needed him? If only he'd stuck around until after she'd started out, made sure she'd be alright.

But then, he'd had no reason to fear she wouldn't be.

She supposed she could call him. He'd given her his business card, after all.

Did this constitute an emergency? She figured she'd better check out the situation herself first.

Kristi grabbed her cane, climbed down from the buggy, and approached Samson from the side. He eyed her nervously and snorted with a toss of his head.

"You aren't going to let me touch you, are you?"

He snorted again, shaking his head from side to side.

Was that his way of saying no?

Of course not. Samson wasn't exceptionally bright. Kristi was simply looking for an excuse to summon Shane to her rescue.

She stepped closer to the horse again. He shied away, his eyes wild.

Too bad if her motives were slightly selfish. It was time to call for help.

Kristi reached inside the buggy for her black bag, pulling out her cell phone and Shane's business card. She punched in the number, her heart rate increasing with every digit. Within seconds, she'd be speaking with Shane. No doubt he'd come to rescue her. That's just the type of guy he was.

"Talk to the Paw Veterinary Clinic, Patsy speaking. How may I help you?"

The voice was too perky. Too feminine.

Kristi swallowed. She hadn't expected to reach his clinic. She'd somehow assumed he'd given her his personal number. Silly of her. And this Patsy person? Kristi pictured a buxom blonde, or maybe a pretty redhead, like his deceased frau. Her heart hurt. "Um, is Sha—Dr. Zimmerman there?"

"I'm sorry, he's out of the office for the rest of the afternoon. May I schedule an appointment for you? Or take a message and have him return your call?"

"Nein. No. I'll…." *What? Be fine?* "I'll, um…." Kristi gulped and snapped the phone shut without completing the thought. Who else could she call? The driver, to come get the horse and buggy and take her home?

The phone made a series of annoying beeps and powered off. Dead battery. She'd neglected to charge it sufficiently.

Now what? She looked around. None of the businesses in this sparsely populated area appeared to be open. Why did she have to have a lame horse on the outskirts of town? She supposed it would have been worse on a busy highway, but still.

There was nothing to do but walk. Somewhere. She needed her exercise, anyway.

Kristi tied the reins to a fence post, then readied her cane. There was no telling how far she'd have to go to find help. The question was, which way should she go? Kristi turned in a circle.

She remembered passing a farmhaus with plenty of pickups in the yard. She turned in the direction in which she'd come and started making her way down the road.

It wasn't long before her left leg started to throb. Without the cane, she wouldn't be standing. Even with its help, she moved slowly. Painfully. Like a cripple.

Which was the truth of it. Like it or not, that's what she was.

When she finally reached the farmhaus, Kristi hobbled up to the bright-red front door and knocked. The home looked welcoming, with window boxes of blossoming geraniums, but such a fancy abode made it clear that the residents weren't Amish.

Moments later, the door was opened by a woman covered in flour. The aroma of freshly baked bread drifted out. "May I help you?"

"I hope so. My horse is lame, and I need—"

"Menfolk in the barn." The woman jabbed a finger to the right.

"Dank—thank you." Kristi turned toward the barn, painted red to match the front door.

"They're delivering a breech calf. Looks like Marc had to call for the vet to come out and assist."

Kristi straightened and surveyed the assemblage of vehicles parked by the barn. She smiled when she recognized Shane's Jeep. He was here.

"No telling when they'll be done, but I can't leave the house. I have bread in the oven and a couple of pies and a batch of cookies to prepare yet. Marc does like his sweets, and

I'm fresh out. Go on out to the barn and let the vet know you need him when he's done."

Kristi took a step back. "Thank you."

"After you talk to him, you can come on back to the house. Door's unlocked. I'll be in the kitchen, and I'd love some help with the pies. You Amish have a special touch with the crusts."

Kristi blinked as the front door swung shut. She wasn't sure how special her touch would be. But she supposed her pies were passable. At least, no one had complained yet.

She sucked in a deep breath and willed herself to move in the direction of the barn. She hated that Shane would see her having such trouble walking, but his presence here was a godsend. As she limped across the yard and into the barn, she could hear bellowing coming from one of the stalls.

She followed the sounds and soon came upon a group of men gathered around a cow. Several men were at the front end, and her heartbeat took off at a gallop when she noticed Shane at the rear, his arm buried in the depths of the bawling animal. And he was bare-chested.

With a short gasp, Kristi forced herself to look away, at the cow. She hadn't expected this kind of a scene. And Shane…should she be seeing him like this? Her heart pounded. But that didn't stop her from sneaking another peek at his rippling muscles.

The clamor of voices dropped off, and the group of men regarded her silently, their eyes wide, as if she were an Amish apparition.

With a grunt, Shane raised his head and met her gaze. Color flooded his face. "Kristi. What are you doing here?"

"My horse…he's lame."

Shane nodded. "I'll take a look when I finish here. Can you wait?"

One of the other men stepped forward. "Go on up to the house. My wife'll make you welcome. I'll send Dr. Zimmerman up there when we finish."

Kristi nodded. "Thank you." She really wanted to stay and watch Shane work, but it was clear she was in the way. The thought of walking back to the haus made her want to cry, especially since what awaited her was the task of rolling out pie dough—a task that required standing.

But she bit her lip, blinked back the tears, and started back to the haus.

What a way to spend her birthday.

Chapter 8

After the calf had been delivered, Shane washed up at the outside shower. Marc sent him over to the house for a coffee and his check, telling him that he and his men would hook a horse trailer to the back of Marc's pickup. They figured he could carry the buggy on the bed of the truck and save a trip.

In the kitchen, several pies rested on the table, cooling. Mrs. Ellis bragged that Kristi had made them all.

Her praise did nothing to buoy Kristi, who stood at the sink washing dishes. Her shoulders sagged, and she appeared to be putting most of her weight on her good leg.

He should have insisted that she take a seat on a hay bale and wait for him. The manner in which she'd limped away had told him she'd reached the end of her physical strength.

Still, he'd been glad when she'd left the stall. The way she'd looked at him, as if she'd never seen a shirtless man before, had made him uncomfortable. Then again, she was Amish. Maybe she never had.

She lived in an Englisch world. She must have.

He didn't feel like analyzing her expression any longer. The fact was, she'd looked at him the way a horse would eye a sugar cube. And he'd liked it.

Too much.

That was what made him uncomfortable.

He accepted a mug of coffee from Mrs. Ellis and sat down at the table, helping himself to a cookie from the plate she held out to him. Then, Mrs. Ellis sat down and talked, allowing Kristi to clean up the kitchen like a servant.

To be fair, she had asked Kristi to join them, and she'd declined.

Shane was glad when Marc came in, stomping his shoes on the rug by the door. "We're ready. Did you pay Dr. Zimmerman, Martha?"

"Oh, heavens, no. I forgot." Martha jumped up and hurried out of the room, then returned a moment later with a checkbook. She handed it to Marc, along with a pen.

Shane wanted to ask for a second check, made out to Kristi for her labors in the kitchen. But he figured it was enough that the Ellises were letting him borrow their truck and horse trailer free of charge. Plus, his demanding payment for her, when she needed to do "good works," might be offensive to her. He'd talk to Marc later in private about the matter. In the meantime, he was going to insist she sit in his Jeep and rest.

Shane stood, pocketed his check, and went over to Kristi, putting his arm around her waist. She inhaled sharply but didn't pull away. Instead, she allowed him to turn her away from the sink and lead her out of the room. "Come on. Let me get you home."

He ignored the curious looks from the Ellises. Couldn't they see she was wiped out?

Kristi's breaths came in uneven spurts. She was grateful for Shane's arm around her waist. Her leg had been hurting so much, she'd wondered how she'd be able to walk out of the Ellises' haus in her own power. For the first time since her release from the hospital, she wished for the wheelchair she'd spurned.

When Mrs. Ellis had insisted she sit down and rest, she'd refused, knowing she wouldn't be able to get up again. She hadn't wanted to embarrass herself, especially in front of Shane.

His grip around her was strong, reassuring. She swallowed her trepidation and reached behind his waist, grabbing hold of one of his belt loops. In her other hand, she carried her cane, rendered unnecessary by Shane's support.

He steered her around to the passenger side of his Jeep and opened the door. Then, he released her waist and lifted her—effortlessly, it seemed—into the vehicle. He helped her to twist around so that she was facing front, tucked her skirt inside, and said, "Buckle up!" as he shut the door.

She secured the gray strap across her chest while he talked to Marc. Moments later, Shane hopped in and started the engine. "Marc's going to follow us in his truck. Where'd you leave Samson and the buggy?"

It was a good thing he was all business. Otherwise, she'd be turning to mush. "I don't know, exactly." She pointed to the road. "Some abandoned plumber's supply store."

Shane nodded, as if he knew exactly where it was.

She sank back into the seat, grateful to be off of her feet.

"The plan is to load Samson into the trailer, lift the buggy onto the flatbed, and take you home. I'll get you inside while Marc unloads Samson, and then I'll help him with the buggy and check Samson's leg. I want you to stay seated and rest. I can see you're in pain."

"Danki, Shane." Tears burned her eyes. "It was a blessing to find you at the Ellises', to be sure."

He reached out his right arm and squeezed her hand. "You could have called my office. I would have called you back and saved you the walk."

"I did. I didn't know what to do when your…assistant… said you were out of the office."

"Receptionist. Didn't she offer to take a message?"

"Jah, she did. I just didn't know what to say. And then my phone died."

"I'll write down my cell number for you to use in the future. I'll always answer it, unless I'm in the middle of something. In that case, leave a message, and I'll call back as soon as I can."

"Danki."

He released her hand and pulled his away. Immediately she missed its strength.

With a twist of the wheel, he steered into the lot where her buggy was parked and stopped the vehicle. "Stay here." He hopped out and slammed the door.

She clenched her fist as she watched Shane get to work. If only he hadn't chosen to end their friendship. Yet, he'd been acting friendly again, cooking her breakfast, sitting with her at McDonald's, helping her escape from the Ellises' haus, and now this. What was going on?

Whatever it was, she couldn't afford to get her hopes up. He might go back to keeping his distance as early as tomorrow.

And she could see herself falling in love with this friendly Shane.

Tears burned her eyes at a fresh realization: maybe that was precisely why he'd acted the way he did. Maybe he hadn't wanted the complications of attracting someone without feeling reciprocal attraction. Especially when that someone was Amish.

Too late. Being around him today had only intensified the feelings she'd started to develop while in the hospital.

She watched as Shane checked Samson's leg and then led him into the trailer. He and Marc loaded the buggy onto the flatbed, strapping it down securely, and then Shane jogged back to the Jeep and climbed in. "Okay, let's get you home." He gave her one of his heart-stopping grins.

Forget mere infatuation. She was definitely falling in love with Shane Zimmerman.

❦

When they returned to the Lapps' house, Shane did as planned: he got Kristi settled inside the house on a sofa and then tended to Samson. He couldn't ignore the whimpers coming from the dog kennel, so he released Chinook for some wrestling in the yard.

After a while, he decided to check on Kristi. Chinook followed him to the porch. Kristi must have been watching out the window, for when he raised his hand to rap on the door, she opened it before he could knock. "Samson is fine," he told her. "He had a rock wedged in his shoe." He stepped back and leaned against the porch railing, while Chinook settled at his feet.

"Danki. I'm glad it wasn't a sprain or something more serious."

He nodded, glancing down at her legs. "Did you rest like I asked you to?"

"Jah, I sat down awhile. Won't you stay for dinner? I'd like to thank you for everything you did for me this afternoon." She held the door open wide, silently inviting him in.

"I wish I could. But I have...a date." Why had he chosen that particular excuse?

"Ach." Kristi's expression fell. "Well then, danki. For everything." She stepped out onto the porch, letting the door close behind her. "How much do I owe for the flatbed and trailer? And Samson's checkup?"

"Not a penny." He wanted to reach out and trace a finger gently over the curve of her cheek. Instead, he petted Chinook on the head, wishing he dared accept the dinner invitation. "You shouldn't be entertaining men alone, anyway. What would your intended say if he knew you and I were alone together?" He tried to insert a note of teasing into his voice, but it came across sounding husky, instead.

"My intended?" Kristi's eyes widened. "I don't have one. I told you in the hospital."

"I thought things had changed. Your da…I mean, I heard you might be getting married this fall or winter."

A shadow crossed her face. "Who would want me?" She lifted her cane, as if it were Exhibit A. "The other women work circles around me. A man wants a frau who can chase toddlers and put in a garden. I'm nowhere near ready for those things."

Ira had lied to him? But then, he'd said he hoped she'd get married. Technically not untrue. Just a deliberate misconception designed to discourage Shane from coming around.

And it had worked.

For a day.

Shane rubbed a hand over his chin, rough with stubble. He decided to level with her. "My date tonight was actually going to be with the TV remote and a microwaveable meal."

Kristi brightened. "So, you can stay for dinner, then?"

He hesitated, then nodded. Hopefully, he wouldn't regret it.

"Gut. It's my birthday, and I'd rather not spend it alone."

"Your birthday?" Shane shifted against the porch railing. Why would her parents leave her alone on her special day? "I can't let you cook on your birthday."

"What, are you going to cook for me again?" She laughed.

"I do know how to cook, I'll have you know. This morning's breakfast didn't count. Someday, I'll show you what I can do in the kitchen. But in my world, a man takes a woman out to eat on her birthday."

Kristi looked pensive. He could almost read her thoughts. If anyone saw her out with him that evening, especially if that person had spotted them having lunch together earlier that day, the ruse of a professional relationship would be ruined. Tongues would wag, and the news would surely travel to Sarasota, or wherever her parents had gone, in no time at all.

"Ach, nein. That's sweet, but nein."

Disappointment ate at him. He knew he should accept her refusal. But he couldn't resist pursuing it further. "Not that I want to encourage you to sin by dating an Englischer, but I could take you somewhere you aren't likely to be known...say, Springfield."

"Dating?" There was a breathiness to her voice that made her tone sound almost hopeful. Or maybe horrified.

He hitched his shoulders. "Wrong word, I guess." He chuckled. "But no one should have to spend a birthday alone. And I would really love to treat you to dinner. As friends. You have plenty of friends who are Englischers—Starr, for example. I've seen you...." He hesitated at the sudden lump that formed in his throat. "It's just me you're not allowed to be friends with."

"Not allowed to be?" Kristi tilted her head. "I thought you were keeping your distance on purpose." She sounded defensive. Hurt.

"No. Your dad…I think he's afraid I'm a danger to you." Shane gulped. He hadn't meant to bring her father into this.

"A danger to me?" Kristi shook her head. "Nein. Not possible. You wouldn't hurt a horsefly."

Shane laughed. "I would. And I have." He scratched Chinook behind the ears.

"Daed never said we couldn't be friends."

But he'd said so to Shane. He still remembered the chat—more like the talking-to—they'd had in the hospital.

Surely, Ira would understand that the circumstances called for a breach of their understanding. Shane couldn't have left Kristi to fend for herself when she'd needed help with her horse. And if she wanted his company on her birthday, well, he wasn't about to disappoint her.

Should he tell her the truth? He didn't want to turn her against her father. But it seemed he needed to say something by way of explanation.

She stepped nearer. "I'd love to go with you into Springfield for dinner. But only if you aren't ashamed to be seen with a handicapped Amish woman."

He smiled. "I could never be ashamed of you. But, your dad—"

"I told you, Daed never said I couldn't spend time with you."

Shane shut his eyes. "He told me to stay away from you." Pain wracked his heart.

She caught her breath. He opened his eyes and saw his pain mirrored in hers. "Daed gave you explicit orders?"

He rubbed his jaw. "I'm sorry I didn't explain earlier. I just didn't want to come between you and your dad."

"He's afraid I'll jump the fence like my brother Justus."

Shane didn't know what to say. He should have wished her a happy birthday and been on his way. Instead, he'd not only hurt her, but, in trying to fix the situation, he'd also destroyed her opinion of her father.

"He should know better." Tears shimmered on her eyelashes. "I'll never jump the fence. And I'm allowed to choose my friends." She raised her chin defiantly. "So, if you want to take me to Springfield, I'll go."

Chapter 9

After Shane had gone home to get cleaned up, Kristi retreated inside. She realized she should probably change clothes, too, after making pies and everything, but she didn't know what to wear for her "date." Should she put on her good dress or an everyday work frock?

It was probably wrong of her to defy Daed, but how many chances would she have to go out with Shane? With him being Englisch and her Plain, she didn't see many. And since he'd offered an opportunity to go to Springfield, where she wouldn't be recognized, she'd jumped at it.

Still, it felt like a flock of birds flapped their wings in her stomach. Fear at disobeying Daed outright warred with excitement about getting her wish—an evening with Shane.

Daed had no right to run her life. When had he told Shane to stay away from her? At the hospital the day he'd first met him? If so, why had Shane come back again to visit the following nacht?

That would explain Shane's hasty departure when Mamm had shown up. As well as his rushed retreats every time he'd seen her over the past four months.

It would be a month before Mamm and Daed returned home with Grossmammi and Grossdaedi. And then what? They'd go back to being strangers? Two people forbidden to associate with each other? She'd be nursing a broken heart. If only he were Amish.

Why hadn't Daed made it simple and told her to stay away from Shane? Why had he left her wondering why Shane had ended their friendship so abruptly?

And if it wasn't okay for her to be around Shane, why didn't Mamm and Daed follow the same rules? Daed often took his morgen koffee outside and chatted with Shane as he returned Chinook to her kennel. And Mamm had, on occasion, taken him a tray of freshly baked cinnamon rolls.

It didn't add up.

But Daed wouldn't explain anything to her. She was his child, not his equal.

She went to her room, her parents' old room, and sifted through her sparse selection of dresses. If only Starr were here to help her choose one to wear. She always made a big deal about dressing for dates. In fact, she usually went shopping for a new outfit.

She heard the front door open and close. "Kristi? Are you home?" The familiar female voice belonged to her best friend, Janna Kauffman.

"Jah. Back in my parents' room."

A moment later, Janna appeared in the doorway. "Happy birthday! I knew your parents were away, so I thought I'd kum over and spend the evening with you. I brought you some whoopie pies and a little present."

"Ach, Janna, you're so sweet." Kristi gave her a hug. "I wish I'd known. I...um...already have plans. What do you think I should wear?"

When it came to fashion, being Amish was easier than being Englisch, in one way. Harder, in another. She was severely limited in her choices: blue, green, gray, or maroon. Her gray dress was in the laundry, and she had worn her green dress today. She untied her apron and looked down. "Is this clean enough?"

"What are you going to be doing?"

After a moment's consideration, Kristi reached for her good dress—the blue one—which she wore for church Sundays and singings. "Another friend is taking me out to dinner." Shane was a friend, ain't so?

"Really? Who?" Janna perched on the edge of the bed.

Kristi shrugged uncomfortably. "Ach, he...um...."

Janna smiled with a wink. "Ooh, someone is coming courting." She stood. "I'm so happy. I know you were naerfich no one would want you. See, you were being a dummchen. I told you the men would see past the cane and the limp. This is wunderbaar gut! I'll leave and try to kum back tomorrow. You can tell me all about it." She gave Kristi a hug, then turned toward the door. "I'll let myself out. The whoopie pies and your present are on the kitchen table."

"Danki, Janna. See you tomorrow." If only the courting part were true. But Kristi couldn't tell Janna it was an Englisch man. She second-guessed herself enough, knowing it was wrong, knowing she'd be in trouble if word got out, but wanting to be with him anyway. Just this once.

Fifteen minutes later, Kristi heard another knock. She hurried as quickly as her sore leg would allow her and flung the door open. Shane looked handsome in blue jeans and a blue shirt that matched his eyes. He'd traded his work boots for tennis shoes. Her pulse sped up.

His color was a bit pale, though. Maybe he had second thoughts about taking her out. She hoped not.

"You look beautiful." He swallowed. "I know this isn't a real date, but I haven't been on one since my wife died. Forgive me if I'm a bit rusty."

Not a real date? Tears sprang to her eyes. She quickly reminded herself that he'd said as much earlier. He was taking her out only because it was her birthday.

She shouldn't set her expectations too high.

She'd only feed her crush.

◦∽◦

This is not a date, Shane had to remind himself. Because, suddenly, it felt like one. He wiped his sweaty palms on his jeans, sucked in a shaky breath, and turned, offering Kristi his arm for support. As he did, he noticed her wheelchair, folded up in the corner of the dimly lit kitchen. "You have a wheelchair. Maybe you'd like—"

"Nein. I wouldn't." She shut the door and tucked her hand into the crook of his arm.

With his free hand, he pinched the bridge of his nose, then released it. "Kristi, there's no shame in being in a wheelchair. If you need it, then you should use it."

"Nein." Her jaw firmed.

"Okay." Case closed, evidently. He swallowed any remaining objections and led her over to the steps, waiting while she maneuvered her way down.

She reached the ground and made her way to his Jeep. He hurried to catch up with her. She was reaching for the handle when he put his hand over hers. "First of all, let's get one thing straight. When I'm out with a woman, I want to treat her like one. You need to let me open doors for you. Pull out your chair. That sort of thing."

With eyes wide, she nodded.

He released her hand and opened the door. Hesitated. Even though she seemed to be moving better after resting, he didn't know if she'd be able to manage the big step up into the Jeep on her own.

His heart rate tripled. But he reached out, grasped her waist, and lifted her into the seat.

"Danki." She didn't quite meet his gaze. Color filled her cheeks.

Then, he noticed where he'd placed his hands, with his thumbs in a rather precarious position.

He released her and stepped away, his face heating, and waited while she twisted around and arranged her skirts. Then, he shut the door and jogged around to the driver's side.

The confines of the car seemed to close in around them. Without glancing over, he could sense her, so close, despite the console between them. Near enough to touch. To hold. To kiss.

He sucked in a breath. He must have been out of his mind to ask her out.

He hadn't started the vehicle, but it was already too late to change his mind. He couldn't plead insanity. Or say he wasn't ready to date again.

She would know as well as he did that both of those statements were lies.

Besides, this wasn't a date.

He stuck the key into the ignition and started the car. The radio blared when the engine turned over, and Kristi jumped. He reached for the knob to turn down the volume.

It was a love song.

He hesitated a moment, then flicked the radio off entirely.

It wasn't a date.

But it sure felt like one.

And she was probably aware of it, too.

Maybe he should have left the radio on. It would have prevented this awkward silence between them.

As he shifted into drive, he glanced over at her. She averted her gaze.

He expelled a breath. "So, where would you like to go to eat?"

"Ach, I don't know. I've never been to any restaurants in the city."

"There's a restaurant for just about anything you're in the mood for: steak, pizza, seafood, Mexican, Chinese, Thai... you name it."

"I've never had Chinese before. Starr says it's wunderbaar."

"Then, Chinese it is."

"But I do love pizza. And seafood. What if I don't like Chinese? You could probably tell at lunch today that Starr's eating habits and mine are vastly different."

He chuckled. "I guess you'll have some time to think about it."

Did he dare hold her hand? Might as well live dangerously. He reached over, loosely intertwining his fingers with hers.

As he merged right onto the highway, her hand tightened around his. He heard her sharp intake of breath as the traffic immediately closed around them. "I hate this road," she muttered. "It's terrifying in a horse and buggy, but I think it's just as scary in a car."

He glanced at her. "You really eat pizza?"

She nodded. "Homemade, so I can control what goes in it. I'm not sure about the greasy stuff Starr likes to eat."

"Authentic Chinese is pretty healthy, I think, but the places in Springfield are more 'American Chinese.' Probably a bit greasier than the real thing, but tasty nonetheless."

"I think I can handle a little greasiness just this once."

When he looked over, she smiled at him.

He grinned back. "You should know, though, some of the dishes are hot and spicy."

"Hmm. Guess I won't know until I try, right?"

He nodded, turning his attention back to the road. "Hot and spicy" was hardly a description he would have imagined using for an Amish girl, but Kristi made his senses come alive in every way imaginable.

They made small talk for the next ten minutes, until he turned onto an off-ramp leading to the 65 bypass and wondered aloud which Chinese restaurant was the closest.

Fifteen minutes later, he pulled into the lot of a restaurant off of Glenstone and parked the Jeep. "Wait for me to get the door for you, okay? Remember, you're letting me treat you like a lady."

"Okay."

When he opened the passenger door, her eyes moved back and forth from him to the ground. "I think I can do this alone. It shouldn't be too different from getting out of the buggy."

"Okay. I'm here if you need me." He stepped back, far enough so he wouldn't be in her face, yet close enough to catch her if she fell.

She readied her cane, shifted to face him, and started a slow slide out of the vehicle. Her skirt rode up slightly, revealing a shapely calf. Not wanting to stare, he focused on her face, instead.

She hesitated, grasping the door handle and looking down. "Maybe I should have some help, after all."

He was more than happy to step closer and grasp her waist. She put her hands on his shoulders. But he wasn't prepared for the small jump she made, and he staggered slightly with the unexpected move. Instinctively, he pulled her against his chest, holding her tight while he regained his balance.

"Danki," she sighed.

He loosened his hold and slid her down the length of his body, then released her and stepped back, searching for

a smile and a normal tone of voice. "Next time, wait for me."
He wasn't quite sure he'd succeeded with the normal tone,
and the smile might have been more of a grimace.

No, asking her out hadn't been a wise move on his part,
as aware of her as he was.

☙❧

After dinner, they got back in the Jeep, but Shane didn't
start the engine right away. Kristi glanced over at him, seated
behind the steering wheel of the dark vehicle, lit only by the
streetlights lining the road and, on occasion, the headlights
of a passing car.

"My leg feels much better." She rubbed at a spot that still
ached a little. "Resting has helped."

"Good." His tone was curt.

He kept his hands firmly on the wheel, his body squared
straight ahead, and didn't reach to touch her at all. He'd
been rather withdrawn during the meal, keeping his distance
physically, too, with the only exception being when he'd
helped her back into the Jeep. Had she done something
wrong? If only she dared to ask.

Come right down to it, why didn't she dare? She sucked
in a breath. "Are you mad at me?"

He glanced at her. Hesitated a moment. Then shook
his head. "Are you ready to go home? It's probably past your
bedtime."

Ouch. She checked the clock on the dashboard. "Not
quite."

Chuckling, he inserted the key in the ignition. "Not quite
past your bedtime? Or not quite ready to go home?"

"Both."

He said nothing for the longest time.

Kristi fingered the fabric of her skirt. As they drove along, every second of silence that stretched out between them tangled her nerves even more.

Finally, Shane whipped the steering wheel to the right, maneuvering the car into the gravel parking lot of what appeared to be a small neighborhood park. Under the streetlights, Kristi could see a swing set, a see-saw, and some kind of elaborate, colorful climbing structure, complete with a slide, that would make any child drool.

He stopped the car and shifted into park. "Why are you doing this, Kristi Lapp?"

She frowned. "Why am I doing what?"

"Going out with me. I know I said I was inviting you out for your birthday, not for a date. But that was a lie. This is a date. There's something between us. Some kind of connection. I feel it. And I know you're woman enough to recognize it." His voice was rough, his tone harsh. "We both know a relationship would take us nowhere."

Kristi didn't know what to say. Any elation she might have felt from his admission of being attracted to her was crushed by his almost surly tone.

As if interpreting her silence as confusion, he pressed on. "Going on a date with an Englischer—is this some part of your rumschpringe? Something to record in your journal? A moment of madness before you settle down with a good Amish man? Or are you looking for a way out of your community? A reason to jump the fence?"

She gawked at him. Hadn't he asked her out? On second thought, she'd invited him over for dinner first. What was she supposed to say? "I...I guess I did ask you out first, offering to cook for you." Because she liked him. Because she didn't want to be alone on her birthday. "I wanted to thank you."

Because she wanted to be near him. And, yes, to her shame, because she'd wanted a date with him.

"You're playing with fire, Kristi Lapp."

Could he read her mind? She sucked in a breath. "Jah, you're right. We should probably head back. Danki for dinner. I...I had a nice time."

"Right." He half smiled. "The thing is, sweetheart, I think I might be in danger of falling in love with you."

Her pulse pounded in her ears. Did he really have reciprocal feelings for her? Did he sense the same bond between them?

"The problem is, I don't really know you."

At least he had some sense. More than she had. She pressed her lips together to keep from blurting out that she wanted to know him better.

He reached for her hand. "But I care deeply for the woman I'm becoming acquainted with."

She could say the same thing about him, but she still wasn't sure where he was going with this conversation. Her muddled mind tried to make sense of it.

His hand tightened around hers. "I'm troubled because...." He sighed. "Because of our differences. In past, present, and future." He paused. "So, I'll ask again: why are you doing this?"

Chapter 10

Shane studied Kristi's face in the warm glow of a streetlight—a glow that illuminated her lovely features. As he looked at her, his question resounded in his mind: *"Why are you doing this?"* He hoped she'd give him a straight answer. If she didn't, he'd ask more questions. He needed honesty. Even if it hurt.

"I don't know."

He shook his head. "I don't accept that." He would try not to leave any excuse for her to hide behind. "Tell me the truth."

Her chest rose and fell. She glanced up at him, then away. "Daed's started talking about marrying me off to this older widower in another district."

"Another district?" Shane frowned. "How many districts are there in Webster County?"

"Twelve. It's the largest Amish community in Missouri."

"Hmm."

"But anyway, this widower...he has seven buwe. They haven't introduced us yet, but there's been talk. Daed thinks this man might not mind having a handicapped frau."

"Are arranged marriages common in these parts?" Shane raised his eyebrows.

"Nein, not usually. But sometimes, in cases like mine, jah. I've heard of it. After all, it's God's will for us to marry and have a family, ain't so?"

107

He grunted. Ira would force Kristi into a marriage with someone. As a permanent way to keep her away from him, probably. He narrowed his eyes, considering this.

"I guess I…well, this is uncomfortable. But you were honest, saying all those things." She tugged her hand free from his. Leaned away from him a bit. "Truthfully, I wanted a memory with a man of my choosing before I got harnessed to someone who wasn't."

"But the arranged marriage…it's just talk, right? Not for sure?" Did he sound as alarmed as he felt?

"With Daed, there's no such thing as 'just talk.' There's always action behind his words. Negotiations behind the scenes."

"So, when he said you might be getting married in the fall, he meant it?"

She shrugged one shoulder. "I don't know anything about it. And whoever he's talked to might refuse me."

Not if the man had any common sense. "You wouldn't have any say in the matter?"

She shook her head. "Nein, not really. I could run away, I guess. But they know I won't do that."

Shane couldn't think of any way to prevent an arranged marriage for Kristi. Even if she left, then what? She'd most likely abandon the area, meaning she'd still be out of reach for him. If she stayed and started a family, at least she'd have some hope for happiness. But a widower with seven children? He shook his head.

She'd wanted a memory. With a man of her choosing. And she'd picked him. He reached for her hand again. "Are you saying I'm a man of your choosing? Someone to make a memory with?"

"Ach, that came out wrong. Made it sound as if I were using you. That isn't true. I really like you, Shane. And if you were Plain, I would be doing everything I could to make you notice me. But you aren't Plain, and I realize nothing can possibly develop between us."

Nothing except heartbreak. He swallowed. Hard. "I'm flattered." After a few seconds of silence, he glanced at her in sudden alarm. "How much of a memory do you want to make?" He wouldn't do anything to make Ira come after him with a sawed-off shotgun, assuming that's what an Amish father did when his daughter's virtue was compromised.

"This is gut. Talking. Being together."

"Oh, Kristi." He squeezed her hand. "I'll try to make the rest of your birthday—our date—pleasant for you."

"It's been pleasant."

Surely, she was just being nice. "Pleasant" could hardly describe her experience at the restaurant. He'd clammed up for most of the meal, making mental speculations about Kristi and her reasons for coming out with him. And he'd seen the hurt in her eyes.

The sound of babbling water reached his ears, and he noticed a brook running along the edge of the park, leading deep into the woods. Beyond peaceful. He released her hand and draped his arm around her shoulders, pulling her gently to his side. Enjoying the opportunity to hold her. This would be as far as he allowed it to go.

She gave a soft sigh and turned toward him with a smile. "This is nice. I can't imagine a better way to spend my birthday."

He closed his eyes and inhaled deeply, his nostrils filling with the scent of spices that always seemed to accompany Kristi. His eyes popped open in alarm at the sudden, inexplicable urge to taste her. All rational thoughts, wisdom, and other objections faded, until he could focus on only one thing. His gaze dropped to her lips. When was the last time he'd kissed a woman? He could hardly remember the last time he'd wanted to.

❦

Kristi closed her eyes as Shane brushed several loose strands of hair away from her face. His hand trembled, as if he was touching a treasure and feared he might break it. Then, he leaned forward and touched his lips to her cheek in the lightest of kisses—so light, in fact, she almost wondered if she'd imagined it.

She wanted to turn into his kiss, but it was probably better this way. Kissing was a privilege reserved for courting couples. For a man and a woman who'd made promises to each other—something she and Shane would never be able to do.

He pulled back, his eyes searching hers. Then, his arm around her shoulder tightened, turning her toward him and drawing her nearer, while his other arm enfolded her tenderly. She could find no words to object, even when his eyes dropped to her lips.

"I shouldn't...." His voice was a low rumble that sent shivers down her spine. "But, happy birthday, Kristi." His lips found hers, brushing against them. He raised his head, meeting her gaze. When her eyes fluttered shut, she felt him settle in, firmly. He tasted like the peppermint candy he'd grabbed on the way out of the restaurant.

She moaned softly as his lips slid away from her mouth and explored her jaw, her cheek, and her ear, then traveled down her neck. She shivered as he pulled her even closer and cupped her face in his hands, angling her head slightly to give him freer access. He kissed a thousand times better than Eli, who'd planted a wet, sloppy smack on her cheek when they'd been courting—before her accident.

Shane's kisses deepened in passion, igniting her desire. While her fingers tangled in his hair, he moved his hands to her shoulders and around to the back of her neck, fingering the strands of hair at the base of her scalp.

Sometime later—Kristi had lost track of time—Shane wrenched away.

Breathless, Kristi stared at him. She still couldn't find her voice.

He sat there, chest heaving, and stared straight ahead. Silence reigned for a minute. Finally, with a strained voice, he said, "I need to get you home."

All she wanted to do was throw herself back into his arms and…jah, they needed to get home. Or at least go somewhere public, with other people around.

He turned and faced her. "I'm sorry. So sorry. I never meant…I didn't intend…. This won't happen again. I promise." Shane reached over and picked up something from the floor of the Jeep. Her kapp, and a handful of hairpins. "You might want to, uh, fix your hair."

Her hands flew to her head and discovered a large knot of unrestrained curls. When in the fog of kisses had that happened?

❧

When they pulled into Kristi's driveway, there was a buggy parked by the house. As he pressed the brake, he looked over at Kristi. "Who—?"

"Onkel Timothy."

Shane returned his gaze to the house. Ira's brother Timothy exited through the front door, carrying a flashlight. He shone the beam directly into the vehicle, blinding Shane for a moment. Then, he turned it off and studied the Jeep as he tugged on his beard, his brow furrowed in concern.

As Shane stepped out of the vehicle, conflicting feelings warred within him. He was disappointed that their time alone was up, yet relieved that their chaperone was already there, which was preferable to his arriving after Shane and Kristi and catching them in the middle of a good-bye kiss.

He knew he should probably feel more concerned at having been discovered with Kristi, but that would come later. When Ira found out. And, judging by Timothy's disapproving frown, Shane doubted that would take very long.

Things had gotten entirely out of hand.

At least Kristi had her memory. Probably a bigger memory than she'd bargained for.

He opened her door and helped her out as Timothy approached.

"There you are, Kristi. Hiram Schultz called looking for you. He said Miriam expected you to kum by today, but you never showed up." He glanced at Shane, evidently holding him responsible for Kristi's failure to make the appointment. "She thinks she's gone into labor. Hiram called me when he couldn't reach your cell phone. She might have had the boppli by now. I've been trying to track you down for over an hour. Your horse and buggy were here, so I figured you must be…courting." Another hard look at Shane. "I checked the local hangouts before stopping here again to see if you were asleep."

"It's my fault," Kristi explained. "My cell phone died—I mean, the battery did. And Samson went lame, so I wasn't able to make it to my afternoon appointments—"

"Get your things. I'll get your stepstool and then take you over to the Schultzes'."

"Danki." She started making her way up the porch steps.

"I can charge your phone for you," Shane offered.

She turned and sent him a heartwarming smile. "That would be wunderbaar. I'll bring it out to you."

She disappeared inside the house, leaving him there in the darkness with Timothy.

"Don't tell me she's playing midwife to cats and dogs now. Or is it cows?" The sarcasm of Timothy's comment was plain. As was its meaning.

"It's her birthday. I took her to dinner." No need to say more.

"Just how did you know it was her birthday?"

Shane ran his hand over his jaw, glad he'd shaved before picking her up. "She told me."

Timothy folded his hands together. "I think you know as well as I do, this wasn't a gut idea."

He wouldn't have put it so mildly, had he witnessed them at the park. Shane looked away and remained silent, hoping this wouldn't spell the end of his veterinary career in Webster County.

Timothy spun around and headed for the barn. He returned a few minutes later carrying a wooden stepstool with a hole in one side of the top. He set it up beside the passenger side of the buggy.

Hearing the front door open, Shane looked toward the house. Kristi stepped outside with her cane, carrying a black bag and her cell phone in her free hand. She'd changed out of her blue dress into the green one she'd had on earlier that day.

Shane moved to take the bag and her phone.

"Danki again for charging my phone, Shane. And for dinner. That was sweet of you to not want me to have to cook on my birthday."

Timothy snorted as he took the bag from Shane.

Shane ignored him. "Would you like me to feed Chinook?"

Kristi nodded. "Jah, that would be nice. Danki."

He opened the door of his Jeep and tossed her cell phone and charger into the console before shutting the door again. "I'll do that before I leave, then. Good night, Kristi."

"Gut nacht, Shane."

He was rounding the corner of the house when he heard Timothy talking sternly. "You need to watch yourself, Kristi. He's not one of us. You'd do better to go to singings and frolics and find yourself a beau. And don't bother telling me you do. I know you haven't gone since your accident. Your daed won't like this development one bit. I won't be at all surprised if I get orders to buy a bus ticket and send you down to Florida there for the remainder of their stay."

Shane's stomach clenched. He'd suspected something would happen, but losing Kristi to Florida hadn't occurred to him. Yet, as much as he didn't want her to go, maybe it'd be easier having her far away. Out of sight, out of mind.

Though he doubted that would be the case.

He reached the kennel and opened the latch, greeting Chinook with a great big hug. "I think I could see myself marrying her," he mused, running his fingers through the dog's thick fur. "But the options are pretty obvious. She'll either leave town to find someone in Florida or stay and marry the widower with seven kids."

Chinook's ears perked up, and she cocked her head slightly. Shane imagined that she was urging him not to give up on the possibility of a relationship with Kristi.

He sighed and shook his head. "It's hopeless, Chinook. She's Amish. I'm not. We may as well be a cat and a dog in love."

But cats and dogs can't choose to change. People can.

He dismissed the thought as quickly as it'd crossed his mind. He knew about the complications that arose when an Amish united with a non-Amish. And he didn't want to go there.

Chapter 11

Miriam Schultz's boppli made an appearance in the early hours of the morgen, about ten minutes after the rooster crowed. Hiram named the healthy, eight-pound-seven-ounce bu Noah, after his father.

After helping Miriam to the bathroom, Kristi stripped the sheets off the bed and replaced them with clean ones. She tucked Miriam under the covers, her boppli in her arms, and showed her how to nurse. Then, she left the first-time mamm to run the soiled sheets through the wringer washer. It was already filled with water, as Miriam had been in the process of doing laundry when she'd gone into labor.

When the laundry was finished, Kristi carried the wet sheets outside and hung them on the clothesline to dry, then went back inside. She needed to fill out the paperwork required to document the birth, and she wanted to help by cleaning the kitchen, doing the dishes, and mopping the floor. As soon as word got out about the boppli's arrival, community members would descend in droves to welcome the newest member of the Schultz family and to shower them with food and baby gifts. Miriam would be embarrassed if her haus didn't meet the Amish standards of cleanliness and order.

Kristi glanced at the battery-operated clock on the shelf. Shane would be on a run with Chinook about now. Hopefully, she would see him today, though he probably would have left for work by the time she returned home.

She peeked out the kitchen window. Today promised to be nice—perfect weather for making soap outside. She needed to, since she was on her last bar. Also on the agenda was a nap, as she'd had another sleepless nacht. She wasn't scheduled to meet with any expectant mamms today, unless she tried to make up the appointments she'd missed yesterday. But once everybody learned about the birth of the Schultzes' boppli, she'd probably be off the hook, as everyone would assume—never mind wrongly—that she'd been with Miriam the whole time.

Maybe Shane would come by and visit with her after he got home.

She sighed, smiling, as she opened the file folder marked "Miriam Schultz." A month with Shane to make more memories. Unless Onkel Timothy interfered, as he'd threatened to do. Her smile faded. What if Daed insisted she go to Florida? She'd have no choice but to obey—either that or go before the bishop to be disciplined for her rebellion.

Her heart heavy, she clicked the pen and started writing. Name of mother…Miriam King Schultz. Name of father… Hiram Schultz. Would someone ever fill out a form like this for her? And, if so, what would her last name be?

Not Zimmerman. That much she knew.

And she couldn't help hoping her future husband would kiss her like Shane had—or better. She didn't think she could settle for less.

Whatever had possessed her to grant Shane such liberties? Their kisses had gone far beyond what was fitting and proper for a courting couple, let alone two people who had never made promises to each other. She must have suffered from temporary insanity at the thrill of his touch. That was the only explanation for it.

She couldn't let it happen again.

Ach, but she wanted it to.

Dressed in his running gear, Shane jogged over to Kristi's with her fully charged cell phone and charger. Instead of knocking, though, he set them both on a rocking chair on the porch. He didn't want to disturb her after what must have been a late night at the Schultzes'. Really, he had no idea how long she'd been gone. He'd lain awake for hours, thinking about their date—about the things he should have done differently, but mostly about the passionate moments they'd spent together. He must have dozed off and missed hearing her come home.

What had gone through her mind when he'd kissed her? Did she regret the exchange, or did their kisses haunt her every bit as much as they did him?

He turned away from her door but kept his senses tuned for the sound of footfall in the hallway or the smell of coffee brewing—any indicator that Kristi was up and about.

Yet the only noises he heard came from the animals in the barn. Moments later, Timothy emerged through the open doors, leading the family's dairy cows. He glanced briefly at Shane and then, without as much as a blink, turned toward the pasture.

His face heating, Shane hurried down the porch steps. If Kristi was asleep, as he assumed she was, then his standing on her porch looked very bad. He remembered his grandfather telling him the importance of avoiding any appearance of evil. This would definitely give the wrong impression.

As he headed for the kennel, he glanced back at the house. No lights. No movement. Nothing.

He sighed. He knew he should stay away from Kristi, but he yearned for her smile, her bright eyes, her warmth. She'd said if he were Plain, she'd be doing everything in her power to make him notice her.

She wouldn't need to try very hard.

If he were Plain, he'd be the guy tossing pebbles at her window at night. Taking her to singings and frolics and wherever else Amish youth went when they were courting.

But he wasn't Amish. Courting her was a nonissue.

Chinook looked up at him, her tail wagging like crazy. He mustered a smile and started his jog, ignoring Timothy, who stood in the cow pasture.

When Shane returned, he was hot, sweaty, and in need of a shower. Chinook was hardly in better shape; she panted heavily, with her tongue hanging out of her mouth. Shane jogged past the house and went straight to the water pump, where he filled Chinook's bowl with cold water.

When he turned around, there was Timothy, standing right behind him.

That didn't help to calm his heart rate. He gulped. "I returned Kristi's cell phone and charger. They're on one of the porch rockers."

"I moved them inside." Timothy met Shane's gaze and held it. "Ira said he told you to stay away. I won't bother with reiteration."

"He knows I exercise the dog every day."

"You know the dog isn't what he's concerned about."

Shane shifted his gaze and scanned the field before meeting Timothy's eyes again. "If she needs me, I'm going to help her. Otherwise, I'll endeavor to honor Ira's wishes." He hesitated a moment. "Take yesterday, for example. Her horse went lame, she walked more than a mile to find help, and, while she was waiting, she baked at least six pies. I wasn't going to abandon her."

Timothy nodded. "Commendable."

"I'm not going to insult your intelligence by lying and saying I'm not interested in Kristi. But I also am very aware that a…a union…between us is not only unlikely, it's impossible. I'm sure neither one of us wants to pursue a dead-end relationship."

"Again, commendable. So, you believe Ira has no basis for concern?"

The kisses they had shared flashed though his memory. There was definitely cause for concern. "Minimal."

Timothy nodded. "We lose many of our young people to the world when they believe they have fallen in love with an outsider. We lost one of Ira's sohns that way. We don't want to lose his only dochter."

"I understand." But what about Kristi's wishes?

Timothy gave Shane a friendly slap on the upper arm. "You seem like a gut man, Shane Zimmerman. And I appreciate your honesty. You help Kristi, if she needs it, with my blessing. But otherwise, stay away." He turned and strode toward the road.

Leaving a wide-open window of opportunity right there.

And Shane's heart warring with his conscience.

Kristi was glad to see Janna when she showed up, around mid-afternoon. She helped Kristi haul the cast-iron kettle out of the barn, hosed it out, and hung it on the hook over the fire. Thankfully, Daed had already laid the fire before leaving for Pinecraft, with the expectation that Kristi would make soap while Mamm and he were away.

Kristi lit the fire, then pulled the recipe out of her pocket to peruse it:

Boiled Soap

32 pounds lard
16 quarts soft water
8 cans lye
Boil 2 hours. Add 1 more gallon of water. Stir and remove kettle from fire and pour into molds.

She'd already gotten out the supplies she needed, including the rubber gloves and safety glasses for handling lye, as well as the rag-lined box she'd pour the soap in to set once it finished cooking.

Janna kept silent while helping her to measure the ingredients, but she was clearly curious about Kristi's date, judging by the way she kept glancing expectantly at her.

For a long time, Kristi pretended not to notice. She didn't know how much she could share safely. She dropped the lard into the kettle and then, hearing Chinook whine, went over to the kennel to release her. The dog trotted back with her to the fire, staying close by—something Shane must have taught her, as she'd never bothered to heel before.

Chinook nosed Kristi's hand, wanting to be petted, so Kristi rubbed behind her ears for a few minutes, until she flopped contentedly on the ground. Kristi checked the lard and added a couple of logs to the fire.

Finally, she turned to Janna. "Last nacht was gut. Great, really. But I don't know if anything will kum of it."

Janna grinned. "If he's smart, something will. You'll make a great frau." Her smile faded. "I hope it wasn't Amos Kropf. I do his shopping, and I can't imagine your marrying him. He approaches all of the maidals, it seems."

"It wasn't anyone named Amos. I've never met him."

"Will you tell me who it was?" Janna took a sip of the soft drink she'd brought with her.

Kristi shook her head and tried not to glance at Shane's haus. "He's wunderbaar, I'll say that much. He's a widower, but not much older than we are."

"A widower...so, he doesn't go to singings and frolics." Janna sighed. "Is he in our district?"

Kristi shook her head.

Seeing that the lard was melted, she donned the safety glasses and gloves and added the lye to the cold water. Once it had dissolved, she poured it into the lard and stirred it with the wooden spoon.

Shane's Jeep pulled into his driveway.

Chinook whined and rose, then looked at Kristi, as if asking permission to go and greet him.

"Stay." She said it halfheartedly, expecting the dog to disobey, as usual. But with another whine, the dog dropped and rested her head on her front paws. Kristi blinked, baffled by her pet. She hadn't known that Shane was doing obedience training with Chinook. He'd never said so, but that had to be the only explanation.

She'd thank him when he came over. *If* he came over.

Kristi's heart rate tripped into a gallop when the driver-side door of the Jeep opened.

And it thudded to a halt when Shane got out, slammed the door, and headed inside without as much as a glance in her direction.

Maybe he wanted to shower before he came to see her.

Or maybe Janna's presence had scared him off.

Half an hour later, when Janna left for home, Kristi fully expected Shane to appear. But there was no sign of him.

What could possibly be keeping him? He usually came over right after work to take Chinook for a run. And, after their date, she'd assumed he had an even greater incentive to stop by.

Especially after they'd both admitted having feelings for each other.

Especially after they'd kissed the way they had.

She returned her attention to the soap she was making. Still, she couldn't stop herself from stealing a glance at his haus every few seconds or so.

Finally, impatience overtook her, and she gave up pretending not to care. With a sigh, she fixed her gaze on his front door, willing him to come out.

Movement in her peripheral vision prompted her to turn toward the road. It was Creepy Guy from across the street. He was dressed in a black zippered sweat suit over a stained white T-shirt. And he was walking up her driveway.

She cringed. What business did he have with her?

Chapter 12

Shane went to the kitchen and poured himself a cup of coffee left over from the pot he'd brewed that morning. He reheated it in the microwave, added some Almond Joy-flavored liquid creamer, and went to stand by the kitchen window, angling himself so that the Lapps' property was in full view. He felt like nosy Donald across the street, spying on Kristi this way. But he was just trying to be neighborly. Making sure she didn't need any help.

Kristi was still working in the side yard at the burn pit, where a cast-iron kettle hung from the hook suspended over it. When he'd returned home and noticed her there, he'd figured she was cooking some of those worthless herbs of hers. She'd had a friend with her, so he hadn't offered to help. Instead, he'd opted to mind his own business until she finished. His run with Chinook could wait.

Kristi picked up a long wooden spoon and started to stir whatever was in the kettle. Shane didn't see her girlfriend there anymore. He glanced at the barn. Sure enough, the extra horse and buggy was gone.

When he looked back at Kristi, a man in a black jogging suit stepped into his line of vision. He stood facing Kristi—too close, in Shane's opinion—with his back toward Shane's house. He reached out, apparently trying to touch her backside. She jolted away, and the creep followed, moving so that Shane could see his face. Rage burned within him. It was Donald from across the street.

Shane slammed his coffee mug down on the table and bolted outside. He could hear the low hum of conversation as he approached, but he wasn't able to make out the neighbor's words. When Donald noticed him, he stopped talking.

Kristi turned around and cast Shane a look of relief.

Donald stepped out of her personal space, his hand falling to his side. "What's up, Doc?" He laughed as if he'd just told the biggest joke of the century.

Shane forced a smile and searched for some topic of conversation to engage Donald. The weather seemed like a safe enough subject. He glanced up at the sky and mentioned the unseasonably warm temperature, especially after the cold snap the day before, which got Donald talking about his garden and what he was going to plant. What he wasn't going to plant might have been a shorter list.

Tuning him out, Shane glanced around, trying to piece together what type of project Kristi was working on. Empty cans labeled "Red Devil Lye" littered the ground—an odd ingredient for an herbal mixture. He sniffed but didn't detect any peculiar odors, which eliminated the possibility that Kristi operated a backyard meth lab. He scanned the remaining items on the ground: lard boxes and several empty plastic milk cartons. He scratched his neck, trying to remember the type of herbs the midwife had given his wife. Red raspberry leaves. Evidently unrelated to whatever Kristi was concocting. What was she doing?

Donald cleared his throat, drawing Shane's attention back to their conversation—if you could call it that. It was more of a monologue. "Well, believe that's the cable guy I've been waitin' on." Donald hitched a thumb over his shoulder, and Shane noticed a white van pulling into his driveway. "Feel

free to come over and watch TV with me sometime, Kristi."
He winked at her and then shuffled away.

Kristi ignored him. When he was back on his side of
the street, she looked at Shane. "Danki for coming over.
He started telling me about these shows he watches on…
pay-per-view, was it? And how he'd like to watch them with
me." She shuddered. "Plus, he tried to touch me. He's just
scary."

What a louse. "Next time you're mixing a 'love potion,'
maybe you should fix a repellent for the men you don't want
to attract."

Her brow furrowed. "Love potion? What's that?"

"Never mind." Shane cast another look at the sky. The
clouds seemed to forebode a coming storm. If he was going to
run with Chinook, they ought to leave soon, before the rain
started.

"I'm making soap. It's almost done; I just need to pour it
into the molds." She gestured at the row of boxes lined with
rags. "I'll give you a bar after it cures."

"You do know you can buy soap at the grocery store,
right?" He winked.

She pulled a couple of potholders out of her apron
pocket and tossed them playfully at him. "Jah, I know.
But if we bought soap, I'd miss all the fun of making it.
Plus, store-bought soap is specially designed for bathing,
so we'd have to buy separate dish soap and laundry soap.
We use this for everything: laundry, dishes, baths. It's more
economical."

"But a lot more work." He frowned at the flowery mitts
in his hand.

"Idle hands are the devil's workshop." She grinned.
"Would you pour for me, please? Fill each box up to about
here." She bent down and pointed to show him.

He slid the mitts on. They were a snug fit for his large hands. Careful not to spill, he lifted the kettle and slowly poured the contents into the boxes she'd prepared, then hung the kettle back on the hook.

"I'll need to wash that out and store it away in the shed. Would you please hand me one of the boxes? You can get the other ones for me, if you would." She positioned her cane in her left hand and reached out with her right arm.

He shouldn't enter her house, he knew. But she needed his help. "I can get all three, if you want."

Kristi shook her head. "Nein, I'll take one. Either that or the trash."

"I'll come back for the trash." He bent down, hoisted a box, and positioned it gently in the crook of her arm. "You sure you can handle this?"

"I need to do something."

Nodding, he stacked the remaining two boxes and picked them up. "Lead the way."

He followed her toward the house and up the steps. On the porch, he moved ahead of her, set his boxes down, and turned to take hers. "Where do you want them?"

"In the kitchen, on the table. It's just me right now, and—"

At the sound of buggy wheels rattling, Shane followed her gaze to the driveway. The driver looked familiar—Shane had seen him around town—but he didn't know his name. He had a beard, which meant he was married. Kristi was probably about to be summoned to another birth.

"I'll put your soap inside and grab your black bag, if you tell me where it is," Shane offered.

Kristi shook her head. "He isn't married to any of my patients. I don't know him."

When the buggy came to a stop, the driver nodded at Kristi, then shifted his gaze to Shane and looked him over. Judging by his scowl, he didn't fancy blue jogging shorts.

Shane sized him up, as well, noting his graying brown hair and his brown eyes. He estimated his age to be about fifty. Too old for Kristi.

Evidently, the Amish man had dismissed Shane as inconsequential, for he looked straight at Kristi and said, "Ira Lapp's Kristi? Amos Kropf. Your daed has arranged for me to have supper with you."

❦

Kristi blinked at the stranger in the buggy. "My daed arranged supper? Between you and me?" She glanced at Shane but couldn't read his expression.

"Hasn't he mentioned me?"

Her throat felt like it was closing up. It was hard to breathe. "Nein. Not by name. Are you the widower with seven kinner?"

Amos smiled, apparently oblivious to her trepidation. "Jah. All buwe. Youngest is a wee one, just turned five. Oldest is seventeen."

She tried to keep from wilting. What was Daed thinking, setting her up with a man whose oldest child was a mere five years younger than she? Judging by Amos's graying hair, he was at least as old as her daed, if not older. Daed must really be desperate to marry her off. "This supper...is it tonight? Here?"

"Jah, tonight. That's why I've kum."

"But...I have nothing prepared." She searched for an excuse that would send him on his way.

She glanced over at Shane again. With arched eyebrows, he chewed his lip as he surveyed Amos Kropf. Then, he looked at his wristwatch. "Wow, look at the time. I need to be going." He backed up a step.

Kristi's eyes filled with tears, and her throat seemed to close the rest of the way. She tried to swallow and reached for Shane but stopped short of touching him. That would be wrong, especially with Amos Kropf watching. She found her voice. "Actually, Dr. Zimmerman, I would like you to join us tonight, as payment for taking care of my horse. Besides, Herr Kropf and I will need a chaperone."

One of Daed's rules was that if a suitor came to visit Kristi, the two of them were not to be alone unless Daed had decided they'd earned that right. It struck her as odd for him to have scheduled what Starr would call a "blind date" while neither Mamm nor he was around. If she admitted Amos Kropf without a chaperone present, and someone noticed, her reputation would be ruined. And then she might have no other choice than to marry this stranger with seven buwe. To be truthful, there was no "might" about it. She would have no other choice. Period.

Eyes wide, Shane shook his head. "Oh, no. I couldn't impose on a date."

Kristi held her breath, panic welling inside her chest. "You must!" She cleared her throat and calmed her voice. "Please."

He blinked at her.

Please, Shane, she pleaded silently, praying he'd sense her fear and get the message.

Finally, he gave a slow nod. "Fine then, Miss Lapp. I would be honored. But I'm not dressed appropriately. Give me a minute to run home and change."

Kristi's gaze dropped to his blue shorts and well-toned legs. She forced her eyes to meet his again. "You're fine. Really." She didn't want to be left alone with this stranger, even for just a minute.

"No, I'm not." Shane started to turn. "I'll be right back."

"Maybe you could borrow some of Daed's clothes. He didn't take all of them to Florida."

Shane chuckled, and Kristi felt her face flush. What had she been thinking? Shane was much slimmer than Daed, not to mention taller.

Amos frowned. "Won't do to have an Englischer impersonating an Amish."

"Maybe some of my brothers' clothes would fit you," Kristi suggested. "They left some of the jeans and T-shirts they wore during their rumschpringe."

He hesitated a moment, then nodded. "I guess I could try them."

She smiled, relieved.

"We don't need a chaperone," Amos stated, glaring at Shane. "I'm a gut man with honorable intentions." He raised his chin, dropped the reins, and got out of the buggy.

But Kristi *wanted* a chaperone. Daed had something planned, and she wasn't about to let him succeed. She forced a smile. "Nevertheless, I invited Dr. Zimmerman to join us, and he accepted. I don't appreciate being taken by surprise like this. I'd planned on having a light supper. It's lucky I put some chicken out to thaw." Three pieces, exactly—one for supper tonight, one for lunch tomorrow, and the other...it didn't matter now. Three would be enough to feed these men. Especially since she didn't think she could manage to eat one bite.

How could Daed do this to her?

Shane's stomach churned as he entered the Lapps' farmhouse. It felt more than strange. Weird. Wrong. A violation of Ira's trust. Especially since Shane had never been invited in when Kristi's parents had been home. At least they had a chaperone—even if Amos was oblivious to the part he was really playing.

Yet Kristi had never objected to being alone with Shane. They'd spent hours together, unsupervised, on her birthday. Helping her make a memory. So that she could face an arranged marriage with Amos—a man old enough to be her father.

Shane drew in a breath. The house smelled like Kristi. Whatever those spices were, they smelled good. Very good.

The scent also reminded him of the moment of passion they'd shared—not that he needed something specific to trigger the memory. He relived it often enough on his own.

He glanced around the kitchen, slightly dismayed to see so many jars of dried herbs lining the open shelves. There were more herbs drying on a clothesline strung up in the corner. He shook his head.

He hadn't planned on seeing her tonight. He'd intended to keep the promise he'd made to Ira and to Timothy. Kristi needed to find her own love—an Amish love. He didn't want to lure her away from her family and friends. Well, truthfully, he wouldn't mind, except for the high price she'd have to pay: shunning.

Shane's father had been shunned when he'd left, though his grandparents had welcomed Shane and his sister. His dad had never visited his parents. Never talked to them. It hurt both parties, but they'd accepted it. Somewhat.

As for Shane, while he appreciated the business of Amish farmers, he had an ever-growing client base of non-Amish people—plenty to keep his clinic afloat.

He didn't want to be here tonight, posing as a chaperone so that another man could take Kristi's measure as a potential wife. Not when he wanted her for himself. But Kristi had seemed desperate for him to stay.

"My brothers' room is at the top of the stairs, third door on the right," Kristi said. "There are a couple of dressers, so you'll have some options."

"Thanks." As Shane walked to the steps, he spied Kristi's black medical bag on the floor beside the hutch. Yet another point of contention between them. Kristi had no idea he was opposed to midwives, but it broke his heart every time he remembered that she shared a profession with the woman he held responsible for Becca's death. Maybe it was insensitive, but he couldn't marry someone if he lacked all respect for her vocation.

Why was he even thinking like this? He didn't have a chance with Kristi. Yes, she was pretty. Yes, they'd formed a bond while she'd been hospitalized, and their friendship had picked up again, effortlessly, after four months without any contact. And, yes, they'd succumbed to a spark of fiery passion for a moment in time.

He pushed the memory away. That was as far as they would go. It had to be.

Aging widower or not, the man seated at the kitchen table was the better choice for her by far.

Shane counted three doors down and turned the knob, pushing his way inside. The room was very stark, with whitewashed walls, bare wood flooring, an antique-looking iron bed frame with a sagging mattress devoid of any bedcovering, and a dresser that had seen better days.

The floorboards creaked underfoot as he crossed the room to the dresser. He opened a drawer and found several T-shirts stacked inside. Selecting a blue one, he unfolded it to assess the size. It would work.

Next, he closed that drawer and opened the one beneath it. Bingo—blue jeans. He sifted through the selection. None of them was the right waist size, but he found a pair that would stay up without a belt. They were a tad short, but they would work for the short time he'd be wearing them.

He folded his workout clothes and stacked them neatly on top of the dresser, dressed, then carried his things downstairs. Whenever Amos left and Shane was free to go, he'd take Chinook for a run, provided it wasn't raining.

Shane left his pile of clothes on the bottom step and returned to the kitchen, where Kristi stood at the sink, peeling potatoes; a long string of skins dangled over the plastic bowl on the counter beside her.

She turned around and surveyed his outfit with a grin. "Not the best fit, for sure."

"Where'd Amos go?"

She nodded toward the door. "Putting his horse in the barn. It's supposed to rain, he said."

"I thought I noticed some storm clouds gathering." He moved closer to her and leaned against the counter.

She shook her head. "I know next to nothing about Amos Kropf. How can I be sure Daed even arranged this dinner? I'm not sure what to think. All I know is, I don't want to be left alone with him."

He gave her an empathetic nod. If only he could tell Amos to go home. Then, he could take Kristi in his arms, and...no. It would be far better for Kristi to fall in love with someone else—not Amos, maybe, but a young Amish man. Her lameness might hinder many potentially acceptable suitors, but Shane had an idea that might remedy the problem, at least somewhat. A church friend of his was a physical therapist. Shane would give her a call and try to arrange for her to work with Kristi. She would walk without a limp in no time. Why hadn't he thought of it sooner?

He straightened. "Anything I can do to help?"

"Hmm." She looked around, then nodded at the counter. "You could empty that can of green beans into the kettle. I need to get them warming."

"Sure." He moved around her and picked up the glass jar. It'd been a long time since he'd eaten home-canned vegetables. His Amish grandmother had put them up, but his mom didn't have quite the same knack. She'd made a couple of weak attempts with homegrown tomatoes but had since allowed her garden to become overrun with wildflowers.

"Shane." Kristi's voice sounded strangled.

Startled, Shane turned around.

She looked up at him, tears in her eyes. "Why...why would Daed choose someone as old as Amos?"

Shane swallowed and set the jar of beans back on the counter.

"Is he the only one he could find who would have me?" A tear trickled down the curve of her cheek.

Shane reached out, wiping it away. Then, praying Amos would be occupied in the barn for a few minutes more, he opened his arms and drew her into an embrace.

Chapter 13

$\mathcal{K}$risti wrapped her arms around Shane's waist and burrowed her face in his chest, sniffling as she tried to stanch the flow of tears. She was ashamed at this display of weakness, especially when she'd thought she was ready to accept her fate after making a memory with a man of her choice.

Shane tightened his embrace, cuddling her closer to him. He made shushing sounds, like a parent comforting a young child, while his hand rubbed her back, gently yet reassuringly.

"I'm sorry." She lifted her head, blinking the tears away.

He released her with one arm and brought his hand to her chin, lifting it gently with his fingertips. With his thumb, he brushed one cheek and then the other, then moved to her mouth, tracing her lips. Her breath hitched as her heart rate increased, until it felt as if a swarm of butterflies had taken flight in her chest.

"He's not the only one who'll have you," Shane whispered. "What's not to like? You're beautiful, smart, hardworking... any man with eyes should be able to see what a treasure you are."

"But—"

He shook his head, his thumb pressing against her lips. "If I were Amish, I wouldn't hesitate."

"But you're not," she whispered.

"No. But that doesn't stop me from being attracted to you." His gaze dropped to her lips.

Kristi inclined her head and crossed her arms around his neck. Her lips had barely reached his when she heard the stomping of boots on the porch, followed by the rattling of the doorknob.

Shane released her and stepped back, snatching the jar of green beans in the same movement.

Kristi pulled in a shaky breath, wishing Amos Kropf were a million miles away. She returned to her bowl of peeled potatoes, picked up the knife, and started slicing them. When the door closed, she glanced over her shoulder at Amos. "Please, make yourself at home. By the way, when did you speak to my daed?"

"He called this morgen. Left a message on the answering machine in the shed. I might have misunderstood, but I thought he said tonight. He didn't leave a number to call back, and I didn't want to pass up a gut meal. Wasn't sure if the invitation included my buwe, so I sent them to their grossmammi's." There was a scraping sound as Amos pulled out a kitchen chair. "Guess I didn't think they'd be needed as chaperones."

Shane popped the seal on the jar and dropped the beans into the pot Kristi had indicated.

Amos cleared his throat. "You've got to admire a man who isn't afraid of the kitchen. I never could get comfortable cooking, even between fraus, so I had to hire help. Made me wish I'd had a dochter or two instead of all buwe."

"Between fraus?" Kristi set the knife down and rinsed her hands. "How many were there?"

Amos remained silent. When she glanced over her shoulder at him, he appeared to be deep in thought.

Not a gut sign.

Kristi filled two infusers with dry mint leaves and lowered them into two mugs, which she covered with boiling water from the kettle. Then, she set the mugs on the table, one in front of Amos, the other where Shane would sit.

Amos looked up at her absently. "It's kind of a blur, but I think there were three. The last one wasn't with us long. Just a couple of years. She was the mamm of the wee one. She fell…." He lowered his head and blinked at the greenish liquid in his mug.

Shane sat down next to him, a sympathetic look on his face.

"I'm sorry." Not knowing what else to say, Kristi turned around and stepped over to the stove, preparing to pan-fry the chicken.

"So, Amos." Shane broke the heavy silence. "Tell us about yourself."

❧

Amos didn't look at Shane much while he talked. Instead, he kept his eyes locked on Kristi, evaluating. Assessing. Shane could see the admiration in his eyes as he watched her at the stove. But when she stepped to the side to reach for a spatula, Amos scowled.

Her limp was not extremely pronounced. Yet Kristi was probably right to count it as a turnoff.

Funny, it didn't bother Shane. Not like the mug of tea sending steam in his direction. It smelled like mint. Probably from Kristi's garden. Hopefully, she wouldn't be offended when she realized he hadn't touched it.

Shane leaned back in his chair and stretched out his legs under the table for a few minutes as Amos droned on.

Finally, in the middle of the older man's monologue, Shane stood and walked over to Kristi, who was carving up the chicken and forking each slice onto a platter. "How can I help?"

She nodded at the stove. "You could drain the potatoes and beans and put them into those serving dishes. Danki." Kristi set down the knife and picked up the platter, balancing it on one arm. With the other hand, she gripped her cane.

"I'll get everything on the table." Shane took the dish from her and carried it the rest of the way. "You sit down. You've been working hard."

She stiffened. "I'm not helpless." Still holding her cane, she turned around and reached with one arm for some plates stacked on a shelf.

"I didn't mean to imply you were. I want to help." Shane glanced at Amos.

Amos frowned and shook his head slightly. It appeared that he had judged Kristi and found her lacking, largely due to Shane's interference. He had caused her to appear less capable than she was.

With a sigh, Shane set the platter of chicken on the table and went to drain the beans and potatoes. He'd thought Kristi would be grateful for any help in discouraging Amos's affections. But it seemed otherwise. Would she rather he attempted a hard sell? Praise everything about her, so as to renew Amos's interest?

He'd never felt so confused. The only thing that seemed certain was Kristi's frustration with him.

For now, all he could do was let the evening run its course. To make it up to her, he'd talk with his physical therapist friend and see about having her work with Kristi. Of course, Shane would need permission to bring in outside help first. It would be pointless to talk to his friend if Kristi's family was bound to disapprove of her undergoing therapy. He'd start with Timothy.

❧◦❧

Kristi bit her tongue to keep from ordering both men out of her haus. She might have limited mobility, but she didn't need to be coddled. Shane should realize that.

And Amos Kropf might be Daed's choice for her to marry, but he wasn't her choice for a husband. She would try to give him a chance, but, deep down, she knew she could never marry him, even if he were the last man on earth.

Right now, she wanted to be left alone. Crankiness had reared its ugly head. Maybe it was because she'd been out all nacht delivering a boppli and hadn't rested much since then. And Daed's underhanded orchestration of this dinner had hardly helped. She knew how desperately he wanted to marry her off, but if he expected success, this was not the way to go about securing it. Moreover, her left leg had begun to ache, confirming her doctor's jest that she would be able to predict the weather forecast with her limb. She hadn't laughed then, and the memory only caused her mood to sour even more.

Her mind wandered down the path of all the work she needed to do before she could sleep, but she made herself gather three plates, hand-stitched cloth napkins, and silverware sets and then carry them to the table.

Shane had already brought over the three serving dishes, poured himself a glass of water, and settled in the chair next to Amos. She walked around to the empty chair across from Shane—her usual place—and sat down.

When Amos bowed his head for the silent prayer, Kristi hesitated a moment, surveying the table. No bread, no jam, no chowchow, no pickled eggs. He was going to think she was a skimpy hostess. Should she stand up again and get those things? She didn't even have a measly pie to serve for dessert.

On second thought, there might still be some cookies from the batch Mamm had made just before leaving. There were Janna's whoopie pies, too, but Kristi didn't want to share them with Amos. *Selfish.* She'd get them if there weren't any cookies left.

She glanced at Shane. His head was bowed like Amos's. Probably praying, as well. Maybe he wouldn't miss dessert. He hadn't ordered any when they'd gone to dinner in Springfield, and she was pretty sure the Englisch weren't as big as the Amish on having dessert with every meal.

She bowed her head for a quick prayer, then grabbed her cane and went over to the cookie jar and lifted the lid. She was in luck. There were six peanut butter cookies left. She set them on a plate and carried them over to the table.

Amos forked a piece of chicken onto his plate. "So, can you work? Can you handle laundry okay? What about gardening?" He speared her with a glance as sharp as the prongs of a pitchfork.

She set the plate on the table and stood there a moment, trying to tame her tongue. Then, she lowered herself into her chair and glanced across the table at Shane.

He kept his eyes focused on the green beans he was piling onto his plate, as if the task required all of his attention.

"I can work just fine." She hoped her voice hadn't betrayed any of the bitterness she felt.

"Jah, but I have seven buwe. We generate a lot of laundry. Right now, I have a maud who does the washing, but if you become my frau, you'll take that over, along with the cleaning, the cooking, the gardening, and—"

"I spent the afternoon making soap," Kristi pointed out. "I finished just before you showed up."

"Jah, but you needed help, ain't so?" Amos's eyes locked on Shane as he passed him the platter of chicken. "I saw your friend, here, helping to carry the supplies into the haus. I have to assume you would need help with even the most basic of chores." Amos helped himself to a scoop of potatoes, then commenced shoveling food into his mouth.

Shane's lips quirked, but he remained silent.

Kristi wrapped her foot around the chair leg and shifted positions. How to prove she was self-sufficient? "I can do basic chores just fine. By myself."

"Can you get down in the dirt and weed around the base of plants? Chase after a five-year-old who doesn't want a bath?" Amos pushed his empty plate away. "I think Ira understated your injuries considerably. Tell your daed I'm sorry, but you don't suit." He grabbed three cookies and stood. "Danki for the meal." He nodded, turned, and walked out the door, letting it slam behind him.

"He's right," Shane said. "You don't suit."

Kristi's jaw nearly dropped.

"You can do better."

So, he was trying to be sweet. "Danki, but you heard him. The list of chores? If I get down, I won't be able to get up again. Any Amish man knows better than to choose a frau like me."

Shane reached across the table and took her hand, giving it a gentle squeeze. Then, with a look of discomfort, he released her and stood up. "I guess I need to go. We shouldn't be alone. Just this morning I promised your uncle Timothy I'd stay away, unless you needed help."

"But—"

"Kristi. I promised."

"You should at least stay and finish your meal. It isn't as if we'll be alone that much longer." She was grasping at straws, she knew, but it was worth a try. As frustrated as she'd been with him for making her look helpless in front of Amos, she didn't want him to go.

"We'd be asking for trouble, sweetheart. And as much as I want to stay, I need to do the honorable thing." He picked up his plate. "Thank you for dinner. I can't remember the last time I had a home-cooked meal. It was delicious. If it's okay with you, I'll just finish at home. I'll bring back the plate and your brother's clothes later tonight and leave them on the porch."

"Okay" was all Kristi could think to say.

After Shane disappeared through the door, she sat there in stunned silence, staring down at her dinner, cold by now. She hadn't eaten a bite. And she still wasn't hungry. She pushed herself to her feet and began cleaning up the kitchen.

Once the dishes had been washed and put away, Kristi headed for her bedroom. She was exhausted, and her leg was screaming for rest. But she felt a rush of energy at the sight of Shane's jogging clothes on the bottom step.

With the handle of her cane, she hooked the top item—his shirt—and pulled it up high enough to grasp with her other hand. Leaning again on her cane, she hugged the shirt to her chest, relishing his signature scent.

The kitchen door opened, and she whirled around. She'd be mortified if Shane saw her cuddling his clothes.

But it was Onkel Timothy who stood in the kitchen.

Shane filled a plastic grocery bag with the remaining garbage from Kristi's soap-making project, then tied it securely shut. He'd already washed the kettle and stirring spoon and put them back in the shed, trying to save her as much work as possible—no matter how much she might protest.

As he turned to survey the area for additional trash, he spied Timothy Lapp leaving Kristi's house, carrying something in his arms. Shane hadn't seen him arrive, but he might have come while he'd been busy cleaning up.

When Timothy spotted Shane, he made a beeline in his direction. News traveled fast, judging by the anger that radiated from his face.

Was he upset with Shane for accepting Kristi's dinner invitation? She'd said she needed a chaperone. And it'd been more than a little uncomfortable for Shane, having to sit by and watch while a woman he wanted for himself was courted by another man.

Timothy marched up without a word and shoved the bundle he carried against Shane's chest. Shane looked down, his eyes widening in recognition. His jogging clothes. He hadn't meant to leave them at the Lapps'. He hoped he hadn't gotten Kristi in trouble.

His tongue tripped over itself as he searched for the right words to say. Yet, to be honest, he was tired of explaining his every move to these people. Clearly, they didn't trust him, and he doubted he could say anything to change that.

On second thought, why should they trust him, when he couldn't trust himself alone with Kristi?

Timothy huffed, his chest rising and falling. "Amos Kropf stopped by to tell me she wouldn't suit." He nearly spat his words.

So, Shane wasn't the object of Timothy's anger. Relief washed over him, and he nodded.

"He said she needed your help getting dinner on…and making soap."

Shane sighed. "Not exactly. She could have managed on her own. I came over because I saw a neighbor guy making a move on Kristi, and I wanted to make sure she was safe." He paused, holding Timothy's gaze. "When Amos Kropf showed up without warning, she begged me to stay and chaperone."

Timothy was the first to look away. "I figured Amos must have been mistaken. She's pretty capable. But I called Ira, and he's given me orders to get Kristi on the first bus to Pinecraft. He seems to think he'll find her a husband down there. I imagine she'll go, but not without some fussing." He shook his head. "I told Ira he should give up on Kristi marrying. There's no shame in her remaining a maidal."

Shane tucked his workout clothes under one arm. "With your permission, I think I could help."

Timothy grunted. "You know some desperate Amish man who's willing to marry an 'almost worthless' frau?"

"She's not worthless. And, no, I don't." He took a deep breath. "However, I do know a physical therapist who could help her to strengthen her leg and improve her mobility."

Shane had been planning to make this proposition to Timothy, but the opportunity to talk had come sooner than expected—and he hadn't yet discussed the situation with his physical therapist friend. Could he convince his friend, as well as Timothy, to go along with the plan before Kristi was carried off by bus to Florida? He'd never been much of a salesman.

Timothy appeared pensive. At least he hadn't rejected the idea outright. Shane continued. "This physical therapist… she and her husband raise pedigreed show dogs, and I tend to the animals' medical needs. The couple has an open account at my clinic. I'm sure that if I offered to forgive some of their debt, this therapist would be more than willing to work with Kristi. But I would need your permission, since Kristi would probably require assistance with some of the exercises, and it would make sense for me to be the one helping her."

Timothy's eyebrows drew together as he considered the proposal. After a few moments, he shook his head. "I don't think this is a gut idea."

Shane forced composure into his voice. He didn't want to beg. "I just thought it might improve Kristi's chances of finding a husband if she were able to move more easily, without assistance. Walk without a cane."

"Hmm. Physical therapy would enable her to do all that?"

"It would." *I hope.* "You and I both want the best for Kristi. We both want to see her settled with a man who will love and respect her." If only he could be that man. It pained him to make this argument. But he cherished her enough that, if he couldn't have her, he wanted her to be with someone who made her happy.

Timothy whipped off his straw hat and slapped it against his leg. "Okay. I'll grant you permission to talk to your physical therapist friend and see if she can help Kristi. But if she can't, then you tell me, and I'll put her on a bus bound for Florida."

Chapter 14

The following evening after dinner, Kristi had her arms elbow-deep in sudsy dishwater when she heard a sharp rap at the kitchen door. She hesitated, wondering who it could be. All of her friends and clients knew better than to knock; they always opened the door and hollered her name if she wasn't in the kitchen.

She dried her hands on a towel and then turned toward the door. "Kum in."

The door opened, and Shane stepped inside. Her heart skipped a beat. He met her eyes and winked, still holding the door open.

Seconds later, a petite Englisch redhead walked into the haus, carrying a manila folder and a big black bag that resembled the one Kristi used to carry her supplies for delivering boppli.

The woman smiled. "Wow, it smells great in here."

Kristi blinked at them.

Shane's brow furrowed in concern. "You really should keep your door locked when your parents are gone, and not let anyone in unless you know who it is."

Kristi shrugged. "There's nothing here worth stealing. Besides, Daed always says that anyone who's desperate enough to steal something must need it more than we do, and we ought to pray for him."

146

"And your safety?" Shane's voice sharpened. "Your virtue?"

"I'm safe. Besides, I know you. Her, I don't know." She studied this woman with flaming-red hair styled in spikes and brilliant green eyes. She was beautiful. And she reminded Kristi of the woman pictured with Shane in the photo she'd seen at his haus. His frau. "Your girlfriend, jah? Pleased to meet you. Have a seat while I finish up here."

"No, this is—"

"Kristi, I'm Lisa Davids. Shane and I are friends, as well as business associates. I'm a physical therapist."

Kristi eyed her warily. "Physical therapist?"

"Yes. Shane didn't tell you about wanting to arrange for me to work with you?"

Kristi looked at Shane. "No. We never discussed this." And if they had, she would have objected. She'd endured more than enough therapy in the hospital. She was done with these "specialists" who seemed to take pleasure in torturing people.

Shane stepped forward. "I talked to your uncle Timothy last night. He told me your father had asked him to ship you off to Florida, in hopes that you would find a husband down there. But Timothy doesn't want to see you condemned to a loveless marriage, and—"

"Loveless marriage?" At this point, any union would be loveless. She was falling in love with the man who stood in her kitchen, and he wasn't an option.

"And he agreed that it might help your chances to regain at least a degree of your former mobility," Shane continued. "He said I could talk to a physical therapist friend of mine and see about having her work with you."

Lisa set her bag on the kitchen table. "Shane filled me in on your accident and the operation you had. Let's see what you can do, and then we'll talk about what you'd like to be able to do."

"See what I can do?" She hated sounding like a parrot.

"I assume you walk with a cane most of the time, seeing it there beside you, and considering that your wheelchair is folded up in the corner, with your walker parked next to it." Lisa nodded at the cane. "Let's get your shoes on, and then I'll have you walk into the other room, sit down on a chair, and stand up again. I'll be right behind you."

Kristi glanced at Shane. "Can you hand me my shoes, please? They're by the door."

He grabbed them and passed them to her with an encouraging smile.

Kristi sat down at the kitchen table to put on her shoes. Then, following Lisa's instructions, she stood and walked into the other room. She started to head to a chair with armrests, but Lisa said, "No, that one," pointing to an armless chair. When Kristi had lowered herself into the chair, Lisa motioned for her to hand her the cane. "Now, try standing up."

Kristi reached for her cane, but Lisa smiled and shook her head.

It was a struggle, but Kristi managed to make it to her feet.

"Good job." Lisa grinned. "Sit down again. I want to show you something."

When she was seated again, Lisa showed her a different way to position her feet. "Try standing now."

Kristi did, and found it a little easier.

"Can you walk without the cane?"

"Not easily."

"Try. I'll be right here, and I won't let you fall."

Suppressing a sigh, Kristi started forward and struggled across the room.

"Okay, that's good. Sit for a minute while I go grab my folder." Lisa waited until Kristi got settled, then went into the kitchen.

Tears burned Kristi's eyes. She wanted to be back to normal, but it'd taken so much effort to get to where she was. She didn't know if she had what it would take to get any further.

❦

Shane towel-dried another dish as Lisa walked into the kitchen. He turned to face her. "Well?"

Lisa shrugged. "It's going to depend on her and on what she's willing to work for. From what I've seen so far, she can walk without a cane, but she relies on it to the point of being afraid not to use it. Getting up is a struggle, but she's worked around that by only sitting in chairs with arms. I need to talk to her yet to see what she wants to accomplish, then give her some exercises to do on her own. If she's willing to work, then someone should be with her when she walks to encourage her and assist her, if needed."

Shane nodded. "I'll help as much as I can."

"Good. She's lucky to have a friend like you." Lisa scooped up her folder and the bag and headed back to the other room.

Shane followed her, then stopped in the doorway and leaned against the frame. Kristi met his gaze, her eyes wide, as if she were unsure what to say or do. He gave a slight nod. "Your uncle said I could help you."

That must have been just what she'd needed to hear. Color filled her pale cheeks, and she visibly relaxed.

Lisa sat down in a chair across from Kristi, opened her folder, and reached for the pen clipped to the top. "Okay, Kristi. What are the goals you want to accomplish through therapy?"

Kristi squirmed and glanced at Shane again before meeting Lisa's gaze. "I don't know…I guess I'd like to be able to climb stairs better than I do. It's kind of awkward, and I need help going down if there isn't a handrail. I'd also like to be able to crouch and kneel, and get back up again, without help, so I can tend the garden more easily. And I'd rather not have to use the cane all the time."

Her gaze flickered back to Shane, and he nodded, hoping to encourage her.

Lisa scribbled something in her folder. "Great. We'll start there." She closed the folder and looked up at Kristi. "I'll stop back in two to three days, depending on my schedule. In the meantime, I want you to practice walking without the cane, without holding on to things. Try doing this as much as you can—all the time, if possible—unless you're in a lot of pain and absolutely need it. You can do it. I just watched you. But you need confidence. Shane said he'll work with you until you feel more secure. In your case, I think fear is holding you back more than physical inability. You have to use it, or you'll lose it. The next time I'm here, we'll see how you do with stairs."

Kristi nodded. "Dank—thank you."

Shane straightened, taking a step into the room. "Thanks for coming, Lisa. I know you're busy, and I appreciate your taking the time."

"Sure thing." Lisa rose to her feet, then hesitated, studying Kristi. "I encourage most of my clients to set short-term goals and then reward themselves for reaching them. In your case, if you walk across the room and over to the kitchen counter without holding on to anything, you could treat yourself to…well, not a movie or a manicure, I guess, but maybe a slice of pie? Something small that you want. It'll encourage you to keep going. And then, plan a larger prize for when you get where you want to be. For instance, one of my clients rewarded herself with an Alaskan cruise." She shrugged. "Think of something you'd really like, and then reward yourself when you reach your goal."

Kristi turned to Shane and arched an eyebrow. Was she hinting at what he thought? It wouldn't be a good idea. Then again, if kissing her would speed up her progress, who was he to deny her his "help"?

Lisa snapped the folder shut. "I'll let myself out. Shane, if you have time, maybe you could spot Kristi while she takes a walk up and down the driveway. Be there for support, but try not to help unless it's absolutely necessary." She smiled at Kristi. "I'll see you in a few days."

"Thank you again."

Lisa strode past Shane into the kitchen and out the door. Moments later, he could hear her car engine start, followed by the crunch of gravel as she backed out of the driveway.

Kristi struggled to her feet from the armless chair, then took a couple of hesitant steps toward the table where Lisa had propped her cane.

Shane snatched the cane and held it behind his back. "No, Kristi. You heard her. Try to walk without holding on to anything." His gaze drifted down to her feet. She was still wearing tennis shoes, but no socks. "You should put on some socks."

"I don't need them."

"I don't want you to get blisters."

With a sigh, Kristi turned around, then made her way across the living room. She disappeared through a door and reemerged seconds later, carrying a pair of thick black socks. "I hate for you to see me like this."

"I've seen you in worse shape. You've made great progress."

"Danki." Her smile was mischievous. "So, what will be my reward for walking down the driveway, with socks, shoes, and all?"

"Hmm. I don't know. What do you have a hankering for?"

She thought for a moment, and then her lips formed a mischievous smile. "You could take my shoes and socks off again and massage some lotion into my heels."

Becca had loved having her feet pampered. Shane had lost count of the times he'd fixed her a tub of hot, soapy water to soak her feet. Afterward, he would dry her off with a plush towel and massage her heels, ankles, and calves with scented oil. The ritual had usually led to other, more pleasurable activities….

❦

"Shane?" Kristi waved a hand in front of his face. "Didn't realize my smelly feet posed such a threat." She hoped he wasn't disgusted with her suggestion. But her feet would have smelled worse if she'd worn socks all day. Instead, she'd gone barefoot, as was her custom in warm weather.

"Sorry about that." Shane smiled. "Here, let's get your socks on."

Reluctantly, she placed them in his open palm.

He fingered the material. "Wool?"

"Jah. Mamm made them. She buys the yarn from a farmer in our district who spins it from his sheep. But they're heavy and itchy."

He nodded. "Sit down somewhere and I'll help you put them on."

"I really don't need help, you know." She lowered herself into a straight-back chair.

"Yes, but we might get outside a little sooner if I help you. Maybe I can get Chinook exercised before the next storm system comes through. There weren't any tornado cells in the ones last night, but, last time I checked, the forecast said there might be some tonight. The system passed through Oklahoma and Kansas earlier today."

"Tornadoes?" She shuddered.

"Possibly." He sat on the floor in front of her, untied her shoes, and pulled them off. He picked up a sock, then hesitated. "You have pretty feet."

She snorted.

"No, really. They're small and…dainty." He lifted her right foot and ran a fingertip along the sole, sending shivers down her spine.

She jerked back, her toes curling.

"Don't worry. I'll be good." He slid one sock on, and then the other, followed by her shoes, tying the laces snugly. "We need to get moving. Can you stand up on your own?"

The chair she was seated in didn't have arms. She hesitated. "I should try." She felt a twinge of fear she wouldn't do it right without the therapist there, but slid to the edge, positioned her feet, and pushed up. She hated this whole idea of therapy stuff, but since Shane would be the one helping her, she'd do it. For him.

"Great." Shane grinned at her. "I'll help you down the porch steps, but you'll be on your own to the end of the driveway and back. I'll stay with you the whole time."

Kristi pulled in a deep breath. *Lord, help me do this.* She walked toward the kitchen door.

Shane held it open for her, then moved slightly ahead, holding her hand as she navigated the stairs, one at a time.

"It's a little uneven here." Shane released her as soon as she was safely down. "I'll be right beside you, so grab on to me if you need to."

Lightning flashed overhead. She grimaced. "Looks like the storm's coming in soon."

"I may not get to take Chinook out." He lifted a shoulder. "You come first. Do you have a basement or storm cellar, in case it gets bad?"

"No. But there's an interior closet. I'll be fine. What about in your haus?" She started down the driveway.

Shane kept pace beside her. "There's a basement, mostly used for storage at this point. My brother-in-law keeps nagging me to finish it and have a pool table installed."

Kristi's breath caught. Brother-in-law? Was he still close to the family of his deceased frau? What would they think of his spending time with an Amish woman?

"But he doesn't live near here," Shane continued. "In fact, he's a Marine, and he's about to be deployed overseas. My sister is expecting a baby in eight weeks or so, and he wants her with family. She will be coming to stay with me for a while."

Kristi felt a small wave of relief. Shane was talking about his sister's husband, not his late frau's brother. Still, she wasn't sure she liked the prospect of having to share him with another woman, even if it was just his sister. "Wouldn't she rather stay with your parents?"

Shane shook his head. "They live in a one-bedroom apartment, and she'd have to sleep on the couch. I actually have a spare room for her. Mom said she'd come closer to the time the baby is due." They were nearing the road. "You're doing great, Kristi. Make a wide arc when you turn back. Might be easier."

She made the turn. "Will this be your sister's first child?"

"Yes, her first."

"Does she have an obstetrician? I'd be happy to help with the bir—"

"We'll find her an ob-gyn when she gets here," Shane cut in. "She'll deliver the baby at the hospital in Springfield."

"Ach." Kristi was taken aback at his vehemence. "Of course. That…would be best."

"Yes. It would."

Did Shane's sister have a problem with midwives? If so, why hadn't he said anything? Kristi couldn't help feeling deflated—and confused. She glanced over at him and lost her footing in a slight depression in the ground. She reached out to grab Shane's arm but missed.

Shane immediately grasped her upper arm to keep her from falling. "Easy, there." He held her until she found her footing again, then released her.

"Danki." She hated how she immediately missed his touch.

As they reached the porch, Shane tucked Kristi's hand into the crook of his arm to steady her as she climbed the stairs.

Kristi stopped at the door, holding on to the knob for support. She'd make it inside on her own. She hoped. Maybe she could do this. "Danki for taking the time to work with me, Shane."

He smiled warmly. Maybe she'd misinterpreted his reaction. "You're welcome. You did great. So, how are you going to reward yourself?"

Part of her wanted him to kiss her as he had in Springfield, but the rest of her was unsure how to proceed, given his outburst earlier. She lifted a shoulder. "I don't know. I probably won't."

"You deserve something." His voice dropped in pitch, and his gaze lowered.

Was he studying her lips? Kristi pretended not to notice. She shrugged again, opened the door, and took a step back. "It's really not our way."

His eyes glinted with regret. "I'm sorry I was so adamant back there. It's just…well, my sister wants a hospital birth, and I've always been overprotective of her."

"That's okay. Midwives aren't for everyone. Even some Amish women choose to give birth in the hospital."

He reached out and brushed her cheek. "Thanks for understanding."

"When will your sister kum?"

"I'm not sure. Soon. It depends on when Michael is set to ship out. He and Sylvia live on base, and their plan is to pack everything up and store it in my basement until they can be together again."

"Well, you'll have to let me know when you expect her. I'd like to prepare a basket of herbal teas and ointments to welkum her."

"Don't...please." Shane looked angry, but his expression quickly softened. "I'm pretty sure Sylvia's allergic to a lot of that stuff. She would feel guilty not being able to accept your gift."

Kristi had never come across an herbal allergy before, but she decided to take Shane's word for it. Especially since she didn't want to ruin her chances of getting a reward for walking up and down the driveway.

As if he'd read her mind, Shane stepped closer and cupped her cheek with his hand. "Speaking of gifts, how about that reward I promised you?"

Her heart fluttered as he traced a finger over the curve of her cheek, working his way toward her lips. She leaned into his kiss, even as her conscience and sense of social propriety screamed for her to stop.

Lisa had suggested setting "small" rewards at the outset. Kristi needed to pull away now if this kiss was to count as a petty prize.

⚬⚬⚬

Shane hated lying to Kristi. After they'd said good-bye and she'd gone inside, he stood on the porch for several minutes, debating whether to knock on the door and tell her the truth. Explain his reasons for mistrusting midwives and spurning herbal remedies. Reveal how Becca had died.

But he wasn't ready to do that.

With a sigh, he turned toward home.

Fifteen minutes later, he was back in Kristi's yard, letting Chinook out of the kennel. Thunder rumbled softly in the distance, and the sky flashed with lightning, but it wasn't raining yet. He wasn't about to risk taking a run, but he figured the dog could use a little loving. They played in the yard for a few minutes, and he tossed Chinook a milk bone from his stash.

Hearing a door open, Shane glanced at Kristi's house. Timothy marched down the steps and strode across the lawn in his direction. He must have stopped in for a visit while Shane had been inside.

Timothy nodded in greeting. "You had therapy with Kristi today, ain't so? How did she do?"

"Good. She walked without her cane. The therapist thinks she's afraid to try, and she should improve with practice."

"So, she did okay?"

"Fine. Great, actually."

Timothy exhaled. "Gut, gut." He paused. "What isn't gut, I'm afraid, is that you violated the terms of our agreement. I said that you could work with Kristi, provided you went no further. And I saw you…on the porch."

Timothy had seen them kissing? Shane held his breath. He'd thought Donald was the only spy in the neighborhood.

"Kissing is verboden unless a couple is courting—impossible, since you are Englisch. Even then, it is done in private. Never in plain sight."

Shane doubted Timothy would have preferred his retreating with Kristi into the privacy of her house, away from the public eye. Shouldn't he get some credit for keeping his advances out in the open? For not taking advantage of the situation?

A wave of panic pulsed through him when he recalled the consequence Timothy had laid out for him: loading Kristi on the next bus to Florida.

Kristi would have it worse, though. She would suffer the wrath of Ira. And maybe the bishop, if Timothy reported her.

"I should send Kristi away, but I want her to continue meeting with the physical therapist." Timothy spoke slowly, as if reasoning aloud. "I'll talk to my frau about coming over to help Kristi with her exercises."

Shane's heart thudded in his chest—whether from relief that Kristi would remain in Seymour, or from regret at being forbidden from working further with Kristi, he couldn't tell.

"Ira would be more comfortable with that setup, anyway," Timothy went on. "I didn't tell him all of the details of our arrangement, but, based on our previous discussions, I know how he would react." He paused again. "You can still take care of the dog, but stay away from the girl. Understand?"

Shane pinched the bridge of his nose as he tried to generate some explanation that would overturn Timothy's decision. But nothing came to mind. And he was tired of lying. Shane nodded. "I understand. Completely."

Timothy smiled briefly, then turned and walked back toward the house.

Shane stood there, as if cemented to the ground by his disbelief. So, this was it, then.

But maybe it was for the best. It wasn't as if Kristi and he could really end up together. Shane should have kept that in mind from the start, instead of leading Kristi along with compliments and kisses. If he made himself scarce, she would have more time and attention to spend on a legitimate suitor. An Amish one.

The rationalization brought little relief to his aching heart. With one last glance at Kristi's house, Shane gave Chinook another pat, dropped the latch on the kennel, and headed toward home. Chinook began to whine, but he ignored her.

When the whines turned to howls, he couldn't resist glancing back for a second. The dog stood on her hind legs with her front paws propped against the fence and, if he didn't know better, a woebegone expression on her face.

Shane sighed. *I know just how you feel, girl.*

That nacht, Kristi tried to sleep, but in vain—Chinook wouldn't quit whining. Finally, for the sake of the neighbors, as well as herself, Kristi grabbed her cane and went outside to check on her. She ended up bringing the dog inside to sleep with her. Daed would have been upset, but what he didn't know wouldn't hurt him.

The next morgen, Kristi woke up next to a big ball of fur. For a moment, she was startled, but she quickly remembered how the dog had gotten inside. She dragged herself out of bed and took Chinook back outside in time for her early run with Shane. After that, she scrambled a couple of eggs for breakfast as she tried to plan out her day.

There were a couple of expectant mamms she wanted to visit. Today might be a good time, even though none of them had an appointment.

As she was cleaning the breakfast dishes, she heard footfall on the porch. She turned just as the door swung open.

Aenti Deborah, Onkel Timothy's frau, burst inside, bearing a plate of sweet rolls. She glanced at the sink. "Ach, I'm too late for breakfast. Your onkel sent me over to help with your exercises. He told Dr. Zimmerman I'd handle it, to appease your daed." She set down the platter of rolls and got herself a plate.

Kristi managed what she hoped sounded like a sincere thank-you to her aenti, but her heart sank. Shane hadn't said anything about handing off the duty of helping with her therapy. She filled a mug with koffee and set it on the table. Then, while her aenti ate, she finished washing the dishes. As she watched the dirty water drain from the sink, she envisioned her chances with Shane swirling down and away. Taking with them his companionship. His kisses.

She peeked outside and across the yard, at Shane's haus. His Jeep was gone. He must have started his day early, or maybe he'd been called out to assist with the delivery of a calf or a foal.

Had Shane even protested this latest edict of Onkel Timothy? Kristi wouldn't blame him if he hadn't. She'd been foolish getting her hopes up about a relationship with him. Still, fool or not, she couldn't help it. She'd fallen in love.

Chapter 15

Shane eased his foot off of the gas pedal, resisting the urge to speed to work. He'd been summoned out to a ranch in the early hours of the morning to help deliver a baby calf whose mother was having difficulties. Afterward, he'd stopped at home just long enough to shower and change before heading to the clinic.

He walked into a waiting room filled with dogs and cats and their owners, not to mention an overwhelmed receptionist. Patsy put down the phone and followed him back to his office. "Where've you been? I've been trying to call you all morning. I don't know how many messages I left on your cell phone."

"Sorry. I had an emergency call this morning from Mr. Johnson—his cow was having a difficult labor—and I left my phone at home. I didn't get a chance to check the messages till I was on my way here."

Patsy raised her eyebrows. "Whatever you say, Doc. I'm still not convinced you aren't recovering from a late night." She put her hands on her hips. "I just made a fresh pot of coffee. It should be ready."

"Thank you." He ignored the implication that he'd given a false excuse for his tardiness. "Go ahead and send my first patient to the exam room, please."

"You realize we'll be working through lunch to get caught up." She huffed. "I'll order in. Pizza?"

"Sure. With onions and pepperoni?"

"Pepperoni, yes. Onions?" She wrinkled her nose. "Only if you want stinky breath."

He shrugged. "Then, order half without. Makes no difference to me. My breath is still better than most dogs'."

"Suit yourself. I'd rather not have onion breath, just in case. You never know when you're going to lock lips with someone."

Shane immediately pictured Kristi on the porch last night, leaning into his kiss....

Enough daydreaming about the impossible. He had work to do.

He looked up at Patsy with a dismissive nod. And that's when she winked at him, then spun around on her impossibly high heels and clicked down the hallway.

If her sights were set on kissing him, she had the wrong idea. "Double onions on mine," he called after her.

❧

With Aenti Deborah spotting her, Kristi walked the driveway twice that morgen with no mishaps. Maybe this therapy stuff was actually working.

After her aenti had gone home, Kristi fetched her cane, then got the horse hitched to the buggy so that she could make her visits. Later, she would stop by the grocery store for a few items.

It promised to be a beautiful day. The sky was clear blue and cloudless, and the whole world seemed to have been washed clean by the heavy rains they'd had the previous nacht.

She smiled as she climbed up into the buggy seat. Only one thing could make the day more perfect…nein. She wouldn't go there.

Samson plodded down the driveway at his usual pace and obeyed the slight tug of the reins by turning toward town. As they passed Shane's driveway, Kristi heard a popping sound, like the firecrackers her brothers used to set off in the back field.

Samson fell to the ground, shrieking.

Stunned, Kristi sat there a few seconds, staring at her fallen horse. What had just happened? Had he been hit by a burning firecracker? By a bullet? She scrambled out of the buggy as fast as she could and checked the writhing animal. His right shoulder was bloody. She looked around frantically, seeing no one but sensing danger.

She knew Shane wasn't home, but she double-checked his driveway, just to be certain. Still no Jeep. Still no Shane.

Kristi turned again and spotted Creepy Guy running toward her. "Are you okay? What happened?"

"I'm fine, but Samson…my horse…he's hurt. I…I don't know what happened." She swallowed her tears.

"Wrong season for hunters." Creepy Guy looked around, as if to check their surroundings for would-be ambushers.

"W-would you get Onkel Timothy for me, please?"

"Sure thing." He dashed in the direction of Onkel Timothy's haus.

Danki, God, for sending Creepy Guy—I mean, Donald. Please take care of Samson.

Minutes later, Onkel Timothy barreled down the road, rifle in hand. Kristi flinched. Was he planning to put Samson down?

Donald followed on his heels, huffing.

The two men stopped next to Samson and looked at his wound. Onkel Timothy turned to Donald and pointed toward Shane's haus. "Do you know how to reach Dr. Zimmerman?"

Kristi opened her mouth to say that she had his business card at home, but Donald said, "I know where his office is. I'll find him."

He turned and shuffled hastily across the street, disappearing inside his haus. A minute later, his car squealed out of his driveway and sped up the road.

❦

Cup of coffee in hand, Shane listened to his latest voice-mail messages, deleting the ones from Patsy. The rest he'd return when he had a free moment. Then, he set down his coffee and went into the exam room.

"Good morning, Mrs. Hunt." He picked up the dog's chart and glanced at it. "Time for Patches' rabies shot." He patted the Pomeranian on the head and then walked around the table to the counter, where a tray was arranged with the necessary supplies.

As he picked up the needle and stuck it into the vial, a high-pitched screech jarred him. "Sir, you are not allowed back there!"

The door to the exam room burst open.

Shane looked past Mrs. Hunt, who clutched her chest, and saw Donald Jackson in the doorway, panting. He bent over, gasping for breath.

"Donald. Are you okay?" Shane pulled the needle from the vial and walked over to the table. He rubbed the dog's neck a moment, then plunged the needle in.

"I'll call the police if you don't leave this instant!" Patsy clicked into the room and wagged her finger in Donald's flushed face.

"Doc," he wheezed, "you need to come now. It's an emergency."

"Sir!" Patsy pushed her finger against his chest. "This isn't how it's done. If you need to see the vet, you make an appointment, and—"

"Patsy, it's okay. Go back to your desk." Shane frowned. "Donald, what's the emergency?"

"There was a shooting. Horse is down."

Shane nodded. His mind raced as he projected the proper course of action. How would he transport the animal for surgery, if necessary? He tried to think what supplies he had in his Jeep, mentally making a list of what he'd need to grab on his way out. He gave Patches a dog treat, then looked at Mrs. Hunt. Her hand was still pressed to her chest, and her eyes were wide, as if she were being forced against her will to watch a horror film.

"Forgive me, Mrs. Hunt, but I need to go. If you'll see Patsy, she'll give you the paperwork you need to fill out before leaving." He smiled at the older woman, then grasped Donald's shoulder and directed him out of the exam room. "I need to grab my kit and a few supplies. Meet me in the waiting room, okay?"

Shane collected what he needed, then raced down the hallway. He paused by Patsy's desk and addressed the people in the waiting room. "I'm sorry, folks, but I need to tend to an emergency. You're welcome to wait, if you want. Otherwise, please see Patsy to reschedule." With that, he followed Donald out the door to the parking lot.

"Where's the horse?" he called to Donald as they raced to their vehicles.

"On our street. In front of your house, in fact."

"You're kidding! Whose is it?"

Donald stopped and gave him a grim look. "Kristi's."

Shane's pulse beat triple time. Whispering a prayer, he shoved his hand in his pocket, pulled out his keys, and jumped into the Jeep.

Chapter 16

Kristi sat inside the buggy and waited for Onkel Timothy to return with one of his horses, named Taffy, for her to use to run errands. He'd already unhitched Samson, who still lay in the road, screaming. But she didn't want to leave her horse. She wanted Shane to save him, or at least try. And, if Shane would be there, she wanted to be there, too.

She saw dust rising on the road and then Donald's brown car drove into view, followed by Shane's Jeep. She sighed in relief, even as her heart began to pound.

Shane pulled over to the curb and parked about ten feet away from Samson. A moment later, his four-way flashers started blinking, and he jumped out.

He glanced at the squealing animal, and then his blue eyes fixed on her. "Kristi. Are you alright?" He strode past Samson to reach her, as if she were top priority.

Yet he didn't wrap her in a protective hug, as she'd hoped he would. Even so, she was grateful for his presence. It strengthened her. Made her feel safe. "I'm not hurt," she assured him. "But I don't know who shot my horse, or why."

He eyed her tenderly. "I'm sure it was an accident, but I asked Donald to call the police." Then, it was as if a shutter closed over his face. His expression became detached yet determined. Professional mode. A suffering animal needed his attention.

Shane jogged back to his Jeep and grabbed a black bag from the back. He slammed the door and dashed over to Samson, crouching down to check him out.

Kristi looked on but made sure to stay out of the way, so as not to interfere with his work.

Soon, Onkel Timothy returned, leading Taffy by a rope tied around her neck. Hopefully, he wouldn't argue when she insisted on staying. Whether he liked it or not, she wasn't leaving until Shane did.

"Looks like the bullet entered here"—Shane pointed to a spot she hadn't noticed, in Samson's chest—"and exited here." He motioned to the shoulder. "Timothy, if you would help me, we can get Samson up and take him back to the barn, and then I'll get him stitched up."

Timothy grunted. "That horse is a wimp. I've had a horse shatter a bone, and still it stood there on three legs, with nary a sound. This animal just lies there and screams."

Shane chuckled.

"Ira always starts his kinner out with worthless animals. Kept the buwe from racing, I reckon, but it's past time for Kristi to get a real horse. She needs a reliable means of transportation to get to her patients."

Kristi nearly gasped. Finally, someone else agreed that she needed a faster horse!

Shane hesitated and looked up at Timothy. "What are you saying? Do you want him put down?" He studied the horse again. "I think Samson has a good chance of surviving."

Onkel Timothy shook his head. "Not my call. Ira's horse. But if it were my decision, I'd put him down and give Taffy to Kristi."

Shane glanced at Kristi. She stood there, silenced by indecision. She loved Taffy. She was a good horse, sweet-tempered, and she moved faster than Samson. But she'd hate to end Samson's life. He'd served her faithfully, and, despite his unpredictable temperament, they got along well. Besides, couldn't she have both? She could use Taffy and find Samson a good home after he recovered. Just because she wouldn't use him with her buggy again didn't mean he had to die.

Kind of like her own situation. Just because she had a limp and moved slowly didn't mean she should be "put down," either.

Besides, if Shane treated Samson, and the horse lived, he would need to come over from time to time to check on him. Right?

"Kristi will need Taffy anyway while Samson recovers." Shane stood. "And since Ira isn't here to make a decision, I'll go ahead and treat the horse, in hopes that he'll live. If Ira lets you know otherwise, we'll go from there."

Onkel Timothy nodded. "Kristi, you hook up Taffy to your buggy and tend to your errands, then. Dr. Zimmerman and I will take care of the horse."

She nodded, her mind scrambling to find an excuse to delay her departure. "I just realized I forgot something at home." *Untrue.* "So, while I'm at the haus, why don't I make some koffee for everyone? I'll set out some cinnamon rolls, too."

Donald shuffled over. "I called the police. They said it's probably too late, but they're gonna come out and look around. See if they can find a shooter." He pointed at Samson. "He gonna be okay?"

"I believe so."

Kristi took the rope from Onkel Timothy and led Taffy over to the buggy. In minutes, she had her hooked up. As she climbed into the buggy, she heard Shane say to Donald, "Want to give us a hand? Heard you get paid in cinnamon rolls."

Once Samson was settled in his stall, Shane drove his Jeep up to the barn so that his supplies would be easy to access. He asked Donald to fill a bucket with water for him to use to disinfect the wound. After the horse was bandaged, they left him to rest in the barn.

Timothy directed Shane to the outdoor shower Ira had rigged up, where he scrubbed his hands and arms. Then, he followed Timothy and Donald to the farmhouse and into the kitchen, where Kristi had set out a plate piled high with cinnamon rolls. She handed each of the men a steaming mug of coffee and set out a pitcher of cream.

She seemed completely in her element, working around the kitchen—which smelled wonderful, as usual. And she wasn't using her cane. She didn't even seem to need it, maybe because she wasn't thinking about it. There was still a limp, but it wasn't bad.

Shane resisted the impulse to wrap her in a hug, just as he'd avoided any shows of intimacy in the street. He wouldn't risk it, under the watchful eye of Timothy.

Yet nothing about Kristi's treatment of him had changed. That probably meant Timothy hadn't lectured her as he had Shane. Wise man, making Shane out to be the "bad guy." The fickle friend.

Shane sucked in a breath to pull himself together, then sat down at the table.

Kristi tugged out a chair and sat down next to Shane. "Samson…he'll be okay, jah?"

Shane kept his gaze focused on his coffee mug. "I hope so. I've done all I can, at this point, and I'll certainly keep an eye on him. I'll change his bandages the next time I come to take Chinook for a run."

"Danki."

He glanced up and saw that her expression remained downcast. "Hey, don't worry about him. Really. As long as he's kept quiet and allowed to rest and heal, he should be fine."

"Worthless piece of horseflesh," Timothy muttered. "Not like Kristi was ever the type to go racing, like the buwe. But Ira could have bought a decent horse to begin with."

Donald took a bite of his cinnamon roll; Timothy closed his eyes and bowed his head, probably praying. After a moment's hesitation, Shane closed his eyes, too. *Lord....* But nothing more would come.

All he could think to pray about was the impossible: Kristi and him, together. Courting. *"It's supposed to be done under the cover of darkness."* Her words echoed in his mind as if she'd spoken them just now. What would she do if he tossed pebbles at her window? If he spirited her away to Springfield for another date?

He knew what her uncle Timothy would say. Rather, what he would do. Bus tickets weren't hard to come by. It wasn't worth the risk. Best to let things be.

Still, he couldn't keep from watching her. Studying her. Memorizing her features.

After devouring a cinnamon roll and downing two cups of coffee, Shane decided to make his exit. Any longer in Kristi's presence, and his charade of indifference would become impossible to keep up. Sighing, he stood. "I need to get back to the office. It was a madhouse when I left. Who knows how many people are waiting at this point?"

Kristi grasped the edge of the table and got to her feet. "How much do I owe you?"

Shane shook his head. "No charge."

"Danki, Shane."

When he moved for the door, Timothy opened it and led the way outside.

After Shane had shut the screen door, Timothy turned to face him. "I appreciate your taking the time to kum out here the way you did. Just dropping everything. But we mean to pay you for your services."

"Please, no. I don't want to take her money." Shane started down the stairs.

Timothy followed close behind him. "I think the word 'minimal' was a considerable understatement."

Blinking, Shane stopped and looked over his shoulder at Kristi's uncle. "Excuse me?"

"Last week, I asked you to confirm that Ira had no basis for concern about your relationship with Kristi. 'Minimal' is what you said. I guess I should have taken you seriously. After yesterday, I know better."

"At least I didn't deny it," Shane said, leaning back against the kennel fence. "I was trying to be honest."

Chinook got up from where she'd been napping and trotted over. He reached down and rubbed her head.

Timothy came to stand beside him. "I thought I made myself clear yesterday, after witnessing your...moment." His face flushed. "But I noticed the way you were watching her in the kitchen." He kept his gaze straight ahead, on the barn.

Shane gave Chinook another pat. Amazing that the mention didn't trigger feelings of guilt or an abrupt denial. For some reason, he didn't fear Timothy as much as he'd thought. "I said I'd stay away. Stop helping with her exercises. Not change the way I feel about her."

Timothy kicked his boot against the wire enclosure. "Let me remind you of a couple of things. If you continue down this path, she will be shunned, losing all ties to family. And you will probably lose a lot of your clients. Pursuing her will hurt both of you. More than you know."

Shane felt his throat tighten. "I'm well aware that I'm about the worst choice possible for Kristi. And I have no intentions of interfering with her marrying a good man. I want what's best for her."

Timothy's expression sobered even more. "That's the thing, Zimmerman. I'm not so sure you are the worst. I think you'd be better than most, actually. And I believe Ira knows it, too, and that's why he's so desperate to find someone— anyone—for her, before he loses her completely."

Chinook yipped, as if she agreed.

Shane's thoughts whirled. "I…I'm not sure what to say."

Timothy frowned. "Nor am I. What I am sure about is that forbidding a relationship will probably have the opposite effect of its intent. Yet I can't sanction it, either. Ira left her in my care, and I will not countermand his wishes."

Shane turned to face Timothy. "You can rest assured I'm a man of my word. I've already made promises to you and Ira, and I intend to keep them, to the best of my ability." Already he had failed miserably. "I care deeply about Kristi. Love her, in fact. But I don't want to destroy her life."

Shane realized this was the first time he'd admitted having deep feelings for Kristi. He'd known he was in danger of falling for her, but his reaction to the shooting of her horse had cemented his feelings.

He also realized how much he loved her—enough to desire her happiness, at the expense of his own. Her being shunned and forced to give up everyone and everything she loved was not the answer.

"You're a gut man, Zimmerman." Timothy straightened. "And I won't tell you what to do. Let God guide."

Shane nodded, then glanced toward the house, where Kristi was probably still in the kitchen. With Donald. "For now, in Kristi's best interests, I think you should go back inside. I don't trust our neighbor alone with her, despite his helpfulness. And I need to get back to work. I'll stop by later to check on the horse."

"It'll be dark when you kum back. There's a lantern and matches on the shelf by the door." Timothy turned away.

Shane walked to his Jeep, his thoughts more jumbled than ever.

⚯

Gazing out the window above the kitchen sink, Kristi watched Shane drive away after what had appeared to be a serious conversation with Onkel Timothy. She wished she could have listened in. Or maybe not.

Her emotions had never been so tangled up. Only yesterday, Shane had kissed her tenderly. Today, he'd seemed distant. At first, she'd attributed it to "professional mode." But after Samson had been treated, Shane had remained standoffish. Almost cold. And he'd sent Aenti Deborah in his place to help with her exercises.

Kristi's musings were interrupted when the door opened and Onkel Timothy came back inside. His gaze fixed on Donald and the platter of cinnamon rolls, which the neighbor had been inhaling as if they were his last meal on earth. "Want to take the rest of those home with you, Donald?"

Donald's eyes widened. He scrambled to his feet, a half-eaten pastry in his hand. "Oh, no, I couldn't do that."

"Why not?"

"Oh. Well, if you're gonna insist. You sure do cook good, Kristi."

"My aenti Deborah made them." Kristi mustered a smile. "Let me wrap them up for you." She found a paper plate, to which she transferred the remaining rolls. Then, she wrapped the plate in tinfoil and handed it to him.

Onkel Timothy hovered by the door. "I hate to rush off, Kristi, but I know you have errands. I'll walk you home, Donald."

"Thanks for the rolls," Donald said. "Me and my wife'll enjoy them. I hope your horse is alright, Kristi."

"Thank you for helping. I'm glad you were around when it happened."

Donald nodded and went for the door, then turned around. "Speaking of helping, I'd be happy to take you on your errands."

Kristi's eyes widened. "Ach, nein. That wouldn't be... um...."

Onkel Timothy shook his head. "As her temporary guardian, I have to refuse. But thank you."

She didn't need a guardian. She was legally of age. But, as a woman, she remained under her father's rule until she married, at which point her husband would assume that role. Sometimes, she envied the freedom her friend Starr enjoyed. Her own apartment. Her own choices. Her own life.

Onkel Timothy reached for the door and opened it. Two policemen stood on the porch.

Chapter 17

Shane couldn't keep his focus at work. Thankfully, most of his appointments that day were routine—cats and dogs in for their shots, mostly—meaning they didn't require too much thought.

He kept thinking about what had transpired that morning. The shock was just now settling in that someone had shot Kristi's horse in broad daylight—and right in front of his house, no less. Who could have done it? Had it been an accident? It seemed so odd. And the only thing that didn't surprise him was Donald's having been the first responder. The man had basically admitted that he spent a lot of his time spying on Kristi.

When he'd left for the clinic, Shane had passed a police car parked down the street. There had been two officers, as far as he could tell—one had been walking along the curb, poking around a grove of trees and shrubs on the edge of the road; the other had been snapping pictures near where Samson had gone down. But Shane doubted they'd found anything. Within seconds of the incident, the shooter—or shooters—would have been long gone.

Maybe one of Timothy's sons had shot the horse, by accident. It was possible that a round could have gone off while someone was cleaning out a rifle, for example.

As quickly as the idea had dawned in his mind, he dismissed it. Timothy would have educated his sons about gun safety and taught them to empty a gun of all ammunition before cleaning it. Moreover, if they had been cleaning their rifles, Shane doubted they would have deliberately ignored the sound of a horse screaming in the neighborhood.

Maybe Donald had fired the shot, on purpose, hoping to switch roles and be the hero who saved the day. Aiming to win Kristi's gratitude and trust. The bullet's entry and exit points would support a shot coming from the direction of his house....

Whoever had fired the shot, Shane was just glad he'd missed Kristi. The outcome could have been a lot worse. One foot higher, and the bullet would have cleared Samson's shoulder and hit Kristi head-on. His blood ran cold at the thought of losing another love to premature death.

As if these thoughts weren't distracting enough, there was the matter of Timothy's cryptic words. If only Shane could decipher the true intent of Timothy's message. He'd warned Shane to stay away, only to confess that he believed Shane was the best match for Kristi. Completely contradictory. It made no sense.

And what would Timothy have him do? Propose to Kristi, on the condition that she jump the fence and be shunned by her family for the rest of her life? Or, jump the fence in reverse, exchanging his Jeep, his job, and his religious convictions to join the Amish community?

He snorted. Despite his proficiency in Pennsylvania Dutch and his relative familiarity with Amish customs, he had no desire to drive a slow-moving horse and buggy. Nor did he want to give up the modern conveniences that made his job, not to mention his life, so much easier.

The weight of a scalpel in his hand brought his mind back to the present, and he shook off his musings, not caring to analyze the situation any further. For now. He needed to focus his full mental capacity on his job, especially now that a sedated cat lay on the table, waiting to be spayed. The owners would hardly appreciate a jagged-looking scar on the feline's belly. It would be upsetting enough to see Fluffy neatly shaved and stitched-up after the procedure. He didn't need to complicate matters by doing a shoddy job.

He took a deep breath and attempted to rid his mind of any thoughts that were not work-related. Right now, it would be easier to unravel a decades-old unsolved mystery than to try to understand the Lapp family.

After questioning Kristi about what she'd seen and heard, the police officers turned their attention to Donald. He basically echoed what Kristi had said, although he claimed he hadn't heard the gunshot because his television had been blaring. Onkel Timothy reported hearing what he'd thought were firecrackers but said he hadn't seen anything.

Next, the officers followed Onkel Timothy and Donald out to the barn to take a look at Samson. Kristi stayed inside and straightened up the kitchen. Then, feeling somewhat restless, she went out to the barn to ask permission to run a few errands.

Minutes later, she set out in the buggy, pulled by the ever-energetic Taffy. After visiting several expectant mamms, Kristi went to the grocery store. She needed to pick up some tomatoes and lettuce, as it was still too early to plant either in the garden, let alone harvest them. The tomatoes were growing in a southern window in the haus, waiting for the danger of frost to pass. By the time that happened, Mamm would be home, and she could transplant them.

Or maybe Kristi would be able to kneel in the dirt and do it herself. The therapist was supposed to come by that evening. She would be able to assess whether that was a realistic expectation.

Shane had been sweet to set her up with Lisa Davids for the purpose of recovering her physical abilities and, ultimately, attracting a suitable man. But Kristi didn't want a suitable man. She wanted Shane.

Yet he wasn't an option, unless she decided to jump the fence and leave the Amish. It was hard to conceive of becoming Englisch—of leaving her family, her career, and, more important, her salvation.

She wouldn't *have* to give up her career, she supposed. She could still practice midwifery.

But she was getting ahead of herself. Not once had Shane told her he loved her. "In danger of falling in love" was how he'd described his condition. There was a big difference.

And, given his odd behavior of late, it was hard to gauge his feelings for her. What if she left the Amish, only to have him cast her off? Mamm had warned her that men tended to lose interest once they got what they wanted.

Forgive me, Lord. I shouldn't even be thinking like this, especially about a worldly man. Never mind how well he treated her. How good he looked. Kissed. Kristi picked up a head of lettuce to inspect its freshness, but she couldn't see it clearly due to the tears filling her eyes.

Someone touched her upper arm. With a squeal, Kristi jumped.

Starr stood there, looking equally startled. After a moment, she frowned. "Why so deep in thought? I said your name at least five times, and you never answered."

Blinking the tears from her eyes, Kristi tried to formulate a greeting, but she couldn't quite get the words out. "You... you did?" Her voice sounded like a whimper.

Starr grinned. "Just tell me this: Is he marriage material or not?"

"What?" Was she really that transparent?

Her friend snickered. "Your attention is on some guy, I just know it. Some dreamy Amish guy." Starr snapped her fingers. "No, wait—it's that gorgeous vet who joined us for lunch the other day. I saw some definite sparks! So, is he marriage material?"

Kristi considered her question, wondering how to answer honestly without baring her true feelings. "He is… for somebody, someday." Her throat swelled. "Maybe for someone like you."

Starr cocked her head. "But not you?"

Kristi turned her attention back to the head of lettuce and gave a slight shake of her head, the only response she could make without crying.

"Are you almost done shopping? I think we need to discuss this further, over a milkshake at McDonald's."

Kristi blinked as fresh tears filled her eyes. "There's nothing to talk about." She placed the lettuce in her basket and moved on to the display of tomatoes.

"There absolutely is. You're in love with a man who isn't Amish. Don't tell me you aren't. This is huge, Kristi. Absolutely huge."

Kristi shrugged as she selected a couple of tomatoes. "Not so much. And I'm not…well, I shouldn't be…."

Starr gasped. "Oh my word! I knew it. I knew it!" She eyed the tomatoes in Kristi's basket. "What are you having for supper?"

Kristi brightened, glad the subject was moving away from forbidden love. "Bacon, lettuce, and tomato sandwiches."

"Yum! I haven't had a BLT in ages." Starr considered the plastic basket in Kristi's hands. "Well, it looks like you have everything you need. I know you have bread at home, and bacon, too, if there's still some left from the hog your dad butchered last fall."

"Jah."

"Okay then, let's go for milkshakes. My treat. You're more talkative when you've overdosed on chocolate."

"Exactly why I try to avoid it."

At five o'clock, Shane went out and leaned on the receptionist's desk. Patsy was just filing the last folder away and the waiting room was blessedly quiet and empty.

"I need to hire an assistant."

Patsy turned and stared at him. "What?"

Shane shook his head. "I've been going alone for the past year, trying to build my business, but it's too much for me to handle. I keep getting called out of the office, even though I have abbreviated office hours. Can you write a want ad tomorrow?"

"Yeah. While I'm at it, can I advertise for more help at the front desk, too? Sometimes I'm pulled in three different directions at once. Part-time help would be fine, even from a high-school student—you know, with that program that lets them work a couple of hours a day while attending school?"

"Okay. You can write up an ad for that, too." Peering at Patsy, he noticed that her eyes were puffy and red, as if she'd been crying. "Is something wrong?"

She shrugged her shoulders. "My best friend did something incredibly stupid. You know how Missouri has those no-wait laws on marriage? She met this guy yesterday at a bar in Springfield, and they hit it off, so they went and applied for a marriage license and got married in front of a judge today. I can't believe she did that. She's on the rebound from a bad relationship, and this one isn't going to be any better. I've met this jerk—now her husband—before. He's hit on me at the same bar where she met him."

Shane frowned. He wasn't familiar with Missouri's policies on marriage. And, quite frankly, the idea intrigued him.

Patsy picked up a notepad, scribbled something on it, and slammed it down again. "I'll be the one who has to pick up the pieces, next week, next month, or whenever the magic wears off."

"I'm sorry."

"There just aren't enough good guys out there. Believe me, I should know. I've been in too many dead-end relationships." She shrugged again and glanced at her watch. "Speaking of good guys, would you like to join me for happy hour?"

"No, thank you. I don't drink. Plus, I have to go check on a horse."

"You know what they say about all work and no play."

"I guess I'll just be a dull boy." He chuckled and stepped back. "Sorry about your friend. I'll see you tomorrow."

Chapter 18

$\mathcal{K}$risti slid into a window booth and waited while Starr ordered them chocolate milkshakes. She should have refused what was probably the most caloric and cholesterol-laden item on the menu. But the milkshake Starr had ordered on Kristi's birthday, topped with a tall swirl of whipped cream drizzled with chocolate syrup and a dainty maraschino cherry, had looked so tempting. So different from the milkshakes she'd enjoyed as a teenager.

The lines of customers were long. A lot of people were probably stopping to pick up dinner on the way home from work, judging by the number of them dressed in tailored suits and other professional outfits.

Peeking out the window, Kristi saw that the drive-through line looked just as busy. She did a double take when she saw a blue Jeep pulling away from the pickup window. Sure enough, Shane was behind the wheel. Had he picked up supper or just a koffee? She watched his vehicle until it disappeared around the corner of the building.

If only she could be eating with Shane tonight...though maybe he had seen her through the window and would park and come in. That would be a nice treat. She turned in her seat and watched out the windows across the restaurant. There went his Jeep, turning onto the highway. She sighed.

Another fifteen minutes passed before Starr brought two chocolate milkshakes to the table and dropped onto the bench across from Kristi. "Whew. Who knew waiting in line could be so exhausting? It must have been the busy day I had at work. I think every citizen of Webster County came into the library today."

Kristi smiled, then studied the concoction in front of her. Probably loaded with as many preservatives as calories—not that she counted calories. She made an effort to eat only homemade meals with organic ingredients, so that she knew what was in them. But she supposed the occasional splurge wouldn't kill her.

It seemed splurges were an everyday occurrence for most Englischers, including Shane. She couldn't help wondering if that would become true of her, too, if she married him. She didn't think she could live that way. Maybe she could be the exception. Or he could adopt the Amish diet.

Her face heated when she realized Starr was watching her expectantly. "Okay. Time to talk." Without looking down, she slid a straw across the table toward Kristi.

Kristi picked it up and peeled off the wrapper. "There's really nothing to tell."

"Sure, there is. He's a modern man, and you're…well, no offense, but you're a girl who's, like, trying to recreate life in the nineteenth century."

Ouch.

"So, would you become 'fancy,' like me? I could take you to the mall and help you pick out some new outfits. I could even teach you to drive a car! You can't possibly think he'll give up his lifestyle and join the Amish just for you."

Surely, Starr didn't mean to sound so harsh. "Nein." Kristi plunged her straw into the milkshake and took a sip. "Wow. This is sweet." Drinking much more would send her into a sugar coma, for sure. Could she discard the rest without hurting Starr's feelings?

She took another sip. Well, it wasn't so bad. In fact, she could see herself indulging in another on her next trip into town. It wasn't like she came here that often.

"Don't change the subject." Starr sounded concerned.

Kristi sighed. Why couldn't she let it go? "I do like him. Too much. And we both know that a relationship would reach a dead end, sooner or later."

"Hold it." Starr raised her eyebrows. "The two of you have discussed the possibility of a long-term relationship?"

"Well...." Kristi lowered her head and took another sip of her milkshake.

"Have you kissed?"

"Starr." Kristi's face heated. "We don't talk of such things."

Starr gasped. "Oh my word. I can't believe this. So, is kissing, like, a sin? Do you have to go confess to the church and everything?"

"The point is, there's nein relationship. Nein."

"So, you wouldn't mind if I went after him?"

Kristi sucked in a sharp breath. She couldn't take this any longer. She slid out of the booth and snatched her milkshake. "I need to go."

"Just as I thought. This is so huge!"

"Danki for the milkshake."

"If you change your mind, you know where to find me. I'd be glad to take you shopping!"

"Danki, but nein." Kristi turned and stalked off. She ignored the curious looks from the people waiting in line, which only intensified when Starr called after her, "What? Are you seriously expecting he'll go back to the nineteenth century?"

❦

When Shane got home, he stashed his cheeseburger and fries from McDonald's in the fridge for later. Then, after changing into his workout clothes, he went over to the Lapps' to check on Samson and rewrap his bandages. Finally, he released Chinook from her kennel and took her on a jog.

When he returned home, he saw a moving van maneuvering backward into his driveway. A small red sedan was already parked near the garage door. Sylvia and Michael were here already? They must have sent an e-mail to let him know, because they certainly hadn't called. But he hadn't checked his personal e-mail for weeks, preferring instead to spend his downtime doing something quiet, like reading. The way he imagined Kristi spent her downtime, whatever little of it she had.

It was long past time to check his inbox. His mom would be expecting to hear from him, too. He picked up the pace, eager to greet his sister.

When she stepped out of the car, his breath hitched at the sight of her basketball-shaped abdomen. He had a flashback of Becca smiling as she rubbed her swelling belly, just a few days before…. He couldn't help wincing. He'd never imagined what his sister might look like pregnant—or how much seeing her might hurt.

Sylvia smiled as he approached, still holding Chinook's leash. "Oh, you got a Siberian husky! She's so cute." She stepped forward, then stopped, wrinkling her nose. "Don't expect me to hug your sweaty body, big brother. Eww." She waved a hand in front of her face, as if to dispel toxic fumes.

Shane smiled and wrapped her in a hug anyway. "I'm glad you're here. The dog's not mine. I'm just…dating her." His grin widened as he remembered when Kristi had coined the term for his relationship with her dog. "I need to get her home. I'll be right back." With a wave to his brother-in-law, who paced in front of the moving van while talking on his cell phone, he jogged into Kristi's yard. After securing the dog in her kennel and refilling her water bowl, he strode back across the driveway.

Sylvia gave him a puzzled expression. "Dating a dog? Are you sure you're okay with me staying here? I don't want to cramp your love life or anything."

At the sound of horse hooves clip-clopping, Shane glanced toward the road and recognized Kristi's buggy. All his senses came to life. He gave her what he hoped looked like a casual wave, then forced himself to look back at Sylvia. "What love life?" His voice sounded choked. He hoped his sister didn't notice. Or that, if she did, she would attribute it to his lingering sorrow over Becca's death.

"Exactly." Sylvia nodded at the buggy. "I think it's so neat that you live in Amish country. But I don't think you ever mentioned having Amish neighbors. I'd love to meet them!"

Shane shrugged. "Sometime, maybe." But he would put that off as long as he could. Sylvia would sense in no time how he felt about Kristi Lapp. And what if she found out Kristi was a midwife? He cringed as he remembered how supportive Sylvia had been of Becca's decision to consult an Amish midwife. How enthusiastically she'd claimed she wanted to do the same when she was ready to have children.

He couldn't—wouldn't—allow that to happen.

He stepped back. "If you'll excuse me for a few minutes, I'll take a quick shower and then give you a proper greeting. Oh, and please don't go introducing yourself to the neighbor just yet. She's…a little standoffish. I'll be sure to introduce you later."

Hopefully, that would deter Sylvia from trotting over to make Kristi's acquaintance.

❧〜❧

As Kristi maneuvered the buggy toward her haus, she gathered that Shane's sister and brother-in-law had arrived. This conclusion was based on the moving van parked in his driveway, not to mention the manner in which he'd hugged the shorter, dark-haired pregnant woman. Kristi hadn't expected them so soon. And she didn't think Shane had, either. Did he have any food in the haus for them to eat? Maybe she should fix a platter of BLT sandwiches to take over, to welcome them to the neighborhood. Not as an excuse to see Shane.

Though that would be a nice bonus.

She unhitched Taffy and led her into the barn, where she brushed her down and replenished her food and water. She also checked on Samson and saw that Shane had changed his bandages.

After putting the buggy away in the barn, she grabbed her midwife bag from the seat and carried it inside. She wanted to be ready, in case Shane had been wrong about his sister and she wanted a consultation. Plus, Kristi needed to replenish some of her supplies. A couple of boppli were due within the next several weeks.

She savored the final few sips of her chocolate milkshake, but the sweetness couldn't mask the sting of Starr's callous comments about her feelings for Shane. It wasn't rare for an Amish girl to fall in love with an Englisch man. Or vice versa. But Starr was right—whenever that happened, if the couple was to remain together, it was the Amish one, usually the girl, who was likelier to make a switch. To leave the faith and lose her family.

Kristi remembered the pain her family had felt when Justus had jumped the fence. She wasn't about to put them through that agony again.

She stuck the empty plastic McDonald's cup in her bag to carry into the haus. Then, she grabbed her cane, but she resisted the inclination to use it. The therapy was helping already. In most cases, she could walk without leaning on anything or anyone, provided her leg was not in great pain or especially prone to buckling.

She was halfway across the yard when she noticed the Englisch woman approaching her. She had Shane's blue eyes. Kristi blinked, wondering if Shane had told her about them. He must have, or else she probably wouldn't have come over.

"Hi!" The woman waved as she approached. "I'm your newest neighbor. Shane Zimmerman's sister."

Kristi smiled as she tried to conjure Shane's sister's name. She pulled it out of her memory. "Welkum, Sylvia."

Sylvia's eyes widened in surprise. "You know my name! That puts me at a disadvantage. Shane didn't tell me anything about you, other than that you were kind of standoffish. Oops! I shouldn't have said that. But I wanted to meet you. Maybe make a new friend."

Kristi sucked in a sharp breath. Why would Shane tell his sister that she was standoffish? She blinked back the tears that sprang to her eyes. Maybe he didn't want his sister to find out about their relationship, no matter that she wasn't sure how to classify it. Maybe he was ashamed of her.

"So, Shane says he's dating your dog." Sylvia grinned, apparently oblivious to Kristi's hurt.

Kristi forced a chuckle. "Jah. Their 'courtship' began after I was injured in a buggy accident in the fall and couldn't give her the exercise she needed. I'm still recovering." She held up her cane. "I'm Kristi Lapp."

"It's a pleasure to meet you, Kristi. And you aren't standoffish at all. I'm not sure why Shane would have said that."

Kristi sighed. "I'm sure he has his reasons."

Out of the corner of her eye, Kristi saw Shane and his brother-in-law hauling boxes into the haus. "Would you like to kum inside? Or maybe you need to help them." Kristi gestured at the moving van.

"I'd love to come in!" Sylvia smiled. "And they wouldn't let me lift a finger, for fear I might hurt the baby. I'll just trust their judgment when it comes to organizing everything."

Kristi couldn't help laughing. "Unborn boppli are tougher than they seem. And so are expectant mamms." She sucked in a breath, wondering what Sylvia would make of her statement. "Kum on in."

Sylvia followed her up the porch steps. Any observations she might have made about Kristi's awkward climbing were left unspoken.

As they stepped into the kitchen, Sylvia inhaled deeply. "Mmm. It smells absolutely marvelous in here." She eyed the bowl of cinnamon sticks on the table, then inspected the early mint drying on the clothesline strung across the kitchen. The shelves stocked with jars of herbs and spices.

Kristi remembered Shane's mention of his sister's allergies. Yet she seemed quite at home among spices and herbs.

"You're into herbal medicine, I see." Sylvia turned and faced Kristi, tilting her head again. "Are you a healer?"

Chapter 19

When Shane came back upstairs after helping Michael carry a sofa to the basement, he peeked in the living room, expecting to see Sylvia sitting in his recliner, feet up, watching TV. She wasn't there. "Where'd Sylvia disappear to?" His stomach clenched as he anticipated the answer. She hadn't listened to him. But then, had he really expected her to?

"I think she went next door, where you took the dog." Michael shrugged. "Guess she couldn't wait to meet the neighbors."

Shane felt his heart constrict. He dashed outside and looked around, seeing no sign of either Sylvia or Kristi. He raked his fingers through his hair. "I told her to wait."

Michael laughed. "You know Sylvia's insatiable curiosity. That was basically an order for her to go over and introduce herself. Don't worry, I'm sure they'll be fast friends."

"That's what I'm afraid of," Shane muttered. He resisted the urge to march next door and demand that Sylvia come home. Besides, she never listened to orders; she did what she wanted. Always had. He should know that by now.

He took a deep breath and willed himself to calm down. Kristi was aware that Sylvia planned on a hospital birth.

Still, he was haunted by a measure of doubt. Sylvia was gifted at getting to the heart of other people. She very well might have already found out that Kristi was a midwife. That she dabbled in herbal medicine. Or, that her relationship with Shane was more than neighborly.

Shane forced his attention back to the remaining boxes in the moving van. Michael and Sylvia had taken him seriously when he'd offered to store everything they owned. They'd brought not only their personal items but also furniture, appliances, cookware, and even pantry items. Good thing he had plenty of available space in his basement. The food items they'd store in the kitchen and put to use. He didn't want to attract mice or risk anything spoiling.

On his next trip out to the van, Shane spied Lisa Davids' car in Kristi's driveway. Time for a therapy session. Surely, Sylvia wouldn't stay there much longer.

But it was another twenty minutes before he saw his sister exit Kristi's house. That meant she'd probably befriended the therapist, as well. His tongue burned with at least a dozen questions, from what Sylvia had learned about Kristi's profession to what sorts of exercises Lisa was having Kristi do. *Show no interest,* he told himself. It was hard.

Sylvia took her time crossing the yard. She bent down to sniff some daffodils, then paused to peer at Kristi's patch of "weeds." She carried a plastic baggie in one hand. As she came closer, Shane identified the contents: tiny green leaves. And an infuser.

He tried to keep his rapidly soaring temper under control as he marched across the yard toward his sister. "You just couldn't wait for me to introduce you." He hoped he didn't sound as upset as he felt. "You aren't planning on using that garbage, are you?"

"Of course, I am. It's just tea. Kristi says it's extremely beneficial for pregnant women. How cool to live next door to a healer!"

Shane stared at her, but he couldn't respond. Not with the lump in his throat.

Sylvia went on, unfazed by his silence. "Well, she said she isn't a healer, per se; she didn't say anything about making formulas and ointments, like some other Amish. But she knows all about the medicinal properties of herbs. Fascinating stuff. And this 'garbage' is red raspberry leaves."

Shane nearly choked. That was the same stuff Becca had taken, at the insistence of her midwife. The very herb he blamed for her aneurysm. "How do you know they aren't poisonous?"

Sylvia rolled her eyes. "I drank some at Kristi's, and I'm not dead yet." She gasped and covered her mouth. "Oh, Shane. I'm so sorry. I wasn't thinking. I shouldn't have said that."

"No. You shouldn't have." Shane turned away to hide his frustration.

"But Kristi sure knew a lot about me," Sylvia prattled on. "How come you've never mentioned her? I knew nothing about her, except that she was 'standoffish.' Which isn't true at all. Neither of us could figure out why you would have said that."

Shane cringed. Kristi must have been so hurt. He glanced toward her house, wishing he could take back the words. But how could he have known that his sister would waltz over there and blab as she had?

"I'm pretty sure Kristi's a midwife, too. She has this black medical bag. I peeked inside it when she left me alone for a minute. And I told her—"

"No! Absolutely not." Shane cleared his throat and lowered his voice. "Whatever you told her, the answer is no."

Sylvia looked alarmed. "What's the big deal? I was going to say that I told her I was thinking about having a home birth, with a midwife."

"And? What did she say?"

"She said that the hospital in Springfield has a good reputation for its maternity ward."

"She didn't offer you her services?" Maybe Shane had overreacted just a little.

"No. She actually seemed very hesitant to talk about what she did. And she kept trying to change the subject. But I pieced together the clues. I'm pretty good at solving mysteries. Ask Michael. I almost never finish a mystery novel because I figure it out long before the truth comes out."

Shane released a sigh, along with some of his anger. So, maybe Kristi had been deliberately vague about her profession out of respect for Shane's wishes. But it frustrated him to no end that she'd given her a stash of tea leaves—*red raspberry* tea leaves.

Sylvia frowned. "She offered to bring some supper over after her therapist leaves. I insisted that she join us. You will be nice."

If Sylvia felt the need to say that, then Kristi also must have given her no indication of how well she and Shane knew each other. How they had kissed—multiple times. That secret was safe, at least for now.

Sylvia smiled. "I think Kristi and I are going to be great friends. Whether you like it or not."

Shane groaned.

Ignoring him, Sylvia rambled on about the instant bond she'd formed with Kristi and how much she liked her.

Sylvia would make friendship happen. It seemed Kristi Lapp had charmed his sister just as easily as she'd charmed him. He pinched the bridge of his nose. "No herbs and no midwife, Sylvia. I mean it." He nodded toward the bag in her hand. "That stuff goes. Give it back to her when she comes over."

"My decision, *ain't so?*" Sylvia aimed a smirk in his direction, then turned and headed inside.

Shane waited a moment. Two. Then, he went back to the moving van for another load. When Lisa's car was no longer parked in Kristi's driveway, and when Sylvia and Michael were busy unpacking in the spare bedroom, Shane snuck across the yard to Kristi's house for a conversation that was long overdue.

If only he knew what he was going to say.

Kristi was frying bacon when she heard the knock on the door. It had to be Shane. She still smarted over his recent coldness. Even so, when she opened the door and saw him standing there, she wanted him to take her in his arms and kiss her senseless.

Shane smiled, but she thought she read concern in his eyes. "Hi, Kristi. I see you met my sister. What all went on between you two? Sylvia came home with a bag of tea leaves and all sorts of information about you."

Kristi grinned. "We had a nice visit. I was glad to meet her. And it turns out she isn't allergic to herbs. In fact, she loves tea. I brewed us each a cup."

Shane hesitated, then nodded. "She didn't enlist you as a midwife, did she?"

"Nein. I didn't even offer, remembering what you said about her wanting a hospital birth."

"Good."

"But, Shane? She's actually interested in a home birth… with a midwife." She could tell that he wanted to say something, but she pressed on, somehow feeling the need to defend her profession. "Home births are completely safe. I haven't lost a single mamm yet."

"What about a baby?"

"Just one. It was stillborn, so, technically, I wasn't responsible." She hesitated. "But I did send a woman to the hospital in Springfield when I didn't feel I could handle things. I would do the same for Sylvia, if I—"

"You won't. At least, I'm pretty sure Sylvia said she wanted to consult a doctor at the hospital."

"Understood. She's your sister." She stepped back and started to shut the door, but then she held it open. "Your supper's almost ready. If you'll wait a minute, I'll finish it and load it into a basket for you to take home."

"Awfully nice of you to fix us something to eat. My pantry's pretty bare."

She nodded. "My pleasure."

"You'll come over to eat with us, right?"

"Ach, nein, danki. I'm not hungry. I had a milkshake with Starr earlier."

"That shouldn't stop you from eating whatever you fixed. It smells delicious."

"Danki." She closed the door and went to finish packing the basket. Once the lid was shut, she carried it to the door and passed it outside to Shane.

"Thanks." He accepted the basket. "How'd today's session with Lisa go?"

"Pretty well. We practiced going up and down the stairs. She wants me to keep working on that, with someone spotting me. She seemed pleased with my progress, but she said I may never be able to climb stairs without needing to hold on to a railing. And I may never be able to get down, say, to dig in the garden, and get up, without assistance." She smiled, remembering something else Lisa had said. "She did recommend a contraption I could kneel on for gardening. It has handles, like my walker, so I'd be able to pull myself back up. The next time she comes, in two or three days, she's going to bring me some information and an order form. But I'm thinking Onkel Timothy or Daed could make one for me." She shrugged. "We'll see."

Shane grinned. "Keep practicing. You're going to do fine."

"Danki."

He hoisted the picnic basket. "Sure you don't want to join us?"

She hesitated. It would be nice to get to know Sylvia better. But she really had no appetite, and it would be awkward to sit there while everyone else ate. Not to mention the fact that his sister might inquire about their relationship—something neither of them was prepared to discuss with each other, let alone define for an outsider.

She pulled in a breath and nodded. "Jah. I'm sure."

Shane was surprised to feel a measure of relief that Kristi wasn't coming for dinner. He needed time to sort things out. To keep his distance, at least for now. They had some serious obstacles to overcome before they could even discuss a relationship that had any hope of enduring.

But who was he kidding? It wasn't as if they would end up together. Cultural differences aside, Kristi was a midwife. Who peddled herbs. Shane couldn't live with that.

He should have kept that in mind from the start, instead of leading Kristi along with compliments and kisses.

It was time for a clean break. Past time, really.

Shane let his eyes rove over Kristi's features once more. "I'll be sure to return your basket. Thank you again. Goodbye, Kristi." He walked down the steps, away from her. A clean break. But it hurt like a broken heart.

Everyone agreed that Kristi's BLTs were the best they'd had. After dinner, Shane wished that his stomach felt more settled, but he blamed emotional turmoil instead of the BLT. It had occurred to him that a true "clean break" would mean no more jogging dates with Chinook. And, rather than talk to Kristi, he decided to take the easy way out. He wrote a note, tucked it inside the picnic basket, and snuck over to Kristi's, where he left the basket on a rocking chair on the porch.

Kristi—

I'm sorry, but I won't be able to exercise Chinook anymore. I'll talk to Timothy about having one of his boys take charge of her daily exercise.

Thanks for understanding.

—Shane

Chapter 20

Early April

Kristi opened the door and stepped onto the porch. The weather had warmed significantly over the past month, as the world had started to spring back to life after the winter. She wished her heart would do the same. Soon, Mamm and Daed would return from Florida, bringing Grossdaedi and Grossmammi with them. She expected a letter any day, telling her when they planned to arrive and asking her to air out the dawdi-haus.

Glancing next door, she watched as Shane's Jeep backed down the driveway and turned in the direction of town. Aside from a rare glimpse of him in Seymour, she never saw Shane anymore, unless he was coming or going like this.

No longer could they call themselves even casual acquaintances.

Kristi wandered out to the kennel and released Chinook. She played with her for a few minutes, then refilled her water dish and food bowl. Her younger cousins had been faithful to come over and make sure the dog got exercise. But instead of twice daily, they came once a day, right after school. And they didn't take her for runs or even walks but merely played with her in the yard.

Chinook needed to get more exercise, and Kristi was determined to make that happen, with or without Shane's help. She clipped a leash to Chinook's collar and started toward the dirt road, leaving her cane behind. It was the first real walk she'd taken since her accident. If Chinook decided to run, Kristi would have to let go of the leash. She hoped she wouldn't trip and fall in the road.

As she passed Donald's haus, she thought again about the incident with Samson. Hopefully, the fate of her horse wouldn't befall her dog, as well. If only she knew who'd shot Samson. She still felt uneasy every time she took her buggy out. Onkel Timothy had told her that Donald had been taken in for further questioning, but that seemed to be as far as it had gone.

Through his big front window, she saw him sitting in front of the flickering blue light of the television. It seemed he constantly had it on. For noise? Companionship, maybe, while his frau was at work?

Donald turned and looked out the window. When he noticed Kristi, he waved and then stood and walked in the direction of the front door. Seconds later, the door opened. Was he coming outside to talk to her? She hoped he didn't intend to walk with her, although it might help to have someone there who could handle Chinook if she took off.

"Kristi!" A woman called her name.

Kristi turned around, just as Donald's front door slammed shut.

Sylvia waved at her. "We're still on for lunch, right? I'm bringing the meal this time."

Kristi smiled and waved back. Their lunches had become an almost daily ritual over the past several weeks. Kristi usually fixed the meal, but Sylvia insisted, on occasion. Kristi was glad for her companionship, but Sylvia's constant chatter about her brother was at the same time uplifting and unbearable. A combination of water on dry ground and lemon juice on a fresh wound.

"Wait up!" Sylvia called. "I'll walk with you."

Kristi raised her eyebrows. She'd tried countless times to convince Sylvia she needed regular exercise, especially while pregnant. So far, Sylvia had maintained that it was enough to meander back and forth between their homes.

Sylvia crossed the yard at her habitually slow pace. "About time I started joining you. You've been so patient in encouraging me."

Kristi smiled. "I'm glad you finally agree. Have you had any luck finding a doctor?"

Sylvia shrugged.

"You haven't even tried, have you?" Kristi studied her. "You know the importance of having regular checkups, to make sure you and your boppli—"

"I want you to continue doing my prenatal care."

"Really?" This was a departure from the original plan, according to Shane. "Your brother seemed to think you—"

"Forget what Shane said. It's my choice."

Pain knifed through Kristi's heart at the sound of his name, as it did whenever Sylvia spoke it. Apparently she was clueless about their history. Kristi should have known better than to let herself fall for an Englisch man.

Despite the progress she had made through physical therapy, she still didn't have young men flocking to the haus to take her on buggy rides or accompany her to frolics and singings. Of course, she generally stayed away from such events, so the fault was partly her own. As Onkel Timothy had been kind enough to point out.

She didn't know if she could be courted by one man when she was still in love with another.

"I'm over eight months along. I've heard a lot of doctors will refuse to take me this far into the pregnancy," Sylvia said. "Michael is all for my having a midwife, if that's what I want. And he's the only man whose opinion matters."

Kristi smiled. "You're spoiled."

"Rotten," Sylvia agreed cheerfully. "But I want you to deliver my baby. You're my friend, and I trust you."

"Danki. That means a lot." Kristi hesitated. "I don't think your brother is thrilled with the idea. He told me before you came that you wanted a hospital birth."

"I'll handle him." Sylvia smiled. "You can check me out when I come to your house for lunch. I've been craving Mexican food, and I have all the ingredients we'd need to make burritos. Have you ever had them?"

"I don't think so."

"We eat them a lot. I don't understand why Shane never wants to have anybody over for dinner. I've asked him multiple times if I could invite you. He's really missing out, not having you for a friend."

Kristi forced a smile. If only she had an explanation for Shane's refusal to see her. But he hadn't given as much as a hint of an explanation. He'd simply stopped taking Chinook on runs—and, as a consequence, had stopped talking to her.

She supposed it was for the best. Served her right for falling in love with him. It turned out Englisch men were just as fickle as Mamm had made them out to be. She'd get over him. Someday. Maybe.

Someday, she wouldn't lie awake daydreaming about his kisses, his touches, his smile, his tender care.

Her heart lurched. She'd never get over him, at this rate.

Sylvia talked on, but whatever she said went unheard. Kristi tuned in when Sylvia shook her head. "I think Shane is sick. He says he's fine, but he's really listless sometimes. Quiet. If I didn't know better, I'd say he's in love. But he never goes on dates or calls anyone. He's so reclusive. Maybe he's still missing Becca, but it's been over two years. It's time he tried meeting other women."

Kristi realized that she'd never found out how Becca had died. Now didn't seem like a good time to inquire.

"Too bad you aren't modern. I think you and Shane would—"

"Nein," Kristi said quickly. Too quickly. "Let's turn around. My leg is starting to hurt." Minor pain, compared to her heartache.

Chinook yelped.

Kristi glanced at the dog, who had been walking quietly at her heel this whole time. She really owed Shane a thank-you for training Chinook to do that. The dog raised her right front leg in the air and started limping along on the other three.

"Ach, what did you do?" Kristi took the dog's paw and inspected it, but she didn't see anything odd. Maybe Chinook had bent back a toenail or caught it on something.

"I'm sure Shane could help her out," Sylvia said. "I'll drive you to the clinic, if you'd like."

Kristi rubbed her hand on her apron. "Ach, nein, I've never had cause to take her to the vet. Daed always handled it. I'll have Onkel Timothy look at her if she isn't better by tomorrow." She tugged on the leash. "Kum on, Chinook. Let's go home. You're fine."

Chinook hobbled along on three legs, the fourth held up high. Maybe she was really hurt. Kristi looked at the paw again, hoping she'd see a burr, or something else that would be easy to remove, so she wouldn't have to face Shane.

Sylvia studied Chinook. "Aw, the poor dog is hurt. Let's take her to the clinic. I'll drive you there and stay with you the whole time." She reached inside the pocket of her maternity pants, pulled out her cell phone, and pressed a button. "Patsy?

This is Sylvia…. Shane's sister, yes. Is he busy? Oh…okay. I'm bringing in an injured dog. I'll be there in a few minutes." Sylvia pushed another button, slid the phone back into her pocket, and smiled at Kristi. "He's not too busy. And he'll take good care of Chinook."

Kristi's stomach fluttered nervously at the prospect of seeing Shane. "My onkel can do it. Really."

"Nonsense." Sylvia flicked her wrist. "Oh, wait. You won't get in trouble with your bishop for taking her to the vet, will you?"

How easy it would be to lie and say yes. But she couldn't. That'd be a sin. "Nein."

"Okay, then."

With a sigh, Kristi followed Sylvia back toward her haus. Sylvia pulled her keys out of her pocket and unlocked the car.

"It's probably nothing," Kristi objected one more time. But the dog whined, as if in protest.

Sylvia shook her head and opened the back door. Chinook jumped inside with a yelp and curled up on the backseat.

Kristi went around and got into the front seat next to Sylvia, wishing she had some chamomile lemon tea to calm her nerves. How could she possibly act normal around Shane? Her stomach churned.

Seconds later, the engine roared to life, and Sylvia started backing the car out of the driveway.

Maybe Sylvia could take Chinook inside the clinic while Kristi waited in the car. Like a coward.

Nein. She would be brave. And not let Shane see how much she missed him.

Shane led the cocker spaniel he'd just immunized down the hall to reunite with its owners. As he entered the waiting room, he was startled by a big dog jumping on him. Instinctively, he raised his knee to block the animal. But when he recognized Chinook, he relaxed. "Down, girl."

Chinook obeyed, and Shane gave her a treat from his pocket. After handing the cocker spaniel over to a middle-aged couple who were talking with Patsy, he crouched, cooing and scratching Chinook behind the ears, while the dog answered in yips of approval.

After a moment, Shane looked up, first at his sister and then at Kristi, who were seated side by side. He swallowed a sudden lump in his throat. It hurt to see Kristi, up close and personal. He searched for his professional side. "What a... pleasant...surprise. What brings you in?"

Kristi remained silent, her eyes focused on Chinook.

Sylvia spoke up. "We were taking Chinook for a walk when, out of nowhere, she yelped and started limping. Kristi figured she'd caught a toenail or something. I insisted on bringing her in, just in case it was something that needed to be treated."

Shane frowned and studied the dog. "She doesn't seem to be limping now. The toenail theory makes sense—she hasn't been getting regular exercise, which helps keep the nails worn down." And whose fault was that? He'd promised to get Chinook adequate exercise, then backed out of the deal when his feelings for Kristi had gotten in the way. Timothy's boys didn't seem to understand they should do more than just play with the dog.

He stood. "I'll take her for a walk down the hall and check her paw. Kristi, why don't you come, too?" He needed to apologize out of earshot of his nosy sister.

Kristi's gaze darted to Sylvia, her eyes wide with panic. Shane's heart ached at the sight. "Nein, I can't. I...."

Sylvia slid to the edge of her seat. "So, it *is* forbidden to take a dog to the vet? Why didn't you say so? I would have gone to find your uncle—Jim? Tim?—whatever his name is, and insist he check out the dog right then."

Shane shook his head. "It isn't against their Ordnung, Sylvia. Kristi has called me with animal problems in the past." When he glanced at Kristi, he saw that her cheeks flamed a brilliant red.

She pushed to her feet and walked up to him, her head bent, her shoulders slumped. As if she were being called in front of the schoolhouse to get her hand slapped with a ruler for misbehaving.

He inhaled her intoxicating scent, then reached to touch her elbow.

A mistake. She jerked back as if he'd slapped her.

He sighed and rubbed his hand over his jaw. "I don't bite, sweet—Kristi." *Just kiss.* And he wished he could kiss her. But he no longer had that right.

Technically, he'd never had it.

He deserved the silent treatment after dropping her cold and treating her callously, all to protect himself from future heartbreak, and to keep his sister from knowing the truth— that he loved this Amish woman, just like their mother had loved an Amish man.

Keeping his distance, emotionally, had been easier with a physical separation. But now, in such close proximity, Shane couldn't deny the truth: he was still head-over-heels in love with this woman.

As proof, he'd slipped and nearly called her "sweetheart."

He drew in a long breath, and then, without another word, he started down the hall, the dog at his heels. She was limping only slightly, a sign of minor discomfort.

Kristi followed down the hallway but stopped in the doorway to the exam room, evidently opting not to come in.

He did his best to ignore her, despite the strong desire to pull her into the room, shut the door, and take her in his arms.

As he crouched down to exam Chinook's paw, he saw that it was bleeding a little around the base of one nail. He clipped it short. Other than that, he couldn't find any tenderness. He stood up, shaking his head. "She probably did catch her toenail on a rock, or bend it back. She seems fine now, but she needs the rest of her nails trimmed. I'll do it tonight when I check on Samson."

"Danki." Kristi stepped backward. "Kum, Chinook." Her voice sounded strangled, as if this meeting was as hard on her as on him.

If only Shane knew what to say to alleviate the tension between them. It was an uneasy tension—nothing like the invigorating aware-of-each-other type.

The office's resident tabby cat wandered down the hall, brushing against Kristi as she went. Chinook lunged at the feline and took off running, sending Kristi spinning in her wake. Kristi's shoulder slammed into the far wall, and she lost her balance, banging her head against the same wall.

Shane reached to grab her before she hit the floor, but he restrained himself from pulling her against his chest. With effort, he held her at arm's length. "Easy, there."

She stared up at him for a few seconds before her eyelids fluttered, then remained shut, as she went limp.

Kristi awoke on a hard metal table in a small room. It took her fuzzy mind a moment to process where she was. Shane stood beside her, pressing a cold, damp rag to her forehead.

"I'm okay." She struggled to sit up, but dizziness reclaimed her, and her vision dimmed.

"I can see that." With his free hand, Shane took her wrist and pressed the underside, checking her pulse. She could feel it pounding.

"Did you skip breakfast again?"

She shook her head. "Nein, I had a full breakfast." She closed her eyes. "I have a headache."

He removed her kapp, knocking pins askew as her hair fell free of its confining bun, and felt along the back of her head where she'd made contact with the wall. "You've got a knot back here. Look at me." He touched her chin and tilted her head toward him, then peered into her eyes. "I don't see any sign of a concussion, but, just to be safe, what is your name?"

She blinked. "Shane—"

"Wrong." He grinned. "Where are you?"

She sighed. "Your sister's waiting for me. And my dog is terrorizing a cat. We don't have time for this foolishness."

He raised his eyebrows and exhaled. "Wrong again. But you seem to be fine. Rest here while I go round up your dog."

"I didn't know you had an office pet."

Shane nodded. "Mittens is her name. But she's accustomed to dogs—I keep one of those around here, too, for when I need to do a blood transfusion."

Kristi struggled to sit up, ignoring the waves of blackness that threatened to take her down again. The impact of hitting her head against the wall had taken more of a toll than she would have expected.

Frowning, Shane pressed her shoulder gently, holding her down. "I meant it. Stay here while I go get Chinook."

"Sha—"

"Shh." He pressed a finger gently to her lips. Her first instinct was to kiss it. But he moved his finger before she found the courage. "Doctor's orders." He winked, then strode out of the room.

Kristi pulled in a quavering breath, tingling where he touched her and wishing she would have dared to kiss his finger. What would have happened if she had?

She'd never know.

Moments later, Shane came back into the room, leading Chinook by her leash. Her tail wagged happily. "Okay. If you're up to it, I'll help you to Sylvia's car."

"I need to pay first." Kristi reached for her kapp.

"No charge. There wasn't anything wrong with your dog." He helped her sit up.

Once Kristi's vision cleared, she redid her hair, and then, with Shane's assistance, she slid off of the table and onto her feet.

"Heel, Chinook." The dog watched as Shane slid his arm around Kristi's waist. "Okay. Let's go."

Kristi nodded. She'd have to give her dog an extra treat tonight. If nothing else, it seemed this vet visit might have thawed Shane's attitude toward her some.

At the very least, they could have a cordial relationship as veterinarian and client.

"Do you want to join Sylvia and me for lunch? She's making burritos and bringing them over." She held her breath. And her hopes.

He glanced at her, his expression guarded. "Thanks for the offer, but no. I'm too busy to take a long lunch break."

Kristi's heart crash-landed somewhere in the vicinity of her toes.

Shane released Kristi as they approached the waiting area at the front of the building. Like he would be ashamed if anyone saw him touching her. His frown deepened. "And we both know that wouldn't be wise."

If only her heart agreed.

Chapter 21

One morning the next week, Shane came downstairs and found Sylvia standing at the stove, one hand holding a spatula, the other pressed against her lower back, frying up a batch of pancakes. There was already a pile of them on a platter on the counter. Evidently she'd been craving them.

Shane noticed the box of pancake mix balancing precariously atop the nearly overflowing trash can. "I'll take the garbage out after breakfast."

"Thanks. My back is killing me."

"When exactly did the ultrasound tech say the baby was due? You should probably let Mom know, so she can plan her visit. And what about Michael's parents?"

"Michael's parents are on a monthlong cruise. They'll see the baby for the first time over Skype, just like Michael." She sighed. "Babies come when they're ready, not when a doctor says they will, according to Kristi. But my due date is in a week and a half, give or take a few days."

If only Michael could be here. He should have been the one getting the nursery ready. Instead, it was Shane who had spent a weekend setting up the crib and changing table in the spare room. "Are you ready? Suitcase packed?"

"I'm as ready as I'll ever be. I have everything on the list I was given."

"Good." Shane spread a dab of butter on his stack of pancakes, doused them in maple syrup, and took a bite. "Mmm. Delicious."

His sister sat down across from him, laid the spatula on the table, and rubbed her belly. "I'd like to plant some flowers in the bed along the front walk. The ground is ready; it just needs to be worked up."

Shane poured a splash of liquid creamer into his coffee and gave it a stir. "Is this something you're planning to do before the baby comes? I don't think you should overexert yourself like that."

Sylvia stood up again and started pacing. "I'm not helpless, Shane. I doubt I'll do any damage just working the ground."

"Yeah, but you can't even get off the couch unless I help you up. If you were to kneel down to plant flowers, you'd never get back on your feet."

"I could borrow the contraption Kristi's uncle made for her. Haven't you seen her out there, planting her garden? She's got tomatoes and all sorts of things."

Oh, yes. He'd seen her. Felt glad he'd been able to get her the help she needed. And it looked as if she were doing a lot better. Her parents would be pleasantly surprised when they got home.

"Hello? Earth to Shane." Sylvia waved the spatula in front of his face.

Shane blinked. "Sorry about that. I was distracted for a second. I'll be happy to work up the ground for you, Sylvie. If you want flowers, your wish is my command."

Sylvia brightened. "I was thinking marigolds, maybe. I love their cheery color."

"Then, marigolds it is. I'll pick up a flat for you tonight on my way home from work."

"Wait. I should talk to Kristi about it at lunch. She might have another type to recommend."

"But Kristi doesn't live here." *Except in my dreams.* If only those would stop.

Sylvia waved her hand. "I know. But I don't want to plant any flowers that might attract swarms of bugs or anything else that might harm her garden, or be hazardous to the baby."

"Her garden is a good distance from my walkway, and it'll be a while before your baby will be old enough to munch on any dangerous plants."

Sylvia opened her mouth to argue. He could see the disagreement forming in her eyes.

Shane shrugged. "Okay, okay. Just let me know when you decide." He stood. "I need to get to work. See you tonight." He tied up the bag of trash, grabbed his sack lunch from the fridge, and hurried out the door.

As he tossed the garbage into the trash can, he noticed Kristi in her front yard. When their eyes met, he nodded, his heart breaking anew. If only things could be different. If only he'd behaved better. If only she weren't Amish. And a midwife.

She came toward him, tentatively, as if she were afraid to approach him. His heart ached.

She stopped short of his driveway. "Shane? I hate to bother you, but Chinook isn't eating. I'm scared she's sick. I talked to Onkel Timothy about taking her to your clinic, or asking you to stop and check her, but he just waved it off and said she'll eat when she's hungry."

Shane nodded. "I'll be right over. It's no trouble." He opened the driver's side door of his Jeep, tossed his lunch bag on the front seat, and then slammed the door shut. Kristi was already headed back home. He hurried to catch up with her. "How long has this been going on?"

Kristi glanced at him. "She hasn't eaten anything all week. All she does is sit there, looking dejected. She won't even play with my cousins. And she never seems interested in walking, but she'll kum when she's called. She cries to get inside at nacht, but then she wants out right after dawn. Daed will be upset if he discovers I allowed her in the haus while he was gone."

Right after dawn. About the time Shane used to come over every day to take her on a jog. He sighed. "She hasn't been eating grass, has she?"

Kristi shook her head. "Not that I've noticed. It's like she's on a fast or something. She drinks water but turns up her nose at food." Tears pooled in her eyes. "I'm worried about her."

As they approached the kennel, Chinook jumped up to meet them, whining, crying, and wagging her tail. Shane bent down and scratched behind her ears for a few moments, then straightened. With another wag of her tail, Chinook went for her dish and started gobbling down her food.

Kristi caught her breath. "She misses you." She stepped back, blinking. "I think she'd rather be yours."

His head snapped up. "Oh, no, Kristi. No."

"Dogs choose their masters, jah? She chooses you." One tear ran down her cheek. Followed by another.

Shane groaned. He'd never known what to do with a crying female. "I think Chinook would miss you just as much. She loves you, too. But I can start taking her on runs again, if you think that would help."

She nodded, but another tear tracked down her cheek. "Danki. I'll be sure to stay out of your way. You won't even know I'm here."

He pulled in a breath. "Kristi, Kristi. I'm sorry if I've given the impression of not wanting to see you." He paused, trying to compose a coherent explanation. "I allowed our relationship to progress way beyond friendship before. And I'm sorry for that. I'm also sorry for going to the opposite

214 Laura V. Hilton

extreme. Ignoring you completely." He ran his fingers through his hair. "It turns out that absence does make the heart grow fonder. One month without you is too long. Even one week is pretty rough."

She sniffled but didn't respond.

He wanted to reach for her—to hold her and kiss her. But couldn't allow himself that pleasure, especially when he wasn't sure how she felt about him. Hopefully, she'd missed him, too.

"I need you to know that even if you marry someone else, Kristi, I want to be in your life." Shane hesitated. "We can be friends, can't we? Your parents won't object."

She started to nod, then shook her head. "We can never be just 'friends.' Because I fell in love with you."

❧

Kristi couldn't believe she'd just told Shane she loved him.

Apparently, neither could he. He stared at her, slack-jawed, as if she'd just said something shocking.

She had. And now, he was probably trying to find a way out. An avenue to escape her affections.

Should she turn and walk away? Or stay, and deal with the fallout?

Hopefully, he'd let her down easy. At least her heart wouldn't feel worse than it already did.

He rubbed his jaw. Swallowed. Hard. His Adam's apple bobbed. After a moment, he nodded. "I feel the same way about you, Kristi Lapp."

Her heart pounded. "You do?" She fought to keep from grinning but failed.

His mouth quirked. "Yes. I'm just not quite sure where we go from here."

She slumped, disappointed. "Daed and Mamm will be home any day, and Daed will want to resume his search for a suitable husband."

"I would ask his permission to court you, if I could. But I think I know what his answer would be."

Her hopes shattered. "I understand."

He exhaled. "Why don't you join us for supper tonight? Sylvia has been after me to have you over, anyway. I'll call and tell her she can invite you. She'll want to think she talked me into it." He smiled. "We'll go from there."

Kristi's heart sang. "That sounds gut."

"Great." He crouched next to Chinook and rubbed behind her ears. "I need to get to work, girl, but I'll take you for a run as soon as I get home. Promise."

Then, he stood, turned to Kristi, and reached out, letting his fingers trail over the curve of her cheek. Leaving fire in their wake. "I'll see you tonight."

Kristi watched Shane until his Jeep disappeared around the bend in the road. Then, she leaned down and gathered Chinook in a hug. "Bless you. I hope we can work things out. Somehow."

Chinook yipped and wagged her tail.

Kristi straightened and went back inside. She needed to wash a load of laundry and also do some baking. Daed's most recent letter had said to expect them home by the beginning of next week.

She was hanging the wet laundry out to dry when Sylvia rushed over, squealing. "Shane asked me to invite you for dinner! I knew he'd give in, eventually. You'll be there, won't you?"

Kristi smiled and watched Sylvia rub her belly. "You can kum here for dinner, if you'd rather. I'd hate for you to tire yourself with cooking."

Sylvia shook her head. "I feel great. Well, my back was a little sore when I woke up, but I probably slept on it wrong. It's fine now. I've been cleaning all morning. Shane's house never looked so good."

Kristi grinned. "You're nesting."

Sylvia blinked. "Huh?"

"Many women get the urge to clean and redecorate right before giving birth."

"Oh. Well, I'm not going into labor or anything. I still have a couple of weeks to go, remember?"

Kristi opened her mouth to object, but Sylvia held up her hand. "I know. Babies come when they want to."

"That's right." Kristi smiled.

"Well, I'd better get back to work." Sylvia winked. "Lots to do before dinner!"

"I'll see you later, then." Kristi turned back to the clothesline.

"Oh, Kristi? I almost forgot. Please don't mention our prenatal visits around Shane, or tell him I'm planning a home birth. He doesn't know, because…well, I wanted to keep it a surprise."

❧

Shane couldn't wait for dinner. He stopped by the store to pick up the steaks and some salad fixings, along with the additional items Sylvia had requested in multiple phone calls to the office. He had no clue what all she had planned, but she seemed beyond excited to host Kristi for dinner.

How would Sylvia react once she learned that he'd been in love with Kristi all this time? Would she feel betrayed? And would she disapprove? Caution them to end the relationship before it dead-ended on its own?

He'd had enough warnings.

More than enough, actually, if he counted the warnings he was sure to receive once Ira got home. Shane wasn't looking forward to that reunion.

He parked his Jeep in the driveway, grabbed the two plastic grocery bags on the floor beside him, and carried them inside the house. He sniffed. The whole place smelled like Pine-Sol.

He found Sylvia standing in the kitchen, staring into the freezer.

"Hey." He set the bags of groceries on the table.

"Hey, yourself." She grabbed a bag of mixed vegetables and shut the door. "Eww. You reek of animals. Go clean up. Kristi's going to be here soon. How are you going to make a good impression if you smell bad?"

"What makes you think I want to make a good impression?" Shane grinned at her. "I need to take the dog for a run. I'll shower after. Chinook kind of likes the animal smells."

"You and that dog...." She laughed and shook her head. "Maybe you should pay your attention to the dog's owner, instead."

He paused at the bottom of the stairs. "Just concentrate on the meal, Sylvie," he teased. At least he knew how she'd react when she found out. Kristi already had her stamp of approval.

He pondered his sister's words as he headed upstairs to change into his jogging clothes. Would her approval be contingent on Kristi's leaving the Amish? Or on Shane's joining them? He doubted Sylvia had really considered the implications of a possible relationship between them.

After the jog, he hurried home, not having seen Kristi. As he came inside, he heard women's voices in the kitchen. She must have come over already. He scurried upstairs and quickly showered and dressed before going back down to join them.

Kristi had changed into a green dress that made her eyes sparkle. A becoming blush colored her cheeks. Hopefully, it was because of her excitement, and not due to nervousness.

He longed to greet her with more than just a smile. To pull her into his arms and feel the warmth of her body against his. To taste the sweetness of her lips. He repressed a groan.

"It's about time!" Sylvia exclaimed when she noticed him. "I don't suppose I need to introduce you, but I hope you get to know each other better tonight." She gestured at the table. "Look what Kristi brought us! Whoopie pies, for dessert."

Kristi turned her thousand-watt smile on him. His knees went weak.

Suddenly, Shane didn't know how to act. He shoved his hands in his pockets, then pulled them out again. With a brief nod to Kristi, he grabbed the platter of steaks from the counter. "I'll go start the grill." At least that would keep him from touching her. From pulling her near. From kissing her the way he wanted to.

Chapter 22

After dinner, Sylvia invited Kristi to sit in the living room and wait while she went to get something. She didn't say what. The haus had taken on more of a woman's touch since Kristi's first visit. Her only visit. There was a vase of fresh daffodils on the end table. And no sign of the framed photo of Shane and his frau. Kristi hoped it'd been Shane who'd put it away, and that he'd done it because he felt ready to move on.

Sylvia had mentioned she'd been trying to crochet a baby blanket. Kristi noticed a ball of variegated yellow and white yarn lying, discarded, in a heap on the floor. It looked too tight in spots, too loose in others, much like Kristi's early attempts.

Shane came into the room, carrying a couple of soda cans. "Would you like a Coke? If you're allowed to drink it, that is."

She frowned at the beverage. "I don't think I've ever had one, but I know some Amish do." Daed didn't allow it in their home. Once, he had listed all the evils of the drink, claiming it could be used to clean a car engine, among other things. If that were true, it couldn't be healthy for human consumption.

He popped the tab on one of the cans and handed it to her. "Here. See if you like it."

She grasped the cold metal cylinder, brought it to her lips, and took a hesitant sip. The bubbly liquid stung her nose and burned her throat, all the way down. She choked and handed the can back to Shane, her eyes watering.

He chuckled. "I take it you don't." He set both cans on coasters beside him, then settled down next to her on the couch. "I know I said this earlier, but those whoopie pies were fantastic. I don't understand how you Amish stay so thin, with all the desserts you're always making. If I were Amish, I'd have to go jogging more than just twice a day. More like twenty."

She smirked. "I've never seen an Amish man in jogging clothes. We work hard enough; we've no need to run."

He grinned and wrapped an arm around her shoulders, hugging her close. "I don't know where my sister went, but I can't resist holding you a second."

She snuggled against his side.

"Where *did* Sylvia go?" His voice sounded husky. His gaze dropped to her lips.

Kristi repressed a shiver. "I don't know. She said she wanted to get something." She longed for a kiss.

"I'm here." Sylvia came back into the room, holding a thin, black, square-shaped object that looked like a folder, and sat down next to Kristi.

Shane drew back, nonchalantly moving his arm to the back of the couch.

Kristi immediately missed his warmth.

At least he hadn't scooted away. His leg still pressed against hers. And she could imagine she still sat in the curve of his arm.

The folder-like object was opened sideways, but pictures flashed across the one side. A keyboard, similar to one on a manual typewriter, except much smaller, was on the bottom half. Kristi blinked. "What is that?" She reached out and touched the edge of the black thing.

"What?" Sylvia looked up, then pointed to the flashing pictures on the screen. "This? It's what I wanted to show you.

Bakersville Pioneer Village. It's south of town, near the Laura Ingalls Wilder Museum. Have you ever been there?"

"It's a notebook computer," Shane explained, answering Kristi's question.

Sylvia shifted. "I thought it looked interesting."

Kristi pointed to the screen. "That's where the Baker Creek Heirloom Seed Company is based. I've ordered from their catalog, but I've never actually been there." She hesitated. "Is this what's called the…the Internet?"

Sylvia gave her a look that seemed to say, "Are you really so sheltered?" Then, she nodded. "Can you take some time off tomorrow, Shane? I know it's Friday, but they aren't open Saturday. I'd like to go before the baby comes."

Shane raked his fingers through his hair. "I don't know, Sylvie. Do you think that's wise? Maybe after the baby comes would be better."

"Well, if you don't want to, that's fine. Kristi and I will go. Right, Kristi? I'll drive, since you can't." Sylvia clicked a button on the keypad and then started typing. "I'll pull up the directions."

Kristi noticed that the screen now displayed a map of Webster County.

Sylvia leaned forward and met Shane's gaze. "It's less than thirty minutes away. If I go into labor, you'll have plenty of time to get me home—to the hospital, I mean. Right, Kristi?"

"Usually." Kristi squirmed in her seat. "Maybe you should just leave me out of this. I don't want to kum between you two." The last thing she wanted to do was ignite an argument.

"You're already between us." Shane ran a fingertip along the side of her neck, out of his sister's view. She shivered.

He grinned and then reached around her and patted his sister's shoulder. "Since it's so close, I guess we can go tomorrow. I'll let Patsy know. Kristi, I hope you'll still join us."

"Ach, I probably shouldn't. Daed and Mamm are coming home next week, and I need to clean the haus. I'd love to finish putting the garden in. Mamm will be so pleased that I'm able."

Sylvia shut the lid of her notebook computer. "Your house is spotless already. And if you come with us, you can get seeds for your garden." She clapped her hands. "Oh, this is so exciting! Help me up, Shane." She scooted to the edge of the sofa.

Shane stood and pulled Sylvia to her feet.

As she waddled off to the kitchen, he grinned and sat back down next to Kristi. "Okay, where were we?" His eyes darkened as his hand curved around the back of her neck, drawing her head closer to his.

She wouldn't…she shouldn't…but she closed her eyes.

When Shane's lips brushed against hers, her senses flared to life. She whimpered, her arms going around his neck, pulling him to her when he started to move back.

His mouth settled in firmly, prodding, exploring. Then, with a low groan in his throat, he deepened his kisses.

She had no idea how long they were wrapped in each other's arms, lost in the moment. It could never be long enough.

Someone gasped.

Her fingers froze, tangled in his hair.

Shane's hands dropped away from her waist, and he nearly jumped off the couch.

There stood Sylvia, covering her mouth with a cupped hand.

❧❧❧

Shane hadn't expected his sister to return so soon. Of course, he hadn't expected their passions to ignite, either. All he'd wanted was to steal a simple kiss. But kissing Kristi was like holding a lit match to gasoline.

If only he could whisk her away to the office where a couple could apply for a marriage license and be wed the same day. And then spirit her away to a place without the distinctions of "Amish" and "Englisch," where they could live happily ever after.

Kristi's face flushed bright red, and she pushed herself to her feet, away from him. "I'm sorry. I need to go." She headed for the door.

"I'll see you home." Shane stood. He needed to apologize for being so physically forward.

"Nein. I'll be fine." She moved a hand to her kapp, apparently double-checking to make sure it hadn't been disturbed during their embrace, then opened the door. "Danki for dinner."

"We'll pick you up tomorrow morning, then. Around eight, if that works."

With a wave of her hand, she scooted out the door and hastily shut it behind her.

Sylvia's eyes were still bulging. "Sorry, Shane. I didn't mean to interrupt, but…well, I guess you can't blame me for being surprised. Why didn't you tell me? Here I was, thinking you and Kristi barely knew each other, when it turns out you obviously…." She sucked in a long breath. "She's Amish, for pity's sake. How long has this been going on?"

Shane walked to the front window and watched Kristi's retreat across the lawn. "Not that it's any of your business, Sylvie, but pretty much since we first met. It was instant attraction." That had quickly turned to love. But Sylvia didn't need to know everything.

"I noticed you'd put away your pictures of Becca. I just figured you were ready to move on. I didn't think you'd already met someone, and I certainly never dreamed that the someone would be Amish." Sylvia came to stand beside him. "I really like Kristi. She's sweet. But…wow. How is this going to work between you two? Is she going to leave the Amish, like Dad did for Mom?"

"I don't know."

She sighed, a frown marring her features. "Who's that creepy-looking man?" She pointed out the window.

"Donald." Shane answered before glancing in that direction. Sure enough, the neighbor man was crossing the road at a jog.

Shane dashed to the door and rushed out.

Kristi felt like a coward for leaving Shane to face his sister alone, but she was too embarrassed to stick around. She'd been a fool to indulge such a heated embrace, especially with Sylvia in the next room. She should have known something like this would happen.

Tomorrow's trip would be awkward, for sure. Maybe she could beg off. Pretend she'd been at a birth all nacht and was too tired to go. *Forgive me, Lord, for even considering lying.* With any luck, one of her clients would go into labor, providing her with a valid excuse.

"Miss Kristi?"

Startled by a male voice that wasn't Shane's, Kristi whirled around. The sight of Donald approaching almost made her cringe, but she forced a smile.

He shoved his hands into his pockets and looked down at the ground. "I need to talk to you a moment, if it's okay."

"Jah, that's fine." She glanced at her haus. "Would you like to sit on the porch? I could bring you some iced tea or lemonade."

"Lemonade sounds good. And some of those cinnamon rolls, if you've got any."

Kristi smiled. "Aenti Deborah brought over a fresh batch just this morgen."

They walked toward the haus, Donald at her side, studying the ground. The sound of gravel crunching caused Kristi to peek over her shoulder. Shane was approaching at a jog, with Sylvia following at a slow waddle.

Kristi winced. She'd have to face them again, much sooner than she'd anticipated. What must Shane think of her wanton response to his kisses?

Shane slowed down as he neared them. "Everything okay?"

Donald looked up. "I just needed to talk to Miss Kristi about something. Guess I might as well tell you both, since I was gonna come see you next."

Kristi held on to the railing as she maneuvered her way up the porch steps. "Please, have a seat, all of you. I'll be out in just a few minutes with some lemonade and a plate of cinnamon rolls."

Once inside, she found Mamm's silver serving tray and loaded it with four glasses of lemonade, a plate of cinnamon rolls, and some napkins. It was a little awkward, trying to carry it smoothly with her limp. As she stepped through the door, she wobbled, sending the tumblers sliding toward the end of the tray.

Shane jumped up and steadied the tray in her hands. Catastrophe averted, he handed a glass of lemonade to Sylvia and another to Donald.

Kristi set the plate of pastries on the small table in the center, then joined Shane on the porch swing, accepting the glass he handed to her.

He took a sip from his own glass, then draped his free arm loosely over the back of the swing.

Donald reached for a cinnamon roll and took a bite. "These sure are good," he said in between chews.

Kristi scooted an inch or so away from Shane, leaning against the armrest.

"Well." Donald frowned. "Guess I should say what I came here to say." He sucked in a deep breath. "That day your horse was shot, I said I didn't hear a gunshot because I was watching TV. Now, it's true I had the TV on, but I wasn't inside watching. I was out back, messing around with my rifle."

Kristi gasped, and Shane gripped her shoulder. She drew from his strength.

"I sure didn't mean to shoot your horse. It was an accident. But I lied. And that was wrong." Donald took another bite of the roll.

Shane leaned forward. "Have you gone to the police?"

"The police already know. I told them the day it happened. I was sentenced to community service, and I've been seeing a counselor. She told me I should confess and apologize to you. Both of you." Donald licked some icing off of his fingers, then looked up again at Shane. "I want to pay for your vet services, too, Dr. Zimmerman."

"Oh, it's alright." Shane shook his head. "Consider it a neighborly courtesy."

"No one ever told me about a horse shooting." Sylvia's frown was more pouty than panicked.

Shane chuckled. "You hate to be left out, huh, Sylvie? I'll fill you in later."

Donald reached inside his pocket and dropped a wad of cash onto the tray. "If you don't want the money, Dr. Zimmerman, buy something for your new niece or nephew. Or get something for Miss Kristi." He lumbered to his feet and mopped his brow with a shirtsleeve. "I'm sorry for making a move on you several times, too."

Kristi rose. "I forgive you, Donald. Thanks for telling us the truth. I've been wary ever since the incident." She picked up the plate of cinnamon rolls and held it out to him. "Please, take these home. I have more inside."

"Are you sure?" Donald gazed longingly at the sweets.

Shane stood and picked up the stack of bills Donald had left on the tray. "I appreciate your honesty, and your desire to make things right. I'll donate this money to the Humane Society in your name, if that's okay."

Donald nodded as Shane stuffed the money in his pocket. Then, he accepted the plate from Kristi. "Thank you, Miss Kristi." He cocked his head to one side. "Do I need to apologize to your folks? I'll ask my counselor." He turned and made his way down the steps.

Shane helped Sylvia to her feet. "We should go, too. We just came over because...." He glanced in the direction of Donald's haus. "We'll see you tomorrow. Looking forward to it." He winked at Kristi.

Her face heated, and she glanced at his sister.

Sylvia gave Kristi a knowing smile. "And I'm looking forward to hearing what's next for the two of you, now that it seems Shane has moved on from your dog."

Chapter 23

Shane pulled his Jeep into the gravel parking lot outside of Bakersville Pioneer Village, then glanced over at his sister. "Well, we made it."

Sylvia gazed out the window, rubbing her belly.

For a moment, he watched her, wishing he could have experienced a moment like this with Becca. She had just started to feel the baby moving when everything had ended.

Shane forced the memory from his mind. He couldn't wait to see his new niece or nephew. Sylvia had told him that she'd instructed the ultrasound tech not to tell her the gender.

"Too bad it's raining," Sylvia whined.

Shane shrugged. "It isn't hard. Just a drizzle."

"But you don't have an umbrella. I keep one in my car."

"Man up." He grinned at her, then turned and winked at Kristi.

Kristi smiled. "Sometimes I'm glad my brothers have all moved out of the haus. No one left to fight with."

Shane reached into the glove box and pulled out a crumpled-up plastic bag. "Here. Hold this over your head."

Sylvia snatched it out of his hand. "I have to visit the ladies' room. I'll meet you up there." She opened the door, slid out of her seat, and waddled off.

Shane got out and pulled the front seat forward to assist Kristi. She'd had a hard time climbing back there, and he knew that getting out would be as just as awkward.

She slid forward far enough for him to grasp her waist and lift her out. Once she was settled on the ground, she looked up at him. "I owe you an apology."

Shane frowned, confused. "What for?"

She blushed. "The way I acted yesterday. Embarrassing you in front of your sister."

His face heated. "Oh, Kristi. It was my fault. I shouldn't have touched you when I knew we weren't a couple, but I couldn't help myself. I'm as bad as Donald. Worse, since I knew better. Please forgive me."

The difference being, he wanted to marry her. If only she weren't a practicing Amish midwife who peddled herbs. How could he work around it? He had to find a way. Pray for a miracle.

Prayer was something he hadn't considered until now. *Lord, please change Kristi's heart—or mine, if that's what needs to happen.*

"Of course, I forgive you," Kristi said softly.

He mustered a smile. "Come on, sweetheart. Let's go up there and join Sylvia."

They walked beneath an archway and into the village. To their left was a hotel; to their right, a seed store. The village center consisted of a barn, a blacksmith shop, and several other shops.

Kristi gazed all around. "Wow. This is more than I'd expected."

As they passed the Ozark Hotel, Shane peered inside. "It looks like they serve lunch, but the sign says they're open for only a couple of hours around noon. If we're still here, we'll plan on it."

Kristi bypassed the hotel and the mercantile next door with barely a glance. "Ach, look! They have an apothecary."

Shane cringed. That would be the first place she wanted to go.

As Kristi made a beeline for the apothecary—a smaller building, painted greenish-blue—Shane looked around for Sylvia. He saw her coming around the corner of the seed building, and he waved to flag her over.

Kristi opened the door of the apothecary and went inside.

Even though he didn't want to, Shane followed her. No time like the present to try to get over his issues with herbs. *Convince me, Lord. Help me to understand.* He hesitated in the doorway, recognizing the scent he associated with Kristi...unidentified aromatics. Looking around, he didn't see anything too odd or alarming. He recognized cinnamon sticks. Cloves. Maybe Kristi's "herbs" weren't all bad.

As he stepped inside, his lungs filled with the wonderful smell. He approached a display table, picked up a random jar, and read the label. "Fennel seeds." He turned to Kristi. "What are these used for?"

She smiled. "Fennel's used in a lot of recipes, from sausages to breads. It's also an anti-colic, anti-bloating herb. Taken as a tea, it settles the stomach. It's also useful for treating bad breath."

"Hmm." He put down the jar of fennel and reached for a different herb. "Catnip. I know this one. It's put in cat toys. They love it."

Kristi giggled. "Yes, but it does more than that. Taken in tea form, it settles the nerves and calms tension. It has a mildly tranquilizing effect on people."

"Hmm." As he set the jar back on the shelf, he couldn't help entertaining the thought of keeping some catnip on hand for his high-maintenance clients who obsessed over their pets. "And this one? Barberry?" He didn't pick it up.

"Helps heal pinkeye."

"Blackhaw?"

"It closely resembles aspirin, and relieves inflammation and pain associated with arthritis. But it tastes really bitter."

Like some of the medicines he kept in his office. Interesting.

She knew her herbs well, and it turned out they served more purposes than he'd imagined. "Clove oil? That isn't used medicinally, is it?"

"It is, actually. It'll numb a toothache until you can get to the dentist. They used to apply it as a topical anesthetic."

The shop door opened. "Mmm, it smells so good in here," Sylvia said, stepping inside. "Like your house, Kristi."

Shane turned toward his sister and remembered the bag of tea leaves she'd brought home. His blood ran cold. He glanced at Kristi. "Those red raspberry leaves you gave Sylvia...what are they good for?"

"They enhance a woman's holistic health, both during pregnancy and after. They improve muscle tone...and do a lot of other things I won't talk about in mixed company." She blushed.

Lord, let me hear the truth. He chewed his lip. "They don't elevate the risk of, say, aneurysms, do they?" He tried to keep his tone casual.

Kristi blinked. "Nein."

He saw the truth in her eyes but pushed just a bit further to make sure she wouldn't endanger anyone. "Are there any herbs a woman should avoid during pregnancy?"

"Well, there are several that shouldn't be taken in large quantities. Parsley, for one."

"Really?" He shook his head. "You sure seem to know your plants. It sounds like...." He pulled in a breath. Was he really coming to accept her herbs? *Thank You, Lord, for opening my eyes and bringing me one step closer to Kristi.*

He started over. "It sounds like God knew what He was doing and provided naturally a number of things I've always relied on science to supply."

Kristi followed Shane and his sister out of the apothecary and over to the mercantile. Other Englisch wandered around in there, looking at the home-canned foods, the candy, and other items displayed in the store. She wasn't sure what the Englischers found so fascinating about the rows of glass jars lining the shelves. After all, similar jars filled the cupboards and pantry in the farmhaus. She knew the work involved in them.

A man walked up beside her. She'd seen him come in with a woman and two small buwe. She nodded, then looked away when she realized he was staring at her. She focused her gaze outside, on the rain falling from the sky.

"Kristi Lapp?"

She jumped. The voice sounded familiar. She turned to look at him again. An Englischer who sounded Amish. But she didn't know him. Or did she? She studied him, detecting a vague resemblance to…no. It couldn't be.

"Have I changed so much?" He smiled. "It's me. Justus."

She took in his blue jeans, leather belt, T-shirt, and short hair, cut in a style like Shane's. She wanted to wrap her arms around her brother and hold on, but that wouldn't be proper. He'd left the Amish after joining the church. He was shunned. Daed would insist she obey the rules and turn her back on him. But she'd be in the same situation as Justus if she left the Amish to marry Shane.

Her eyes burned with tears. For the first time, she got a glimpse of what Justus must have gone through when he'd married a woman whose name Kristi didn't even know. And he had kinner she'd never met. If she were to leave, Daed and Mamm would never know her kinner, either.

"Don't turn away. Please." Justus must have sensed her inner turmoil.

Kristi glanced around, wondering where Shane had disappeared to. She needed his support right now. But she didn't see him or Sylvia. Just an open door at the far end of the mercantile. They must have gone upstairs, where there was supposedly a mini museum.

She pulled in a breath, then reached out to take her brother's hands. "Justus. I've missed you terribly."

With tearful eyes, he reached out and wrapped her in his arms. His shoulders shook. Was he crying?

After a moment, he pulled away. He ran a hand roughly over his face, then surveyed her. "You've grown up. What are you doing here, anyway? I didn't see a van full of Amish arrive. Or did you kum on your own?"

"I'm…with some friends."

"You have to meet my frau." He spoke in Pennsylvania Deitsch. Taking her arm, he steered her over to a woman who stood to the side with two small buwe. "Dori, you remember my sister, Kristi. Kristi, my frau, Dorcas, and our two sohns, Jonathon and Stephen."

Kristi stared. Dorcas Miller? Her brother's Amish girlfriend had jumped the fence with him? She'd wondered what had happened to her, since she hadn't seen her after Justus had left. But no one ever said. Of course, since Dorcas was shunned, no one would speak her name. Or Justus's. It was as if they'd never existed. As if Justus had never been a part of their family.

Dori gave a tight smile. She seemed to fear that Kristi would turn away.

"It's gut to see you again," Kristi said, surveying her long-lost relatives.

Dori wore a blue denim jumper over a white shirt. She'd tied her hair in a ponytail, with a blue bandanna secured around her head, like she made an effort to dress plainly, by Englisch standards. Justus wore a wedding band, and he looked as fancy as Shane.

Kristi tried to imagine herself standing there, an Englischer, dressed like Dori.

She shouldn't think this way. She didn't want to leave the Amish. But she loved Shane. If their relationship progressed, would she really have a choice? It wasn't as if she would be entirely without family if she were shunned. She would have Justus and Dori.

Kristi found a smile, ignoring the pressure of Justus's hand on her elbow, urging her to…what? Embrace Dori? She wouldn't feel comfortable with that, and she didn't think Dori would, either. The tightness around her lips had eased only a little.

Kristi didn't know what else to say to her shunned sister-in-law, or to the two buwe half hidden behind their mamm's skirt. She supposed she could ask them to hug Aenti Kristi. But it would probably scare them.

Family should be close. Not complete strangers.

Shane stepped through the open door at the end of the shop. His gaze rested on her, then dropped down, to her brother's hand on her elbow. He blinked, his mouth firmed, and something flared in his eyes. He turned away to summon Sylvia, and the two of them came over to join Kristi and the others.

As they approached, Shane studied her brother. His shoulders relaxed a little, probably when he determined that Justus wasn't a threat. "Shane Zimmerman. I live next door to Kristi." He stuck out his hand to Justus. "You look like a Lapp."

Justus smiled and shook Shane's hand. "Kristi's brother Justus. My wife, Dori, and our boys, Jonathon and Stephen."

Shane stepped back and gestured to the side. "This is my sister, Sylvia. She's staying with me for a while." His hand closed around Kristi's.

Seeing her hand clasped in Shane's, Justus raised one eyebrow at Kristi and said, still in Pennsylvania Deitsch, "Down in the dirt with the dogs, jah?"

Kristi cringed, remembering when she'd uttered that very statement to Justus upon finding out he was leaving the Amish to get an education. He'd wanted to go to seminary. Had he? She'd ask him later.

She hadn't realized how unkind her remark had sounded. It must have lingered in his mind. Unkind words from his favorite sister—his only sister. She should have been more understanding. Forgiving. "I'm sorry."

He nodded. Gave her a gentle smile. "If you decide to leave, we'll help." Still speaking in Pennsylvania Deitsch. Maybe he assumed neither Shane nor Sylvia would understand, and so their conversation would be kept private.

But Shane and Sylvia did understand the language, at least passably. Her face heated.

Shane squeezed her hand. "Would you like to join us for lunch? I know Kristi's missed you. I'm sure she'd like to catch up."

Kristi wasn't sure she wanted to have lunch with Justus and Dori. She hadn't shunned them as she was supposed to. If Daed found out about the way she'd carried on in his absence, she'd be facing a visit from Bishop Dave, and then would need to kneel and confess. Or be shunned.

But then, if she were shunned, she would be free to marry Shane....

Daed would be home on Monday. Less than forty-eight hours from now.

The day of reckoning too quickly approached.

"If you decide to leave, we'll help." Shane felt his hopes soar at the remark. Would Kristi seriously consider leaving the Amish for him? The idea hadn't really crossed his mind. Or, if it had, he'd forced himself to dismiss it. He didn't want to ask her to make such a sacrifice.

But then, even if he "jumped the fence" in reverse to marry her, she would still be making sacrifices—her career, in particular. Shane had come to terms with her use of herbal medicine, but he didn't think he could marry her without the condition that she stop practicing midwifery. He just didn't believe it was safe for mothers to give birth anywhere but in a hospital.

His hopes took a nosedive. There was so much to consider. And sacrifice seemed inevitable, on both sides, if their relationship was going to work.

He adjusted the hand holding Kristi's so that their fingers intertwined. He looked at her brother. "So, lunch?"

"I don't know. Dori wanted to visit the Laura Ingalls Wilder Museum after this, before heading home. But we were planning to eat lunch out, somewhere." Justus looked at his wife. "Would that be okay with you?"

She nodded, though she looked uncomfortable. As though she would hide behind her skirt with her sons, if she could. Shane figured she must be shy. He wondered how Justus had met her. She didn't seem the type to go cruising dirt roads looking for men. And Justus didn't seem the type to have strayed far from his Amish roots during his rumschpringe.

Maybe it had been a chance meeting, similar to what he'd had with Kristi. Even though they were neighbors, it had taken him happening upon a buggy wreck and finding her critically injured for them to meet.

Who would have guessed that he'd find love again in the wake of a violent accident? He supposed it was appropriate, since his first love had left this earth in a violent way.

He hadn't spoken the words "I love you" to Kristi. But he did love her. With every breath he took.

Right now, with her hand clasped in his, he thought he could even accept her practicing midwifery. Just not on his sister. He needed to start spending serious time in prayer about their relationship and asking God's direction. He should've been doing that from the start.

He shook his head to pull himself out of his musings. It sounded like Kristi and Justus were still discussing the plan. Sylvia must have joined the conversation, as well, for she stood there, gesticulating as she spoke.

Justus nodded at Shane. "We'll see you at the restaurant, then." Turning to Kristi, he added, "Over lunch, you can tell me where you got the limp."

As Justus herded his wife and sons out the door, Sylvia tugged on Shane's other arm. "Let's walk around the farm. I'd like to see the other buildings and the animals before we go to the seed store."

An hour later, they exited the seed store, Kristi carrying a small brown bag of seed packets she'd purchased, along with a free sample of white tomato seeds she'd said she was eager to try.

Sylvia talked excitedly of planting marigolds along Shane's front walk, having gotten the go-ahead from

Kristi. She asked Shane to buy some starters the following afternoon.

Kristi smiled at her. "I'll help you plant them on Monday, before my parents get back." She sobered immediately. "Sylvia, you should know that I won't be permitted to invite you to lunch nearly as often. Their return changes everything, I'm afraid."

A wave of hopelessness washed over Shane. He'd forgotten about how soon he'd have to face Ira.

Lord, I love her. I want to be with her. Forever. But unless You work a miracle.... His spirit groaned when he couldn't find more words. Whatever happened next would be in God's hands.

Chapter 24

Sunday was beautiful—warm enough to go outside without a sweater. It was a church Sunday, and the service would be held at Onkel Timothy's this time, so Kristi chose to walk rather than drive the buggy. As she made her way there, she couldn't help wondering if this would be one of the last times she'd gather with her church family.

In the barnyard, she merged into the crowd, looking for Janna Kauffman. She finally spied her with a group of other maidals.

Kristi made her way over to them, smoothing her sweaty hands over the material of her new teal skirt. *Why so naerfich?* she demanded of herself. *Nobody here knows you're in love with an Englisch man.* To her knowledge, none of them even knew she'd tempted fate by dating one.

Janna grinned at her. "Are you ready for your daed and mamm to get home?"

Nein. How could she be ready? Her fledgling romance with Shane was sure to be dashed by Daed. She forced a smile. "Jah, it'll be gut to see them."

She did look forward to the crates of oranges and grapefruit they'd bring home. And she couldn't wait to see her großeltern.

A lot had happened while Mamm and Daed had been away, in the fall and spring alike, from Kristi's accident to her breakup with Eli, to her falling in love with Shane and making her first forays into the Englisch world.

In truth, they'd been more than mere forays. And she was a member of the church. She really ought to kneel and confess before the bishop—that is, if she decided to remain Amish.

And even if she did follow the promptings of her guilt-stricken conscience, the repercussions were uncertain. Would the bishop forgive and forget? Or would he impose a temporary shunning?

Probably the latter, to give her a taste of what she would suffer permanently if she persisted in her sinful ways.

Everyone filed into the barn in the proper order. Kristi entered with the other maidals, while the single men lined up outside, on either side of the barn doors, and watched the girls as they walked in.

It was customary for the girls to act bashfully, with heads bowed and eyes lowered, and pretend not to notice the attention of any particular man. Yet Kristi didn't join the other maidals in the tradition this time. It wasn't as if any man would be looking at her in that way.

She sat down between Janna and Katie Detweiler. The three of them had been inseparable as kinner. Katie's family had moved away to Ohio for several years and had recently returned. Kristi looked forward to renewing their friendship.

The single Amish men filed in next. If any Englischers were visiting, they would be ushered in afterward. Starr had attended a service once, but she hadn't stayed long, and she hadn't been back since.

Kristi peeked over her shoulder to see if any Englischers were here today. She did a double take at the sight of Shane and Sylvia. Shane met her gaze and winked, ever so boldly.

Kristi snapped her head forward again, her heart pounding.

Janna glanced around, too, then looked at Kristi, eyes wide. "There's a handsome Englisch man back there," she whispered. "And he's staring at you."

Kristi reached over and grasped Janna's hand. She needed to hold on to something, to keep from getting up and going to join Shane. And starting everyone talking. It was verboden for men and women to sit together. And Englisch and Amish were like oil and water.

Janna studied Kristi's face, a quizzical expression on her own. Kristi tried to appear composed, but she knew it was hopeless. She'd always been told she was transparent when it came to her emotions, especially to those who knew her well. Janna had been her best friend forever.

"Ach, Kristi. Nein." Janna shook her head. She glanced over her shoulder again. "He's cute, but…we'll talk later." She turned her attention to the opening song.

Kristi forced herself to wait until they'd sung twelve verses of the first hymn before she peeked behind her again. Shane still stood there, but Sylvia looked uncomfortable in her seat on the other side of the open barn door. They probably wouldn't make it through the preaching service, which typically lasted three hours.

It was just as well. Kristi wouldn't have been able to avoid looking at Shane after church let out. And if she tried to keep her distance, Sylvia would surely hunt her down.

Shane would follow.

And their secret would be laid bare for all to see.

❧～⊙

Shane shifted his weight. He was growing tired of standing there, his back pressed against the barn wall, and only an hour had passed. The service was far from over.

His brain was also tired from the effort of translating from the High German used for preaching. He tried his best but managed to make out only bits and pieces of the message. Finally, he gave up and started praying. *God, I don't know how to handle this love between Kristi and me. It's complicated. Forbidden. And impossible to deny. Should I ask her to leave the Amish for me? How can I ask that of her? Would I even be allowed to continue working as a vet? How would I support her—and an eventual family—if I couldn't? How can I give up the freedom my dad risked everything for to rejoin the very culture he rejected?*

Sylvia caught his eye and nodded toward the open door. Seconds later, she stood up and slipped outside.

He went after her, wondering what was up. Maybe she'd had her fill of immersion in a foreign culture with its unfamiliar language.

"I've got a pounding headache." Sylvia rubbed her forehead. "I'm going home to take a nap, with a heat pack. Or maybe ice."

"Do you need me?" Shane wanted to help his sister, but he also wanted to stay and experience his first Amish church service as an adult. It was so different from what he was accustomed to: short hymns with piano accompaniment. Not these a cappella choruses that dragged on for what felt like forever.

Not to mention the stern-looking preachers with long white beards. The glares they aimed at him were sharp enough to pin him to the wall, as if he'd sinned just by daring to darken the barn door.

Sylvia closed her eyes. "No, I'll be fine. I just need a nap. And some peace and quiet. That music is kind of spooky. The baby's probably having nightmares."

Shane laughed. "Oh, it isn't that bad. Remember when we used to go with Mammi and Pappy when we were little? It's an adventure."

Sylvia scoffed. "You can enjoy the rest of this particular adventure on your own." She waved her hand dismissively. "Do you think you'll be home for lunch?"

"I don't know. I guess I'd be surprised if they let me stay for the meal. But don't worry; I can fend for myself. Feel better soon, okay?"

Shane stood there in Timothy Lapp's barnyard and watched Sylvia until she'd reached his front steps. Then, he turned and went back inside the dimly lit barn. His nose was assaulted with the smell of animals and humans packed into the same warm room.

As he slid back into his position beside the door, he eyed Kristi. If only he could sit beside her. Hold her hand. Maybe drape his arm over her shoulder, like the men at his church did with their girlfriends and wives.

Would she be open to attending a service at his church? Maybe next weekend, since the Amish had church only every other Sunday? It'd be fair, since he'd attended hers. And it could be a starting point in the search for some common ground. Admittedly, though, she had never invited him to an Amish service.

Then, he remembered that Kristi's parents would be home by next weekend. Even if Kristi were willing to go to church with him, they would never allow it.

Shane shifted his attention from Kristi to the front of the barn. The man preaching now was different from the one who'd been speaking prior to Sylvia's exit. This preacher met Shane's eyes and, in a blink, switched from High German to English, to Shane's great relief. He spoke on the importance of being separate from the world. It was a theme not at all unfamiliar to Shane, but it seemed the Amish lived it out to the extreme.

The man seated on the end of the back row made room for him, and he sat. These hard, backless wooden benches were nothing like the cushioned chairs at his church. Shane sighed. He would have much to get used to, if he decided to join the Amish. And make the decision his dad had made—in reverse.

He allowed his eyes to scan the female side of the barn. When his gaze met Kristi's, and she blushed and faced forward again, he realized she must have been watching him.

Shane grinned. Then, sensing the gaze of the man seated next to him, he sobered and stared straight ahead. Flirting with Kristi from across the barn might be fun, but he couldn't afford to put her reputation at risk.

Plus, he needed to keep his focus where it belonged—on God.

❧

When the service concluded, Kristi hurried over to the farmhaus with the other women to help get the noon meal ready. Meanwhile, the men remained inside the barn, standing in small groups and talking. She'd seen several of them, including Onkel Timothy and Janna's father, Bishop Dave, approach Shane, probably to welcome him. Or maybe to ask what had prompted him to attend an Amish service. Most of them probably knew Shane already, as the local vet.

Hopefully, the men hadn't noticed Shane and her making eyes at each other. Their too-frequent glances would get them in trouble, for sure.

Her stomach churned.

In the kitchen, Kristi collected several plates piled with cold sliced meats and carried them outside. Janna led the way, balancing platters of various cheeses.

Kristi set down the plates in the designated space on one of the long folding tables, then went back inside to help carry out the remaining items: pickled eggs, chowchow, bread and butter, jams and jellies, and so forth.

As the men started lining up for the meal, Kristi joined the other women to wait their turn. She looked around, hoping Shane had decided to stick around.

Her breath hitched when she spotted him walking down the road toward home, head bent, shoulders slumped.

She looked back at the group of men who'd been talking to him. None of them looked her way. Had they confronted Shane about watching her and winking, as he had? That would account for his dejected demeanor.

She'd looked at him entirely too often. And, judging by the way her face had heated, her cheeks must have been as red as a newborn boppli. Bishop Dave probably knew her well enough to read her expressions. After all, he was Janna's father. She'd had plenty of sleepovers at their haus growing up.

What had those men said to Shane? If only she could go after him and find out. But she couldn't. She had to stay through the meal, so as not to arouse suspicion.

Still, she couldn't keep from sneaking another gaze at Shane.

Janna jabbed her in the ribs. So much for trying to be subtle.

She got her meal and went to sit under the trees with her friend. Janna turned to her, eyes wide. "Kristi, if there's something going on between you and that Englisch man, you have to stop it now. Amish marry Amish. You can't...." She leaned forward and grasped Kristi's hands. "You just can't. I won't survive without my best friend. Please." Her eyes brimmed with tears. "Dump him, now."

Kristi shook her head. "I love him, Janna. I don't know how we'll work this out or even if it can be. But I have to try." She looked around at all the assembled church members. "Besides, that bu you had a crush on, Hiram Troyer, jumped the fence, ain't so? What would you do if he paid attention to you?"

"He won't. He's long gone. And besides, that's hardly the same thing, Kristi. You're not thinking clearly. I'm going to talk you out of this infatuation, if it takes all afternoon."

Spending time with her friend would be nice, but it would take every bit of forever to talk Kristi out of being in love with Shane Zimmerman.

Chapter 25

*A*fter work on Monday, Shane unloaded the flats full of marigolds he'd bought for Sylvia from the back of his Jeep, then stepped back and studied them. Planting flowers wasn't something he'd ever been keen on doing, and even his best effort would probably fall short of Sylvia's expectations. Kristi would do a far better job planting them.

But a glance at her house dashed his hopes. Ira was leading one of their draft horses into the barn. Kristi's parents must have returned from Florida while Shane had been at work. And Kristi had said not to expect her to be able to help with the flowers once they were home.

Shane went inside to change into his jogging clothes. And to devise a scheme to get Kristi to come over without her father finding out.

He stepped outside and started stretching when he saw Ira again. Might as well be neighborly. "Welcome back! Did you have a good time in Florida?"

"Always do." Ira nodded. "Brought you back a crate of mixed citrus fruit. Timothy told me your sister is staying with you."

"Yes, while her husband's deployed. Thanks for the fruit. We'll enjoy it." Shane glanced over at the kennel. "I should take the dog for a quick run before dinner. My sister and I talked about going out." He would have invited Kristi to join them, if her parents hadn't been back already. "That reminds me. Kristi had offered to help my sister plant some flowers along the front walkway, but my sister is getting closer to her due date, and she isn't exactly in a shape to be gardening. I would ask Kristi if she'd mind doing it herself, but I haven't seen her all day." Hopefully, Ira didn't know the extent to which they'd interacted during his absence. Shane wasn't ready to broach that topic of discussion.

"Timothy told me you've been helping Kristi when she's needed it. Caring for Samson, first when he went lame, and then when he was shot. I can't imagine." Ira shook his head. "And arranging for a physical therapist to work with her. She's improved, far beyond my greatest expectations." He swallowed. "All that is to say, danki for taking care of my girl. I guess it'd be okay for her to go plant your flowers. A small token of our appreciation. I'll send her over in a bit."

Shane smiled with relief. He couldn't wait to see Kristi. Had Timothy sugarcoated the truth about their relationship? Maybe Shane hadn't misunderstood him when he'd said he believed Shane to be the best choice for Kristi. He hoped he was right in counting Timothy an ally in his struggle for Kristi's hand.

❧

"Kristi, I have a job for you."

Startled, Kristi looked up from her dinner at Daed. His statement had jarred the silence that had prevailed for most of the meal. They had exchanged pleasantries and briefly talked about their time in Florida, until the travelers seemed to have become too exhausted to talk any further. All they'd been doing for the past ten minutes had been to move forks from plate to mouth and back again.

"Shane asked if you'd plant some marigolds for his sister. Evidently she isn't in a condition to do it herself. And they're going out to dinner. I told him you'd do it."

Kristi nodded. "Be glad to, Daed. After dinner?"

He nodded and turned his attention back to his meal.

Kristi stared down at the carrot slices on her plate. How had Shane managed to get Daed to agree to that? It must have been divine providence.

Would she be forgiven if she declined dessert? It would allow her to get over there sooner.

Then again, what would be the point in that? Daed had said Shane wouldn't be home. She decided to remain seated and eat slowly, savoring every bite. If she took long enough with the rest of her meal, as well as with the kitchen cleanup afterward, maybe Shane and Sylvia would return before she went next door.

After the dishes had been put away, Grossmammi yawned and rubbed her eyes. "I'm going straight to bed. I'm so tired, I can't see straight."

Mamm chuckled. "I'll be in bed before long. It was an exhausting trip."

Kristi finished wiping the table. "I'm going next door to plant those flowers before it gets too late."

Mamm nodded. "We'll talk more tomorrow. I'm anxious to hear about how you spent the months without us. Lots of adventures, I'm told."

With a smile she hoped wasn't sheepish, Kristi nodded, then excused herself and headed outside to the barn. She retrieved the kneeler Onkel Timothy had made for her, along with her basket of garden tools, and then made her way to Shane's.

She found the flats of flowers waiting on the front walkway. Once she'd set up the kneeler, she grabbed her trowel and started digging a hole in the bed lining the walk.

She'd planted more than half of the flowers when Shane's Jeep pulled into the driveway. Shane got out, nodded at her, and then went around to help Sylvia out of the vehicle. "Go on up to bed," he urged his sister. "I'm sure you'll feel better tomorrow."

Sylvia maneuvered her way slowly inside, one hand on her back.

The way she carried herself indicated to Kristi that she'd probably gone into labor. Adrenaline surging, Kristi glanced at Shane. Did he know what was going on?

He stepped inside, flicked on the porch light, and came back outside. "I'm glad you're still here." He jogged over to Kristi, then glanced back at the haus. "I'm worried about her. All through dinner, she just picked at her food, and I can tell she's in a lot of pain." He shook his head. "I offered to take her to an emergency care center, but she told me it was false labor and insisted she'd feel better in the morning. How would she know how to recognize false labor? Do women just sense these things?"

Kristi bit her lip. Something told her this was the real thing. Should she go inside? Or wait for a signal from Sylvia? She jabbed the trowel into the dirt.

"I'm going to grab the duffel bag and put it in the car, just in case we need to rush to the hospital." Shane jogged up the walkway and disappeared inside.

Kristi placed a flower into the hole she'd just dug and patted the dirt around it. She tried to distract herself with the flowers, but she still blinked back some tears. Why didn't Shane send her inside to check on Sylvia? Didn't he trust her?

Shane returned. "Those look great, Kristi. Thanks."

Kristi leaned back and gazed up at him.

His eyes met hers for a moment, and then he crouched next to her, studying the plants she'd already put in. "They look a little wilted. I shouldn't have left them sitting in my Jeep all day."

"They'll perk up as soon as they get some water and acclimate themselves to the new ground."

"Danki." He grinned.

His use of Pennsylvania Deitsch made her think of the hours he'd spent immersed in the language yesterday at church. Which reminded her of a question she'd wanted to ask. "Shane?"

"Jah?" He touched her hand.

"After the church service yesterday…you looked unhappy when you left."

Shane hesitated. "A little. I hadn't been to an Amish church service since I was a kid, when I used to spend a week or so with my grandparents. Thought I'd see if it was anything like what I remembered." He raked a hand through his hair. "Actually, I wanted to see what your Sunday was like. And I'd hoped to see you some, before your parents came home."

Kristi smiled as she imagined her friend Starr saying, "How romantic." It was. Really. "I went to a friend's haus for awhile, then had to finish getting the dawdi-haus ready for Grossmammi and Grossdaedi." She'd gone to Janna's, and they'd sat by the pond, discussing her "infatuation," as Janna called it, with the Englisch man. Kristi would have much rather spent the day with Shane instead of subjecting herself to Janna's interrogation. "I also saw Bishop Dave and some of the preachers talking to you."

He blinked. "Bishop Dave? Oh, was one of those men the bishop?" He scratched his jaw. Shrugged. "It was nothing. Just talking about my job. What led me to become a veterinarian. If I liked it. Stuff like that."

She nodded. "And did you like the service?"

"Like?" He shrugged. "I don't know. It's been a while. Given time, I suppose I could get used to it."

⁕

Shane wondered how Kristi would interpret that statement. He hoped she wouldn't read too much into it, or get her hopes up.

After Justus had offered to help in the event that Kristi left the Amish, the wheels in Shane's head had started turning. And he'd even considered suggesting she do that, if she felt she could handle it. He'd prayed about it extensively but felt God telling him to wait before talking to her.

Besides, he couldn't ask that of her. She shouldn't have to endure the heartbreak of being shunned.

His joining the Amish, on the other hand, would eliminate almost all of the obstacles in the way of a relationship between them. He would be a member of the church. Accepted. Able to court Kristi.

After church on Sunday, he'd spent the afternoon continuing to think and pray about the situation, as he'd begun in church. It'd made perfect sense to him yesterday: he would pay a visit to Bishop Dave, state his intentions of courting Kristi with the ultimate goal of marrying her, and ask how to go about joining the church.

Today, he wasn't so sure. Well, he was sure he'd do whatever it would take to win her. But did he really want to become Amish? There was so much he'd have to give up—things he hadn't quite resigned himself to losing. But visiting her church again, talking to the bishop, and asking about how to join seemed the obvious next steps.

Everything would be solved, except the matter of her career as a midwife. After what he'd gone through with Becca, he had the right to resent that. Didn't he?

Speaking of midwives.... "I'm going to go check on Sylvia. If she isn't in labor now, she will be by morning." He stood up and went inside. Why didn't he insist Sylvia go to the hospital, just to get checked out?

When he tapped on Sylvia's door, there were a few seconds of silence, and then he heard some shuffling inside. The door swung slowly open, revealing Sylvia, bent over, a grimace of pain marring her features. She'd changed into an oversized button-down shirt that almost reached her knees.

A lump lodged in his throat. "Sylvia? You're not…?" He sucked in a breath. "I'm taking you to the hospital. Just to get checked out. You might be in labor. And not the 'false' kind. I'd feel better knowing. Let me grab your shoes."

"No…time." She made some strange panting sounds and gripped the doorjamb. "Need…to…push."

"What? You're this far along, and you hid it from me?" Shane rammed his hand into his pocket, yanked out his cell phone, and compressed the number 1 to speed-dial the local emergency medical tech service.

When the operator answered, Shane spun around and marched down the hall. "We need an ambulance stat. My sister's in labor." He barked out his address, then hung up the phone and dashed outside. "Kristi, Sylvia's started labor. Would you mind watching for the ambulance and directing them in?" He hesitated. "On second thought, why don't you go sit with Sylvia? Talk her out of pushing?"

Kristi rose to her feet. "Run to my haus and tell my parents what's going on. Ask for my medical bag."

He took off at a sprint. "You won't need your bag," he yelled over his shoulder. "I've called for an ambulance."

Ira met him at the back door. "Something wrong?"

Shane heaved a breath. "My sister's in labor."

"Wait." Ira went back inside. Moments later, he returned, carrying Kristi's bag. "Here."

Shane could only stare at the thing as shock waves of horrific memories flashed across his mind. The eerie silence of the house. Becca's lifeless body.

Finally, Shane mustered the strength to shake his head. "No. Sylvia's going to the hospital. The ambulance is on its way."

"No need for an ambulance." Ira shoved the bag into Shane's arms. "Everything will be fine. Childbirth is as natural as breathing."

He sounded like Kristi. Shane grasped the handles and lowered the bag as reality set in. Sylvia had concocted this whole conspiracy so that she could have a home birth with an Amish midwife. Kristi was complicit. And so was Ira, evidently.

Shane was such a dupe.

"You're welkum to return here, if your sister's a screamer. We have leftover stuffed peppers and a couple of Key lime pies Kristi made for supper. I'll ask Barbie to put on some koffee. The first boppli tends to take a while. We'll sit out here on the porch and visit."

As if Shane would be able to carry on an intelligent conversation while his sister's life was hanging in the balance.

He mustered what probably looked like a sick smile, then turned and ran back home.

He could hear Kristi's voice coming from Sylvia's room. Numbly, he knocked on the door, then passed the bag through the small space when Kristi opened it.

Still numb, he went back downstairs and started pacing in front of the living room window, checking obsessively for the ambulance's arrival. Willing it to arrive before Kristi could do any damage.

The minutes crawled by with excruciating silence. All he could hear from Sylvia's room was hushed conversation. He went outside, but the silence prevailed; no sirens wailed, nor heavy tires crunched along the dirt road.

After a few more minutes, Shane redialed the EMT number. "This is Shane Zimmerman. My sister is in labor. I called earlier about an ambulance."

"The closest ambulance was in Springfield," the operator explained calmly. Matter-of-factly. "It's en route. You should expect its arrival within twenty minutes."

To pass the time, Shane moved Kristi's kneeler off of the sidewalk, along with the remaining flats of marigolds, to make room for a stretcher. It was less than sixty seconds since he'd disconnected, yet he couldn't resist craning his neck and looking down the road again. If he'd taken Sylvia to the hospital himself, they would be there by now. He sighed and walked out to the mailbox so he could see further down the road.

No ambulance in sight. He went back inside, climbed the stairs, and paced the hallway outside Sylvia's bedroom.

He didn't know how many minutes had gone by when he heard a furious squall from inside the bedroom. Was that the baby already? Some unidentified emotion washed over him as he twisted the doorknob and pushed his way in. He needed to make sure Sylvia was okay.

The first thing he saw was an object that resembled a fish scale. Kristi held it in the air. And inside was a red-faced, screaming infant. "Seven pounds, three ounces," Kristi announced in a calm voice. She turned to Shane. "Say hello to your niece."

Speechless, Shane stared at this new little life. He finally tore his gaze away and looked at Sylvia, propped up in the bed. "Are you okay?"

She smiled drowsily at him. "Fine, Shane. Never better. I'm sorry I hid my labor from you, but…." She sighed. "Kristi prayed with me and talked me through the delivery. You should have seen her work. She's wonderful. The cord was wrapped around the baby's neck, and she was so blue. But Kristi got it untangled and then put her in my arms with a blanket and told me to rub her." Sylvia turned to the baby and beamed. "She's fine now. Shane, Kristi saved her life."

Shane turned to Kristi. He didn't know what to say. "Thank you" would have to be adequate.

The baby's screams were music to his ears as Kristi lifted her out of the fish-scale contraption and laid her out on the bed. Gently yet deftly, she stretched her out and measured her length. "Nineteen inches." A soft smile curved Kristi's lips. "She doesn't seem to care for all this attention. But she'll go through all this and more at the hospital."

"What?" Shane frowned. "She still needs to go to the hospital?"

Kristi lifted her gaze to meet his. "You called an ambulance. Since it was an unplanned home birth, they'll deem these conditions 'unsanitary' and insist that she be hospitalized for a few days."

Shane glanced around the room, noticing evidences of Kristi's efforts to make the space a clean, sterile environment. Her actions were professional, as was her equipment. It was hard to conceive of anyone questioning the level of sanitation.

Maybe he'd misjudged midwifery. Just like he had herbal remedies.

"This home birth *was* planned, but my big brother wouldn't listen. Typical male." Sylvia smiled at Shane. "Aren't you going to ask her name?"

"Sorry." He glanced at the baby, now objecting to being diapered by Kristi's able hands. "What's her name?"

"Adriane Kristine, after Mom and Kristi. Though Michael's mom will probably think the middle name was picked because of her. Tina." Sylvia paused long enough to take a breath.

Tears burned Shane's eyes as he watched Kristi swaddle the baby in a blanket. "Can I hold her?"

With a glance at Sylvia for approval, Kristi laid Adriane in Shane's arms. He gazed down, transfixed, at this tiny addition to the family. "She's beautiful."

He cradled her for several minutes before gently handing her off to Sylvia. "Congratulations, Mommy. Michael will be so happy." Then, he stepped around the foot of the bed to Kristi and gathered her in his arms. "You're amazing. I can't believe I doubted you. Or that it's taken me this long to explain why."

Chapter 26

When the EMTs had wheeled Sylvia and Adriane out of the house and loaded them in the ambulance, Kristi got to work cleaning up the "delivery room." She stripped the sheets from the bed, and then Shane showed her how to use a washing machine.

Doing laundry in an Englisch home was much easier—and more efficient—than she had ever experienced with the wringer washer. Kristi smiled to herself, pretending she worked in her own Englisch home, one she shared with Shane.

The idea of living with him as a married couple somehow seemed easier, now that she felt there were no secrets between them. She finally knew the truth about his late frau, Becca: how she had died. How Shane had blamed her Amish midwife and the herbal tea she'd prescribed.

Kristi could understand his concern. And she thanked the Lord for using Sylvia and her "surprise" of a home birth to open her brother's eyes and to settle his fears.

She packed up her medical bag and then sat down at the kitchen table to fill out the birth report. She'd let Sylvia decide what to do with it, since the hospital would file for the birth certificate, and Kristi's records would have no bearing whatsoever on what they included. They would probably document only what they'd observed, but she would go to the hospital later to find out.

Shane came into the kitchen, whistling. He smiled when he saw her. "I'll take you to the hospital whenever you're ready."

She shook her head. "I need to finish planting the flowers and take my things back home. I'll call for a driver later. You should be there when Sylvia fills out the admittance paperwork."

"How about I help you plant the flowers, and then we can go together?" Shane touched her hand. "We'll get it done in no time. In fact, I'll get started now, while you finish in here." He gazed at her a moment, looking as if he wanted to pull her into his arms and kiss her, but he didn't. Instead, he turned and went outside. Whistling again.

She'd never heard him do that before. The sound made her happy. It reminded her of her childhood, when she would go out to the barn and listen to Daed whistle while he milked the cows. But that had been before Justus had jumped the fence. She hadn't heard Daed whistle since.

Kristi sighed, thinking again of Justus. Of how much everyone had suffered when he'd left. The same had been true of Dori's family. Kristi remembered now that the health of Dori's parents had quickly declined. She finally understood why.

If only there were some way they could work around the issue of shunning. But that was unlikely. If she jumped the fence to be with Shane, she'd be living right next door to her parents yet verboden to interact with them. Her kinner would grow up without knowing their großeltern.

She finished making up Sylvia's bed with clean sheets, then went to transfer the wet laundry to the dryer. Another convenience of Englisch life. On her way out, she grabbed her black bag.

Shane had almost finished planting the marigolds.

"I'll drop this at home and kum back to water the plants. Then we can go to the hospital."

"Put it on the porch." He nodded toward her kneeler, which he must have moved there. "I'll help you get them home later."

Seeing him on his hands and knees in the dirt reminded her of their conversation earlier. *"Given time, I suppose I could get used to it."* The memory of his comment about Amish church services gave her a glimmer of hope. It seemed that he was at least entertaining the thought of becoming Amish. At least, she hoped she'd interpreted his statement correctly. It made her feel cherished. Valuable. Loved.

Yet Shane had never told her explicitly that he loved her.

The next day, Shane left the office on his lunch break to pay a visit to Bishop Dave. Kristi had pointed out where the Kauffmans lived as they'd driven past the night before, on their way to see Sylvia in the hospital. He hoped the bishop was home.

He pulled into the driveway and parked between the barn and the house. A dog bounded out to greet him. Shane let it sniff his hand. Seconds later, the dog turned, its tail wagging, and ran off toward the barn. A probable sign Bishop Dave was in there.

Shane sucked in a deep breath, whispered a prayer for favor, and followed the dog. As he entered the dimly lit barn, he heard rustling sounds from the loft. "Hello? Bishop Dave?"

The older man peered down at him. Shane recognized him as the preacher who'd switched from High German to English. Bishop Dave shifted something in his arms. "Dr. Zimmerman. What brings you by?"

The smile on the bishop's face did little to settle Shane's churning stomach. "Please, call me Shane."

"How can I help you, Shane?"

When Bishop Dave made no move to come down, Shane started climbing up the ladder, uninvited. A conversation of this magnitude was not meant to be shouted back and forth. He wanted—needed—to be on the same physical plane as the bishop. The man holding his fate in his hands.

Bishop Dave released a newborn kitten into a pile of hay, where its mother and siblings were nestled. "Precious, ain't so? I just discovered them a bit ago." He grinned. "Seem to be in top health, though, so I doubt they require your attention."

Shane smiled at his humor. Maybe this meeting would go better than anticipated. After all, they'd had a nice conversation after church on Sunday. Bishop Dave had commented that he'd appreciate having an Amish vet, fueling Shane's hopes that he'd be willing to help him join the church.

"Want to kum to the haus for some koffee? Think we have some pie to go with it."

Shane didn't think he could eat a bite. "No, thank you. I need to get back to work pretty soon, so I'll just say what I need to say."

Bishop Dave picked up another kitten and rubbed his big hand over its tiny head. "I'm listening."

Shane cleared his throat. "If I wanted to join the Amish church, how would I go about doing it? I'm a Christian, saved and baptized. And I can get a letter from my church, if you'd like."

The bishop frowned. "What makes you think you want to become Amish?"

A lump formed in Shane's throat, threatening to cut off his air supply. "I'm in love...with Kristi Lapp. I won't ask her to leave the Amish for me, knowing the agony her family went through when her brother left. I want to become Amish so I can marry her."

The bishop raised his eyebrows. "You want to become Amish so you can marry Kristi Lapp."

"Yes, sir. That's about it."

"You want to give up your life, your modern conveniences, to marry Kristi." It wasn't a question, really, but his disbelief came across clearly enough. "Does she know you came here to talk to me?"

He'd asked Kristi where the bishop lived but hadn't given a reason for wanting to know. Yet she might have made the correct assumptions. "No, sir."

Bishop Dave put the kitten down. "If you're being led by your feelings for a girl, rather than a nudge from God, then your reasons are wrong. I'm sorry, but my answer is nein."

"But—"

"Have you prayed about this decision?"

Shane hesitated. He wanted to be truthful. "About marrying Kristi? Yes, lots. About joining the Amish church? Recently, jah. I just want—"

"Nein. You might want to reconsider this decision." Bishop Dave went over to the ladder, climbed down, and strode out of the barn. Shane had been dismissed.

He looked at the mama cat and her kittens. "That didn't go so well." There was a distinct difference between the kitten-stroking bishop and the curt man who'd abruptly stalked off. What had been wrong about what he'd said?

The mama cat meowed. Sympathetically, or so he imagined.

Joining the church he currently attended had been so easy. All he'd had to do was produce a letter from his former congregation—a body of like faith and mind—and state his intentions.

Somehow, Shane managed to make his way down the ladder and out to his Jeep. He drove back to the clinic, his thoughts in a jumble, his mind clouded by confusion and hurt.

He wouldn't ask Kristi to leave. He couldn't do that to her. But if they were to be together, he'd have to.

What now?

Kristi had just cleared the lunch dishes when she heard buggy wheels clattering over the gravel driveway. Daed got up from the table, peered out the window, and then stepped outside without a word. Grossdaedi followed him, but he paused in the doorway and glanced over his shoulder. "Wonder what Bishop Dave's here for. Maybe he has a potential suitor for you, Kristi-girl." Grossdaedi winked, then shut the door behind him.

Kristi filled the sink with water, ignoring Grossmammi's cackle and Mamm's curious glance. Bishop Dave hadn't come with news of a suitor, she was sure. Unless Shane had spoken with him about joining the Amish. For a second, joy bubbled inside her.

But then, since when did bishops have nothing better to do than play matchmaker? Nein. It was likelier he'd come to deliver a reprimand and threaten shunning. Why else would he have come?

Or, maybe Shane had asked to join the church and been denied. She shook her head to chase away the disturbing thought.

The bishop was probably here for a casual visit, to welcome her family home from Florida. If so, she needed to have the kitchen cleaned, and quickly. He'd expect to be invited in for koffee and pie.

She'd washed up the plates and started on the silverware when the door opened again. Daed stood on the porch, his face drawn. "Kristi. Step out here a moment."

Mamm gave her a worried glance, then set down her mug of tea and stood. "I'll finish the dishes."

Step outside? To see the bishop? A rock settled in Kristi's stomach. He must have conjectured—correctly—her love for Shane Zimmerman, based on her actions on church Sunday. A confirmation of her fears.

Dread wrapped around her like a heavy winter cape. She dried her hands on a towel, dropped it onto the counter, and moved to the open doorway. Once outside, she stopped at the top of the porch steps and looked down at Bishop Dave and Grossdaedi. Grossdaedi looked just as upset as Daed.

"Was ist letz?"

Grossdaedi turned and stalked off toward the barn.

Bishop Dave looked up at her, his expression grim. "I've kum to understand your relationship with Dr. Zimmerman is more than mere friendship. He approached me this afternoon wanting to join the church so he could marry you."

Joy flooded through her. But she tempered it. Her imprudence had come to light. What would it cost her?

A lot, judging by Daed's reaction. He sank down on the bottom step, his eyes on her, watching. Maybe expecting her to deny the charges.

But she remained silent. She wasn't really sure what to say. And all she could think to do was beg Bishop Dave to allow Shane to join the church. To plead their case as a couple.

"I refused his request." Bishop Dave frowned, his eyes sad. "And with the reports of your recent behavior…." He paused a second, studying her, waiting for something. Possibly a show of repentance. "You need to confess before the assembly next church Sunday, or face shunning."

Again, she searched for words. But it was no use. The heavy weight she felt was almost unbearable.

Shane couldn't become Amish.

They wouldn't be allowed to marry.

Unless she left.

Her options were simple: have a life with Shane and be shunned, or keep her family and forgo marriage forever. Because she'd never forget Shane. Or stop loving him.

Bishop Dave stood there, his gaze locked on hers. After a few more moments of silence, his features became etched with sadness. "Kristi Lapp, you're walking on thin ice. If you leave, you will be forever shunned."

Daed buried his head in his hands. His shoulders shook.

Tears sprang to her eyes. Her bad leg started trembling. And her lunch threatened to come back up.

She remembered overhearing Daed's long talks with Justus before he'd left. She didn't know if she'd have the strength to sit through the same lectures without breaking down in tears.

Bishop Dave touched Daed's shoulder in a gesture of compassion but kept his eyes on Kristi. "You are the best friend of my dochter, and the dochter of *my* best friend. So I will grant you a grace period, for fasting and prayer. I expect to hear your decision by the end of next Sunday." He squeezed Daed's shoulder before turning around, climbing into his buggy, and driving off.

Kristi watched him go, then turned to Daed. "I'm sorry. I never...."

Daed sat up and mopped his hand over his face. For a second, hope flared in his eyes, but a look of resignation and disappointment quickly followed, replaced by a steely gaze. "Get out."

She caught her breath. "Daed, you can't mean that. Where—"

"You are no longer my dochter, until you kum to repentance." He stood, climbed the stairs, and went inside. The door slammed shut.

A moment later, her black bag landed at her feet. Followed by her cane.

A wail drifted out from the kitchen. He must have told Mamm the news.

No longer his dochter? He'd begged Justus for what had seemed like hours to stay. Wasn't she worth the same effort? Wouldn't Daed at least try talking some sense into her?

Kristi leaned over and hefted her bag and cane.

Given the efficiency of the Amish grapevine, this news would have reached the entire community by nightfall. And no one would agree to take her in, or they'd be guilty of complicity.

She didn't have any idea what to do next.

Chapter 27

At the hospital, Shane went to Sylvia's room, tapped on the open door, and walked in. Sylvia lay in bed, her sleeping daughter curled in her arm. She looked up and smiled. "Hey. You came alone?"

"Yes. I had to run a few errands on the way." After speaking with the bishop, he'd taken a side trip to the park where he'd kissed Kristi for the first time. There, he'd ranted for a while in the solitude, then fallen to his knees beside a park bench and cried out to God until a sense of peace had finally washed over him. He didn't have a solution, but God did. Shane only had to trust that He would make it clear in time.

He put his hand in his pocket and fingered the hairpin he'd found on the floor of his Jeep.

Sylvia smiled at Adriane. "She is so perfect. Did you look at her fingers and toes? All there. See?" She pulled a tiny, red fist out of the baby blankets wrapped tightly around the infant. "They don't let me hold her much. They say I need to rest. Someone should be here soon to check her diaper...that sort of thing."

"She really is beautiful."

Sylvia grinned. "Thanks for calling Mom and Dad. Dad can't get off work, but Mom got a flight leaving tomorrow morning. I did talk to Dad awhile. He'll fly in for the weekend. Mom will need to be picked up from the airport sometime tomorrow afternoon. She'll let you know when." Sylvia glanced toward the door. "Can you hold her for a little bit?"

"I'd love to."

Once Adriane was cradled securely in his arms, Sylvia threw off her covers, slid out of bed, and slowly made her way to the bathroom in the far corner.

Shane turned and carried Adriane over to the window to see outside.

Seconds later, his cell phone vibrated in his pocket. He shifted the baby and pulled out the phone. He didn't recognize the number, but he answered anyway. "This is Shane."

There were a few seconds of silence, and then a slight sniff. "Shane. It's Kristi. They...they're threatening to shun me."

His heart stopped for a moment. He opened his mouth to comment, but she continued before he could.

"The bishop said I have until next Sunday to decide." She paused. Another sniff. Was she crying? "And Daed kicked me out."

His heart stopped again. "Why?"

An interminable silence hung between them. Then, it dawned on him. He gave a harsh chuckle. "Because of me, right? Because I went and asked to join the church so I could marry you?" He rested his forehead against the window pane and stared out the window, seeing nothing.

"Daed said I'm no longer his dochter until I repent." Her voice broke.

He glanced at his watch. "I'm at the hospital with Sylvia, but I'll be there in an hour or so."

"Danki. I'll get my things and wait by the mailbox."

"You can take your belongings over to my house. It's unlocked." He started rocking the baby gently in his arms. Maybe the action would soothe his fraying nerves. "And, Kristi? Have your ID with you."

❦

Kristi stood out by the mailbox, trembling. Her crying had subsided, but she still couldn't believe Daed had told her to get out. Clearly, he was heartbroken, crying as he had. If he'd wanted her to repent, wouldn't he have wanted her to stay? Now, she didn't know what to do. Calling Shane had been the first thing that came to mind. The only thing, really.

He was generous to agree to store all of her things, in addition to Sylvia's. Everything she owned, she'd carted over to his haus, crying the whole time—mostly because she hadn't been allowed back in her haus to retrieve her belongings. Daed had thrown them one by one out the kitchen door.

It wasn't supposed to be like this. Kristi choked back a sob. *Nein more crying.* It didn't matter. The tears hung there, waiting for her to give in to them.

Shane's Jeep approached and slid to a stop, scattering gravel. He got out and pulled her into his arms, holding her close for a moment, then helped her into the vehicle. "I'm so sorry, Kristi. I never meant for this to happen. The last thing I wanted was for you to be shunned, even temporarily." He shut her door, then crossed in front of the vehicle and jumped back into the driver's seat. "I called Justus. I hope that's okay. He agreed to bring Dori and meet us at a restaurant in Marshfield."

Kristi nodded but didn't look at him. "Danki for letting me store everything at your haus. I tied Chinook in your yard. Taffy and my buggy are in your barn."

"That's fine."

They drove in silence. Finally, they arrived in Marshfield, and Shane pulled into the parking lot of a fast-food restaurant. "We're just getting coffee." He glanced at her. "Unless you're hungry."

She shook her head. The food she'd eaten at lunch sat like a pile of lead in her stomach. "I'm so sorry. I shouldn't have bothered you. I should have called Starr. She could've put me up." Probably would have plied her with chocolate milkshakes, given her a driving lesson, and taken her into Springfield to buy Englisch clothes, too. Not what she wanted.

What she wanted was Shane. She wanted him to hold her close again. Tell her it'd be alright. But he couldn't do that.

Then again, maybe he could. She looked up, hoping he still wanted to marry her. She could face the scary Englisch world with Shane by her side. *Lord, I need You to guide me through this mess. Please don't leave my future in ruins.*

Shane glanced around the parking lot. "Doesn't look like they're here yet." He reached across the console and took her hand in his. "I never told you, Kristi, but I love you. And I want to marry you. Whatever it takes."

His words made her spirit take flight. "Ich liebe dich, too, Shane. And I'm so touched that you would become Amish for me. I just don't know what to do, since it seems Bishop Dave won't allow it."

Shane started massaging her hand. "I know." He hesitated, seeming to weigh his next words. "There is one option that would allow us to get married today, if you wanted to."

"Really?" She straightened her posture.

"Yes. That's why I asked you to bring your ID. If you want to elope, I'm all for it. Just remember, you'll be shunned. I don't expect you to inflict that pain upon your family. Or yourself."

"I'm already virtually shunned, remember? Daed kicked me out." Kristi looked away, her eyes blurring with tears.

"Be honest with me." He reached his arm around her shoulders and drew her as close to him as the console would allow. "Are you really willing to leave the Amish and become Englisch? Today's circumstances aside, are you ready to give up your family? Your friends? To live among them but always have their backs turned on you?"

For Shane, she was willing, though it shamed her to admit it. But did she really want to? Nein. She'd wanted him to become Amish. "I never wanted to. But...."

"Let's talk to Justus and Dori, and also take time to pray about this. Just know that I'll respect whatever you decide, whether to get married at the courthouse or to go to Bishop Dave and repent."

❦

He intended to marry her, one way or another. But was it wrong of him to hope she'd decide to make the leap for him? Whichever one of them did would have a lot of adjustments to make. And he'd probably have an easier time of it. He could live without electricity. The house was mostly gas, anyway, and Ira and Timothy both had solar power. They could help him make the necessary modifications.

Shane would keep his business. His new assistant could stay in the office, making it easier for Shane to travel the countryside and visit clients. In horse and buggy.

His Jeep would be the hardest thing to give up.

If Kristi made the switch, she would lose so much more.

A black pickup truck with extended cab pulled into the space next to theirs, and Dori peered at them from the front passenger window. Justus got out of the truck and walked around to Kristi's door. He opened it, then reached for his sister. "Shane told me. I'm so sorry."

She scooted toward her brother, her shoulders shaking.

Justus gathered her close, patted her back, and muttered something in Pennsylvania Dutch that Shane couldn't make out.

He got out of the Jeep and opened the door for Dori.

She climbed out and gave him a sympathetic smile. "The guest room is all ready for her."

"Thank you."

"I would have invited you both to our house to talk, but I didn't want the boys overhearing. We left them with a babysitter."

Shane glanced over at Justus and Kristi. "I doubt she'll need to stay with you long." No matter which way her decision went.

Dori nodded. "Justus and I eloped." She glanced at the restaurant. "Let's go inside and find a private table where we can talk."

Shane glanced back at Kristi, who stood facing her brother, deep in conversation. He started to move in their direction, but Dori touched his arm. "Let them talk. I actually have a few things to say to you. Things you need to know."

Chapter 28

Kristi studied Justus, leaning against the Jeep, his jean-covered legs crossed at the ankles. He looked so relaxed and casual. The exact opposite of Kristi. If only she could exhibit the same peace. Never mind *exhibit*. She wanted to *feel* it.

Kristi paced back and forth in front of him, the overwhelming sense of loss threatening to overtake her. Again. How could she possibly have any tears left, given how many she'd shed so far? "I just don't understand Daed. How could he do this to me?"

Her brother sighed. "The more important question is, what do you want to do? Shane wants to marry you. Do you want to marry him? Do you love him?"

"Jah, I love him, and I know I'd have to be Englisch for us to marry. But maybe I didn't face reality, because I wanted him to become Amish." She ignored Justus's snort of disbelief. "I didn't dream Daed would shun me beforehand. I guess I was naïve to hope he'd be glad that I had found a gut man to marry. I know he likes Shane; I've seen him outside talking with him often enough. And Mamm takes him cinnamon rolls. Daed's only issue is Shane's being Englisch."

"Which is a big deal to the Amish." Justus smiled. "Even if you are shunned, at least your kinner won't be. Mamm and Daed could still interact with them, and Shane."

Kristi felt a glimmer of relief.

Justus uncrossed his ankles and straightened. "If it weren't for Shane, do you think you'd still want to become Englisch?"

Kristi frowned, then shook her head. "I always thought I'd stay Amish. It pains me to think about losing everything I grew up with. My family. My friends. And what about my salvation?"

"Salvation isn't exclusive to the Amish. I learned a lot in seminary. But we'll talk about that later. If you marry Shane and live next door to Mamm and Daed, how will you handle not being able to interact with them?"

Her shoulders slumped. "Not well. But I can't repent for falling in love with Shane."

"You could repent for things being done out of order."

Kristi blinked. "But I haven't done anything out of order." Memories of the passionate kisses she'd shared with Shane at the beginning of their relationship surfaced in her mind. She sucked in a breath. "For the most part."

Justus's mouth quirked. "I left because I wanted to go to school to be a pastor. I know how everyone felt about that. Preachers are ordained by divine calling and drawn by lot. Which kind of contradicts the divine calling part." He smiled. "And hardly anyone wants the responsibility. I knew I was called. And I had to leave in order to fulfill the purposes God had for me."

"How did you know?" Wasn't it prideful of Justus to claim that God had given him a direct, personal revelation?

Justus pointed to his heart and then his head. "When something is right, you know." He turned and glanced over the hood toward his vehicle, then looked back at Kristi. "Dori was determined to marry me. She didn't want to leave the Amish, initially, but she loved me more. I know it hurts her. She looks so wistful whenever she sees our people. And she laments that our kinner are growing up not knowing their großeltern, aentis, and onkels. All because we both jumped the fence after joining the church." He swallowed. "But I can't go back until God releases me. And He hasn't done that."

"I can't believe you claim to know the will of God."

"You're missing the point." Justus sighed. "Have you prayed about your situation with Shane?"

"Jah." *Some.*

"You need to spend more time fasting and praying."

He sounded like Bishop Dave. Kristi shrugged, refusing to allow painful memories to overtake her again. "I don't know why we're standing here talking. I have nein choice. I'm going to be shunned because I can't repent for falling in love with Shane. I'm going to tell him I'm willing to marry him. Today."

❧

Carrying an iced tea for Kristi and a coffee for himself, Shane followed Dori to a secluded booth in one corner of the restaurant.

Dori set down two cups of coffee on her side of the table and slid into the booth. Shane lowered himself onto the other bench but stayed near the edge so that he could slip out and let Kristi slide in when she joined them.

Dori reached for a packet of sugar, ripped it open, and emptied it into her coffee.

Shane watched her stir it in with her spoon. "You had something you wanted to say?" Her earlier comment had sounded almost ominous.

"Yes." She set her spoon on her napkin and met his gaze. "We would like to take Kristi home with us today. Both of you should spend time in prayer before making a decision. And there are a few things you should consider."

"I'm listening." *Ugh.* He sounded like Bishop Dave, the kitten-petting backstabber. Though he supposed the bishop had been right to refuse his request.

"Kristi needs to know that you love her enough to become Amish."

"She knows that already. I talked to the bishop, but he turned me down. He's the reason she's being shunned right now."

Dori waved her hand dismissively. "You told the bishop you want to join the Amish in order to marry Kristi—a selfish reason, don't you see? You need to research the faith. Find out what they believe. Put some effort into understanding them, and then make your decision. If you and Kristi elope, like Justus and I did, you win. You get the girl. And you'll have no reason to consider changing for her." She paused. "To put this in your terms, you need to be willing to trade horsepower for a horse."

Shane reached for the bowl of liquid creamers in the center of the table. He picked one at random, tore it open, and dumped it into his coffee. Then, he picked up a spoon and swished it around as he considered her words.

"If Kristi leaves the Amish, she will be giving up everything for you. I did the same for Justus, and I know firsthand what she'll suffer. It'll be even worse for her, living next door to her parents and remaining in the community. I miss family deeply, but I don't have to deal with it on a daily basis. Do you really want Kristi to face blatant shunning several times a day?"

"Of course not."

She directed her gaze beyond him and smiled. Justus and Kristi were approaching. "Good. Then, make sure she doesn't have to. And pray."

∽∾⋌⋋

Shane stood up, and Kristi slid past him into the booth. She remembered the first time they'd sat in a booth together, side by side, with his leg pressed against hers.

This time, he kept some space between them. What if he'd started distancing himself from her emotionally, as well? She glanced at him, noticing the furrows in his forehead. The troubled frown.

Her stomach churned. What if she blurted out she'd marry him today? Would he change his mind and send her home to Daed? Or, worse, marry her out of obligation and then regret it every day for the rest of his life?

Would she regret it?

The declaration she'd stated so boldly to Justus died on her lips. Maybe it would be best to follow the bishop's orders—and her brother's advice—to fast and pray.

Jah, that's what she'd do. She desperately needed to hear from God.

Chapter 29

Shane parked the Jeep in his driveway, pieces of the conversation with Dori still infiltrating his thoughts. He'd prayed all the way home, and he hoped Kristi had done the same on the drive to her brother's house.

Shane didn't know where Justus and Dori lived, but distancing himself from Kristi, at least for now, was the right thing to do. They needed space and time to pray and think things through before reaching a decision.

As he climbed out of the Jeep, he glanced at the Lapps' and noticed Ira standing with Timothy outside the barn. Ira's shoulders were slumped, his expression one of defeat, as if his world were ending.

For a moment, a bitter gladness swept over Shane. Ira deserved to despair, after punishing Kristi so severely.

Timothy's gesticulations matched the angry tone of his voice as he spoke, but Shane couldn't discern his words.

When both men turned in his direction, Shane averted his gaze and hurried inside. He locked the door behind him.

His cell phone vibrated inside his pocket. He pulled it out and glanced at the screen. *Mom.* He directed the call to voice mail.

Kristi's stuff was stacked neatly in the foyer just inside the door. Including her wheelchair and walker. How many trips had she taken to drag all of it over here? Probably enough that Ira had had ample opportunity to see where she'd taken it.

Shane hoisted the wheelchair and carried it to the basement, stashing it in an out-of-the-way corner. He made a second trip for the walker. No point in keeping them in plain sight. Kristi no longer needed them—she never had, really—and they'd only conjure painful memories.

A knock sounded on the door. "Shane?"

He sighed, wanting to ignore Ira's summons. But then, the temptation to give Ira a piece of his mind took over. He unlocked the door and opened it wide.

Ira and Timothy both stood there.

Ira's eyes were red, as if he'd been crying ever since banishing Kristi. He looked as if he'd aged ten years since Shane had last seen him. "I think I overreacted."

"*Think*"? Talk about an understatement. Shane raised his eyebrows but kept his sarcasm to himself.

Ira glanced at the pile of Kristi's belongings. "Is she here?"

"No. I'm just storing her things."

"Where is she?"

Shane wasn't ready to give him the satisfaction of knowing.

Plus, if Ira found out that his temporarily shunned daughter was with his permanently shunned son, he would only cry the harder.

"She's safe," Shane assured him.

"I want her to stay Amish. Not marry an Englischer." Ira's voice broke.

Timothy glared at his brother. "He went to see the bishop and ask about becoming Amish, remember?" He gestured at Shane. "That's how this trouble got started. And Daed says he knows Shane's großeltern. 'Gut Amish folk,' he said. Maybe the Lord is using Kristi to bring Shane into the fold."

Ira pulled in a shaky breath. "Tell her to kum home."

Shane hesitated a moment. "I don't think that's a good idea."

"I did overreact, and I'm sorry." Ira rubbed his eyes, then turned and made his way down the path, wobbling slightly.

Timothy watched his brother go, then looked at Shane. "She called you, ain't so?"

"Yes."

"I thought you'd bring her here as your frau."

"We agreed to pray about it, rather than rush into a marriage that would sentence her to a lifetime of shunning. I want to prevent her from facing that pain, if possible. I know what it did to Justus and Dor—"

"You know Justus?" Timothy swayed and grasped the doorpost. He shook his head. "There has to be some way around this." He turned and headed down the walkway, still muttering to himself.

❧

As soon as she arrived at her brother's haus, Kristi excused herself and retreated to the privacy of the bedroom Dori showed her. She didn't want to be unsociable, but, at the same time, she needed to be alone.

Her insides were so knotted up. She wondered if they'd ever get this mess untangled. If she'd ever feel normal, or happy, again.

She longed to consult her Bible, but she'd taken it to Shane's, along with everything else she owned. Thankfully, she found an Englisch Bible on the bookshelf by the door.

She knelt next to the bed, propped the Bible on the mattress, and opened it to the book of Proverbs, chapter 3, verses 5 and 6: *"Trust in the LORD with all your heart, and lean not on your own understanding; in all your ways acknowledge Him, and He shall direct your paths."*

She bowed her head. *Lord, I need Your guidance. So does Shane. Please direct us, according to Your perfect will.*

Peace filled her.

After work the next day, Shane went to the airport to pick up his mom. He took her directly to the hospital to visit Sylvia and the baby before heading home.

When they reached the house, Ira stood on the doorstep. What did he want now? Shane hadn't contacted Kristi yet to tell her about her father's apology, knowing that she—and he, too—needed more time to pray before speaking.

With some dread, he climbed out of the Jeep, opened the door for his mother, and helped her out. "Mom, meet my neighbor Ira Lapp. Ira, this my mother, Adriane Zimmerman."

Mom extended her hand. "Nice to meet you."

Ira grunted a greeting, then reached into his pocket and pulled out a white envelope, which he handed to Shane. "I prayed about this last nacht, talked to my daed and Timothy, and made a few inquiries."

Shane opened the flap. "Airline tickets? I thought Amish traveled only by bus."

Ira nodded. "You aren't Amish."

"I see. And I'm going to…Florida?" He couldn't imagine why.

"Jah. Your großeltern are expecting you. A driver will meet you and Kristi at the airport."

"Me and Kristi?" Shane's heart pounded.

"Jah. It'll be your honeymoon."

Shane blinked. "Our...what?" Was he dreaming? Had Ira really just changed his tune?

"Honeymoon!" Mom gasped and dropped her suitcase, her hand going to her chest. "Shane, is there something you haven't told me?"

Ira frowned. "Maybe we should speak in private."

Shane nodded, then glanced over his shoulder. "The front door's unlocked, Mom. I'll be right in."

Huffing, his mom bustled off toward the house.

Ira waited until the door closed behind her. "Timothy and I talked to Bishop Dave, and this is the plan he approved. Your großeltern will help you to understand what it means to be Amish. Then, you'll kum back, give the bishop the right answers, and start preparing to join the church. Kristi will confess her sins and repent, or...." He pulled in a breath. "She'll be permanently shunned and live as an Englischer."

Shane shook his head. "Wouldn't it be better if I went to Florida alone? And unmarried?"

"You'll marry Kristi anyway, ain't so?"

Ira was perceptive. With a slow smile, Shane nodded.

Ira smiled. "Then, nein. This is a decision you and Kristi must make together." He brushed his hands together. "I have to fix this. Kristi is my only dochter, and I love her. I trust that you'll make the right decision."

Who would have guessed that Ira would come up with the solution to their problem?

Chapter 30

The next morgen, Kristi checked her cell phone for any missed calls. None. With a sigh, she wandered out of the bedroom into the living room. The two little buwe looked up from the floor, where they played with wooden building blocks, and stared at her. Dori glanced up from her sewing. "Good morning, Kristi. Are you hungry?"

"Nein." *Only heartbroken.* Why hadn't Shane called her yesterday? Surely, he could have found time. Had he reached a decision? If so, what? Though he had said he'd honor her wishes.

Even so, she didn't have a choice, really. If he wouldn't marry her, she'd remain a maidal. And she would repent, but only for her disobedience. Not for loving Shane.

Trust in the Lord.... She was glad that God had spoken to her through an Englisch Bible.

"Where's Justus?"

Dori looked at her watch. "He's at the office. He usually stays there till lunch, if nothing comes up."

A key rattled in the lock, and then the door opened. "Daddy!" The buwe lunged to their feet and raced to greet Justus.

Dori shrugged, set her mending aside, and got up to give him a kiss. "I just told Kristi you wouldn't be home for a while."

Justus smiled. "Shane called and asked me to bring Kristi to town." He winked at Kristi. "You ready?"

She brushed sweaty hands over her apron. "Jah." Ready as she'd ever be. This would be it, then.

Kristi didn't know where they were going until Justus pulled into the lot of the park where Shane and she had first kissed. Shane was already there, waiting in his Jeep. He jumped out when Justus brought his truck to a stop.

Letting the truck idle, Justus got out and gave Shane a bear hug.

When Kristi came around to join them, her brother turned to her with a gentle squeeze. "I want to be a part of your life, Kristi," he whispered. "No matter what."

She nodded. Even if she returned home, her days of shunning Justus were over. Somehow, she'd stay in contact with him.

After Justus's truck had roared away, Shane reached for her hand, and they walked down the trail, away from the mothers and toddlers playing in the park. Shane stopped beside a relatively private park bench and turned to face Kristi. "I should have told you this before: your dad came over that first night you left to say he was sorry and that he wanted you to come home."

She dropped down onto the bench. "He did?" His rejection still stung.

"I'm truly sorry I didn't tell you, but I thought it would be better for you to stay with your brother, rather than at home, while we prayed and sought the Lord's will."

She nodded. It would have been hard to focus at home, knowing Shane was nearby.

Shane pulled an envelope out of his pocket, then sat down beside her and fingered the flap. "Last night, your dad came by again, with an interesting proposition." He handed her the envelope.

Frowning, she opened it and pulled out several slips of paper. She studied them, but they didn't make any sense. "What is this?"

"Plane tickets. Since I'm ready to marry you, no matter what, your dad suggested we go ahead and get married now—as in today—and then catch a flight to Florida to visit my grandparents. An educational honeymoon, if you would."

"Honeymoon?" Joy flooded through her. *Danki, Lord. How gut it is to trust in You!* And Daed had suggested it, meaning that she had his blessing to marry Shane. She smiled so broadly that the corners of her mouth ached.

Shane fingered the tickets. "You're still shunned right now, technically. But this is how your dad and Timothy worked it out with Bishop Dave: my grandparents will teach me what it really means to be Amish. If we decide to pursue it further, I'll take Amish baptism classes from my grandpa, who's a preacher. And then, when we come home, I'll talk to Bishop Dave and undergo a series of questions. If I pass, and he approves, I'll join the church. At that point, you'll have to repent for disobedience. Because, Kristi, if you agree to be my wife—"

Kristi launched herself into his arms and kissed him. "Jah. For better or for worse."

He smiled. "Then, for the sake of our future, I intend to pass."

About the Author

Laura Hilton graduated with a business degree from Ozarka Technical College in Melbourne, Arkansas. A member of the American Christian Fiction Writers, she is a professional book reviewer for the Christian market, with more than a thousand reviews published on the Web.

Healing Love is the first in Laura's second series with Whitaker House, The Amish of Webster County. Her first series, The Amish of Seymour, included *Patchwork Dreams*, *A Harvest of Hearts*, and *Promised to Another*. Previously, she published two novels with Treble Heart Books, *Hot Chocolate* and *Shadows of the Past*, as well as several devotionals.

Laura and her husband, Steve, have five children, whom Laura homeschools. The family makes their home in Arkansas. To learn more about Laura, read her reviews, and find out about her upcoming releases, readers may visit her blog at http://lighthouse-academy.blogspot.com/.